Cover by Ecila Media

Falling for the Marine

SHIRLEY JUMP

Copyright

Contents

Chapter 1

The pig refused to cooperate, creating a problem bigger than Green Acres and Big Valley put together. Jenny Wright needed to kiss this piece of pork in the next two and a half minutes so she could usher her third graders back inside—before the principal caught her necking with a mammal on the school lawn on a Friday afternoon.

Dr. Margaret Davis was from the old school and didn't think Jenny's rewards program for her students' achievements did much more than waste time. Everyone in town knew the principal was hoping to be appointed superintendent next year, so she'd been cracking down on anything that made her—or her school—look bad. Jenny doubted Dr. Davis would like the pig much.

Heck, even *she* didn't like it much right now, and she'd hired it to be her pucker partner.

"Come on over here, Reginald," she whispered to the rotund pink animal. "One quick kiss and then you can go back to the farm. Nice bowl of slop waiting for you, I hear."

Reginald grunted, plopping down onto the new spring grass. He heaved a sigh and closed his eyes.

The circle of third graders around Jenny began to laugh at the recalcitrant swine. Kissing a pig as a challenge to the kids to read one hundred books before the end of spring term had sounded like a great idea two and a half months ago, when Reginald was wallowing on a farm far away. But now that the pot-bellied, three-hundred-pound beast was actually here, he didn't look very appealing.

She'd never be able to eat bacon again, that was for sure.

"Go on, Miss Wright, kiss him!" Jimmy said.

"Kiss the pig! Kiss the pig!" The chant spread through the twenty-five kids like a verbal wave. The April breeze carried it across the school lawn and into the open windows, bringing a few heads out to see what was happening.

She'd made a promise and she'd stick to it. If there was one thing Jenny Wright did, it was keep her promises. Especially to her students.

She tamped down the wave of nausea in her stomach, then came around to Reginald's face, got down on her knees in her black capris and, before she could think about what she was about to do, pressed her lips to Reginald's velvety snout.

He snarfled, jerked awake, and backed up quickly. Then he let out a squeal and dashed toward the bright pink "Animals Where You Want 'Em" truck. His handler, Ed Spangler, a tall man in overalls and a straw hat, laughed and helped Reginald up the ramp and into the back of the truck. He shut the door, then circled to the front. "Old Reginald hasn't moved that fast in ten years. Must be one heck of a pucker you got there."

"Gee, thanks. I think." Jenny dug her check out of her pocket. "Here you go."

"Oh, no need to pay me, ma'am. I haven't laughed that much in ages. Plus, the paper got a snapshot of your date with Reginald. I'd say that free publicity makes us about even." Ed gestured toward a young man holding a camera and standing across the street. "I thought this might make a good story, so I called the *Mercy Daily News* myself." He thumbed the strap of his overalls and nodded.

"This is going to be in the *paper*?" Oh Lord, her career was now over. Might as well start scouring the Help Wanted section now. If there was anything Dr. Davis disliked more than Jenny's unconventional teaching methods, it was *publicity* about Jenny's teaching methods.

A tension headache began to pound in her temples. She pressed her hands to her head, then tucked her hair behind her ears. She would deal with this later. Preferably after a lot of Tylenol and a huge platter of nachos.

Stuffing the check back into her pocket, she spun on her heel and flapped her arms at her class like a mother goose. "Come on, children, back inside."

"Miss Wright, what'd the pig taste like?" Jimmy Brooks asked.

"Yeah, was he all boogers and slime?" Alex Herman had a fascination with all things nasal. He'd even fashioned a nose for his clay project in art class.

"Eww, Alex. That is so gross." Lindsay Williams made a face and took a step away from him. "Miss Wright wouldn't *really* kiss a slimy pig anyway. She has taste."

"In what?"

Lindsay shrugged. "I dunno. In animals, I guess."

Not in men, Jenny thought. As far as love lives went, she'd be willing to bet Reginald had better luck than she did. Finding a man wasn't high on her priority list right now anyway, not while she was so consumed with her class. All relationships did was complicate her life. Jenny had had enough complications to last her until she was eighty.

"Okay, that's enough. We need to get back to work." Jenny pulled open the outside door to her classroom and led the children inside. They took their seats amid a steady stream of pig chatter and chair squeaking. Then she moved to the front of the room and clapped her hands. After a moment, the children quieted down and faced her. As always, a small thrill of triumph ran through her when her class ran like clockwork. To Jenny, a civilized and orderly class proved she was doing a good job. "Now, you all have done a wonderful job on the first level of the reading challenge. But we still have a ways to go."

The class let out a collective groan.

"I'm willing to make it fun," Jenny said. "If you're willing to put in the work."

"Are you going to dye your hair green this time? I really liked the pink," Jimmy piped up.

"Uh, no. Not this time," Jenny said. Dr. Davis had nearly gone into cardiac arrest when she'd seen the fuchsia hair Jenny had sported as a first-quarter class incentive.

"How about making us another giant ice cream sundae?" Lindsay rubbed her belly. "I didn't eat dinner at all that day."

Lindsay's mother hadn't been happy about that, either. She'd called Dr. Davis to complain, resulting in another black mark on Jenny's teaching record. "Er, no, no sundaes."

"Well, what then?" the class asked.

Jenny put on a bright, work-with-me smile. "We could read just for the fun of it!"

"Nah. That's boring." Jimmy said. "We want a prize." Twenty-five nine-year-old heads nodded in agreement.

She'd created a monster. The children now expected *rewards* for making their class goals.

Maybe Dr. Davis had a point.

No, she refused to entertain that idea. Her third graders needed every boost they could get to raise their reading level. This past winter, Mercy Elementary's scores in the state achievement tests had come back at their lowest levels in years and the school had been placed on probation. Losing their accreditation was a very real possibility if something didn't change. Jenny couldn't change every class, but she could darn well work on her own.

In the last few years, her class had become her main priority in life. It wasn't that she'd set out to become the stereotypical spinster elementary school teacher. It had just happened that way, after too many failed relationships and one broken heart that refused to heal. And it was a heck of a lot easier to concentrate on the children than on why Jenny attracted bad dates like steel filings to a magnet.

"I'll think of something," she said, rubbing at her temples again and returning her thoughts to the class. As long as it didn't involve pigs or hair dye, she figured she'd be fine.

"Miss Wright?" the school secretary blurted over the loudspeaker. "Can you come down to the principal's office please? I'll have Miss Rhodes cover your class."

"I'll be right there," Jenny said.

Jimmy mouthed "Uh-oh." The other kids' eyes got wide. They knew that even for an adult, an impromptu trip to the principal's office meant only one thing—big trouble.

Debbie Rhodes opened the connecting door between the two third-grade classrooms and gave Jenny a sympathetic smile. "Do you think she saw the pig?" she whispered.

"How could she not? He weighed three-hundred-pounds and arrived in a hot-pink truck." Jenny sighed. "Guess I better go down there and face the wrath of Davis, huh?"

Debbie gave her arm a squeeze. "Good luck."

If she could have trudged in two-inch pumps, Jenny would have. It was a bit hard to look as if she was going to her execution dressed in black capris and a white sweater set. So she held her head high, straightened her shoulders, and figured if she was going to get fired, she'd go out looking good.

"Dr. Davis would like to see you in her office. She said to shut the door." Bonnie, the school secretary, gave her a sad smile, as if she knew Jenny was going to enter the lair of the lion and come out like a shredded sock.

Jenny's spine slumped a little. "Okay." She crossed to the principal's office, entered the room, then closed the door behind her.

Dr. Davis sat at her desk, all business and primness. Her gray hair was woven into a tight bun, her brown-checked suit perfectly pressed. She had on dark framed glasses, a chain dangling from both sides of the lenses. Dr. Davis left nothing to chance—not even losing her glasses.

"Sit down, Miss Wright." Dr. Davis didn't bother to look up from her paperwork. "I hear you had a visitor today."

"Uh, yeah. A really cute pig." Jenny pasted on her bright smile again. "The kids loved him."

"It was a distraction from their learning."

The smile fell a little. "It was a reward for reading a hundred books this term."

Dr. Davis raised her head. She dropped her glasses to her chest. "Your class read a hundred books?"

"Yes, they did." Jenny nodded. "They tried some authors for the first time. Even Jimmy Brooks read three and he didn't read at all before the pig incentive."

Dr. Davis leaned back in her chair. "You know the school has been placed on probation because of our achievement test scores this year."

"Yes, I'm aware of that."

Dr. Davis tapped at her lip with her pen, thinking. "We don't have much time to bring up our scores if we want to make a difference. You have mentioned to me, several times, that you'd like more support for your program."

"I do," Jenny said. "I really think it could work. The children have responded well to incentives and fun."

"Be that as it may, I'm not entirely sold on your methods thus far. However, I do have to worry about our accreditation. There's a grant available to the third-grade class that can demonstrate the best growth in reading skills over the school year. It can be used to buy books, computer equipment, whatever you want. I'm quite impressed with what the other teachers are accomplishing using traditional methods...."

Oh no, here it came. She was going to be stuffed back into the plain reading, writing and arithmetic box. No pink hair, no pigs. Nothing fun.

"However, you have done something unusual and had some success," Dr. Davis said, almost gritting the words out between her teeth. "Time will tell if it pays off in test scores, but at this point, I'm ready to try almost anything. Your classroom could use that grant and our school needs to retain its accreditation. If we can raise our status, it also makes us eligible for additional state funding. A winning solution for everyone." Dr. Davis pursed her lips, then released them. "So, with all that in mind...you have my permission to continue with your students."

Jenny blinked. "I do?"

"Yes, but—" Dr. Davis held up a finger. "I don't want any more animals on the school lawn. No giant desserts in the art room. No painted hair. Instead, *I* have come up with your next reward." She gave Jenny a smile that seemed an awful lot like a lion opening his jaws.

Oh Lord.

"Children like heroes," she continued. "And we have a local hero who has returned to town." The smile widened. "Nathaniel Dole."

"N-N-Nate?" Nate was back? He must be on leave. Since when? And why hadn't she known?

Because the days when he'd pick up the phone and call her to say he was coming home had passed a long time ago. And yet, a part of her still leapt at the thought of him returning, like some Pavlovian response to his presence.

"Is there something wrong with him?" Dr. Davis asked.

"No, no, not at all," Jenny said, shaking her head. A little too hard because her hair came out from behind her ears and whipped at her eyes.

I used to be in love with him, but that's not a problem. Anymore.

Besides, she was twenty-nine now. All grown up. It had been, what, ten years since she'd seen him last?

Nine years and three months, whispered the little part of her brain that kept track of those kinds of things.

"Good. I think Mr. Dole would be perfect to come in and work with the kids. He's home on indefinite leave, doesn't have much to occupy his days right now and he loves children. Think of him as a sort of free aide." Dr. Davis leaned forward in her chair and slid a paper across the desk. "Here's his contact information. I'm sure with all those nine-year-olds, you could always use a helping hand."

The principal *had* found a box for Jenny. One she couldn't escape. Not only did she gain tacit approval for her teaching methods, but also a helper for the busy class.

Nate. The one man she'd vowed never to see again. As if by keeping him out of sight, she could expel him from her heart. If the plan had involved *anyone* but Nate...

"Oh yes, this is going to be wonderful," Jenny said. Almost as good as kissing the pig.

***

Nate Dole's mother had been at it again. No one else would have left a newspaper on his front stoop, with a tin of cookies to boot. He loved her for trying, but he wasn't ready to come out of his self-imposed cave. Not yet. Maybe not ever.

He'd bought the small ranch house he was living in now six years ago as a rental property investment. It had been vacant for a few weeks—good timing for a man who'd needed a cave.

Nate had told his family he was on an extended leave and needed some time alone to rest. They'd believed the extended leave story because he'd barely been home in years. He'd always been too busy fighting the bad guys to stop off in Mercy for some R and R. He'd lied to his family, but it was a lie that bought him a little space and some time to figure out the rest of his life. Or what was left of it now that he was down a knee.

He turned and hobbled back into the house, using the despicable cane to help keep the weight off his left leg. It made him feel ninety, not twenty-nine, and the minute he could get around without it, he was going to use it to start a bonfire.

When he'd shut the door, he reached for the cookies and pried off the lid. He paused, a chocolate chip cookie halfway to his mouth, and noticed the picture on the front page of the Sunday edition of the *Mercy Daily News*.

Jenny.

Not just Jenny, but Jenny kissing a pig, of all things. Nate laid the cookies on the hall table, then turned on a light so he could see the paper better. He blinked in the sudden brightness.

How long had it been since he'd had the lights on? That alone was a sign he'd spent too much time sleeping and not enough time—

No, he wasn't going to go there. He rested his weight against the wall and traced the grainy outline of her face.

Jenny.

How many years had it been? Almost ten. He would have thought she'd be married, living anywhere but Mercy by now.

But, no, the caption said "Third-grade teacher Jenny Wright." She was still single. Still his Jenny.

He shook his head. She hadn't been his in such a long time. His brain, though, seemed to forget that fact.

He chuckled a little at the image of her down on her knees, puckered up with Reginald, the kissing pig. The sound of his own laughter startled him, like suddenly hearing a foreign language.

He knew what his mother was up to. Between the cookies and the picture of Jenny, she was hoping he'd come around. Go back to being the old Nate again.

The thing no one understood was that he couldn't go back to being that Nate, no matter how much he wanted to. He'd left that man behind two weeks ago when he'd opted for an honorary discharge from the Marines instead of spending the rest of his service years behind a desk—the only other option the doctors gave him.

The doorbell rang and Nate jumped, dropping the paper to the floor. It fluttered apart, dispersing like feathers. He ignored the cane and hopped the few steps to the door on one foot. Through the glass panel, he could see who it was before he even opened the oak door.

He rubbed at his eyes. Surely, this was too coincidental to be true. Maybe he *had* been alone too long. Now he was starting to hallucinate. Next, it would be pink elephants.

The bell rang again.

Okay, the sound was real. The person on his porch had to be real, too, not a dream come to life.

Nate turned the knob and opened the door. "Hello, Jenny," he said, as if it had been ten minutes, not ten years, since he'd last seen her.

God, she looked beautiful. Even more so now with the sophistication of age. Her straight blond hair fell in a shimmering curtain against her neck and shoulders. She wore a suit of soft peach over a white silk blouse and matching pumps, as if she'd just come from church. Knowing Jenny, she probably had. Family and commitments had always been important to her, no matter the day of the week.

The nether parts of his body could care less how she was dressed. All he saw when he looked at her was a memory from ten years ago—Jenny lying on the back seat of his Grand Am, looking at him with a happy, satisfied smile and a love in her emerald eyes he'd thought would never die.

But that had been a long, long time ago. And he'd been wrong about the love part.

She tucked several strands of hair behind her ear. He knew the gesture well. She was nervous. For some reason, that made him feel better. "Hi, Nate."

"Uh, you want to come in?"

She shook her head. "You're probably busy."

"Not especially. I could put on some coffee." If he *had* any coffee. He wasn't sure what was in his cabinets. He had cookies, though, and he could scrounge up something to drink to go with them.

"Okay, but only for a minute. I just wanted to stop by and discuss the game plan for next week."

He opened the door and waved her in. "Next week?"

She stopped in the hall. "Yeah, that's when you're scheduled to come into my classroom and help out, remember?"

He hadn't been in that deep of a fog, had he? "What are you talking about?"

"Dr. Davis told me you called the school and volunteered to help with my third graders."

He shut the door and leaned against the wall so she wouldn't know how much his knee was hurting him. The last thing he wanted to do was drag out the cane in front of her. "Who's Dr. Davis?"

"The principal." Jenny put a hand to her mouth. "You mean...you never talked to her?"

"No."

"Then how..." Her voice trailed off, confusion knitting her brows.

Nate glanced at the paper on the floor, the cookie tin on the hall table. It didn't take a master puzzler to put the pieces together. "My mother is behind this. I'm sure of it."

"Why would she do something like that?"

"She thinks I need something to keep me busy."

"You?" Jenny let out a laugh. "You're Type-A-plus. I can't imagine you ever sitting around doing nothing." Then she paused, as if her vision had finally adjusted to the darker interior. He saw her note the piles of dirty dishes in the kitchen behind him, the laundry he hadn't bothered to deal with beside the sofa, the discarded newspapers and empty pizza boxes tossed around the room.

"Ah, excuse the mess, I've been—" He stopped. What reason could he give? That he'd been wallowing quite well in self-pity for the last couple of weeks? Lost all sense of direction and purpose? That he'd had a hell of a time knowing who he was since he'd returned to Mercy?

Better to leave the sentence unfinished.

Jenny started backing toward the door. "Well, I'm sorry for bothering you. I'll tell Dr. Davis it was all a big misunderstanding."

She was going to leave. If she did, he had a feeling it would be another ten years before he saw her again. And next time, her last name might not be Wright anymore.

"Jenny, wait." He took a step forward, then saw the cane against the wall, a stark reminder of why he was home in the first place.

She pivoted, her hand on the doorknob. "What?"

He tightened his fists at his side and gritted his teeth. "It was, ah, really nice to see you again."

A strange look flitted through her eyes. Disappointment? Hurt? He couldn't be sure. Half of him wanted to take the words back, to say something that would keep her here, but the other half disagreed.

"Yeah, you too," she said. "Tell your mother I said hello."

And then she was gone. When the door shut, Nate turned off the hall light, yanked the cane up, and retreated to the sofa again. But for the first time, his sanctuary offered no comfort. Like a spring that wouldn't stay down, the memory of Jenny inside his hallway kept popping up and poking at him.

By the time he picked up the phone, he'd already half made up his mind.

Chapter 2

On Monday morning, Jenny came in early. She'd come up with seventeen ways of telling Dr. Davis that Nate had turned her down but rejected them all. Even if the whole thing had been a scheme by Grace Dole to reunite the two of them, or a grand idea to get Nate out of the house, Jenny knew she had to find a way to make the whole thing work out for the sake of her class. If she came up with a good enough excuse for his absence, then it could buy her enough time to convince Nate to change his mind.

David Copperfield moved mountains. Surely she could get one stubborn Marine to agree to help her class—and her career. She'd already kissed a pig. How much worse could convincing Nate be?

But being around him...all day, every day. In the same room, within touching distance. Could she do that? Ten years ago, he'd been the man she'd wanted to marry. The one she had laughed with, cried with. Kissed as if the world was going to end tomorrow.

Their world did. He'd joined the Marines at seventeen and stopped coming home as often. The distance had made their bond weaker, not stronger. And eventually, one of them—she no longer remembered who—had said the words *break-up* and before she knew it, the dream she'd held for so many years had evaporated like summer rain on hot pavement.

It was better that way. She was happier. Granted, she was alone, but she no longer pounced on the mail truck or haunted her email, hoping for note to say that he was okay. That he still cared. She'd finally gone back to normal life.

Well, as normal as life could be with pink hair and a pig for a date.

Jenny pulled out a selection of new library books from her tote bag and set them up on a stand inside the reading circle.

"Miss Wright?"

Jenny wheeled around at the sound of Dr. Davis's voice. Already? She hadn't had time to prepare speech number eighteen yet. "Good morning, Dr. Davis."

"Is Mr. Dole here yet?"

"No, he, ah, he couldn't make it."

Dr. Davis arched an eyebrow. "Really? I was under the impression he was eager to help."

"I think your idea of bringing him in was a wonderful one," Jenny began, weaving speeches number two and number eleven together on the fly, "and I think the kids would really respond to something like that. The boys' top choices in books are almost always hero-related."

The other woman frowned. "I can hear a 'but' in your voice."

"But unfortunately, Mr. Dole—"

"Was running a little late this morning." Nate entered the room, bearing his weight against a cane. A cane? She hadn't noticed one yesterday.

Had he been injured? If so, that would explain why gung-ho, always-another-mission-to-take-on Nate was home for more than a minute.

She'd expected him to wear his uniform and was surprised to see him instead in a light-blue dress shirt and navy pants. He looked good, always had. Her heart, which didn't seem to listen to her head or the warning siren telling her not to notice how he looked, skipped a beat at the sight of him.

"My apologies, Miss Wright—and Dr. Davis." He nodded toward each of them.

"I'm glad you could make it." The principal extended her hand to shake his. "Miss Wright was under the impression you weren't coming."

"Just a misunderstanding." He grinned. "I'm here and ready to help."

"Good. I'll get out of your way then." Dr. Davis gave him a smile, then left the room.

Once the principal was gone, Jenny turned to Nate. His face, she'd realized yesterday, looked older now, more tired, as if the weight of the world wasn't sitting so easily on his shoulders anymore. For a fleeting second, she wanted to reach out and make it easier for him.

She quickly shook off the thought. The days when she'd supported Nate were far in the past, and she intended to leave them that way. "What are you doing here?" she asked.

"Helping you."

"When I left yesterday, you didn't seem interested."

"I, ah, had some time to think it over." He took a seat on the edge of a desk. "I'm here for a week. Do with me what you will." He grinned.

A week. She could last a few days in his presence and not lose her mind or her heart again.

Couldn't she?

Jenny crossed her arms and leaned against the blackboard. "I don't buy it. You're as stubborn as a mule and once you've made up your mind, you never change it."

"It's been a long time, Jenny," he said quietly. "People change."

"Yes, they do." She picked up a piece of chalk and turned it over and over in her palm. "Sometimes."

The silence stood between them like a gate waiting to be unlocked. His deep brown gaze met hers and she had to look away before all the thoughts she'd had over the last ten years came rushing to the surface.

I am over him.

But when she turned again to draw in the face that had once been as familiar as her own, she knew Nate wasn't the only liar in the room.

"Knock, knock." Debbie stuck her head in the room. "Oh, hi. I didn't know you had company, Jenny."

"Come on in." Jenny stepped forward and waved the other third-grade teacher into the room. If she had to, she would have dragged Debbie in. Anything to ease the growing tension between herself and Nate.

It's over between us. Maybe she needed to put that on a sign and wear it around her neck as a reminder.

"I'm Nate Dole," he said, putting out his hand to the slim brunette. "I'm here to help with Jenny's class for a few days."

Debbie's hazel eyes sparked to life and a wide smile took over her face when she took his hand in hers. "Well, if you ever run out of things to do, my classroom's right next door."

"I'll keep that in mind," Nate said. Their handshake—which seemed to last for hours—finally ended.

Jenny shouldn't have felt an ounce of jealousy. Nate had every right to flirt with another woman, kiss another woman, marry another—

No, his left hand was bare. He was still single.

She would *not* acknowledge the relief that flooded her at that thought.

"Well," Jenny said. "Mr. Dole and I need to re-organize the day. The children will be here in seventeen minutes and once they arrive, there won't be any time to breathe.""Yeah, I better get to my own class." But Debbie didn't move.

Jenny opened the connecting door. "See you at lunch."

"Oh, yeah, lunch." Debbie shook her head, then turned to Nate. "Will you be here at lunch?"

"If Jenny wants me to be," he said.

Both of them turned to look at her. She wondered what was on the menu today and if Debbie would look good wearing it, then bit back the evil-twin thoughts. She was *not* jealous. Not one bit. "He doesn't have to stay *all* day."

"Oh, too bad," Debbie said. "I'm sure the...the, ah, students will really enjoy him being around. A big, tall guy like you." She gave him a smile and leaned against the doorframe. "You're a Marine, I hear."

"Debbie?" Jenny said, laying the hint heavy in her voice. "I really need to rework my lesson plan for today."

"Yeah, sure. Me too." Debbie dispensed another smile Nate's way, toothy as a Miss America contestant. "Have a nice day. If you need anything—"

"You're right next door," he finished for her.

Jenny distinctly heard the sound of Debbie sighing as she disappeared into her own classroom. With a firm shove, Jenny shut the door.

"Now, let's talk about the real reason why you're here," she began. "It's not altruism."

He grinned at her, as if he'd seen the spark in her eyes when Debbie had flirted with him. "To help you."

"I know you, Nate. You and children mix about as well as an elephant in a roomful of mice. I don't think so." She tapped her lip with her finger. "There's more to you showing up here than a nudge from your mother. I'd be willing to bet on it."

"Maybe." His grin widened, giving nothing away. "If you want to bet, we could make it interesting."

"This is an elementary school, remember? Nothing R-rated allowed."

"Too bad."

Jenny got out a stack of math fact review worksheets and began putting one on each child's desk for early-morning work. It was easier to do that than to focus on the teasing glint in his eyes. "Believe me, you won't be having any R-rated thoughts in a little while. Once those kids get hold of you, your brain will become mush and your body will beg for a nap."

"I've been through wars. I can handle a bunch of kids."

"A war is nothing compared to twenty-five third graders."

"Jenny, I'm a Marine, remember? I can handle it, believe me."

She paused and turned to him. "I'm going to take such pleasure in saying 'I told you so' later on today." She thrust the pile at him. "Here, finish putting these on the desks so I can get the vocabulary words up on the board."

He slid off the desk and hobbled to where his cane lay resting against the wall. When he'd entered the room, she'd seen him walking with it, but then she'd forgotten about it.

Her attention had been riveted on his face. Those liquid chocolate eyes. The way his hands moved when he talked. And that grin. That damned grin that even now, ten years later, could still cause an odd quiver in her heart.

"What happened to you?" She gestured to the cane.

He shook his head. "Just a little knee surgery. Nothing big."

Once again, she got the feeling he was holding something back, as if he had a bunch of secrets tucked in his back pocket. The Nate she'd known years ago had been as open as a pool of water. But the Nate she saw today had become a darker lake, filled with depths she couldn't see.

"Does it hurt?"

"Only when I let it."

Asking more would mean getting close to Nate. Treading in the personal zone. She didn't want to go there, not again. It had taken her two years to get over their break-up. She didn't have the heart to go down that path a second time.

"As an aide, all you really have to do is help any kids who are struggling." Jenny turned to the board and began writing because it was too hard to watch him wrangle his way through the rows of desks. She knew Nate—help was a four-letter word in his vocabulary. She cleared her throat and got to work chalking the list of words from the books the class had been reading. "Anyway, our theme this week is heroes. You being here is perfect timing."

"Why?"

She turned, the chalk still between her fingers. "Because you're the definition of a hero."

Nate shook his head. "Not in my Webster's." He jerked away, the cane rapping against the tile.

"Nate, what do you mean by—"

"Hi, Miss Wright," Jimmy Brooks said. "My mom dropped me off early. Again." The wiry blond boy disappeared behind the coatroom wall, then poked his head out. "Hey, who are you?" He pointed at Nate.

"Jimmy, this is Master Sergeant Dole. He's going to be with our class this week."

Jimmy dropped his backpack to the floor. His eyes widened. "You're in the army? Like a G.I. Joe?"

"I'm not—" Nate began.

"Mr. Dole is a Marine," Jenny explained before turning to Nate. "Sorry, I didn't mean to interrupt you."

"That's, ah, exactly what I was going to say anyway." Something flickered in his eyes—a shadow passing through—but then it was gone.

"How many people have you shot? Can I see your gun?" Jimmy circled around Nate, rat-a-tatting the questions.

"Later." Jenny said, bending down to the boy's level to get his attention. "Right now, you need to put your book bag away and start your morning work. Sergeant Dole will be here all week. You can talk to him later."

"But—"

Jenny put up a finger. "I said later. And no questions about shooting people."

"Aw, Miss Wright. You're no fun." Jimmy trudged off, muttering about how the class finally had someone cool and the teacher had made it all uncool.

She glanced at Nate and caught him watching her, a bemused expression on his face. Unbidden, the corners of her lips turned up into a smile. His brown gaze linked with hers, and something fluttered deep inside her. Something she'd thought she'd left in the past, like the photo album tucked under her bed.

Before Jenny could consider what that *something* could be, the bell rang and the other children entered the room like gaggles of baby geese, talking and laughing, poking and prodding, complaining and shouting. Each stopped and stared when they noticed Nate, then started up a sea of whispers in the coatroom.

"As soon as you all take your seats and get your morning work done, I'll tell you about our visitor," Jenny called over the clamor. Focus on the class, not Nate. And maybe that quivering in her gut would stop.

The children nearly knocked each other over trying to get to their desks. Pencils flew across papers faster than cars zipping around the Indy 500 raceway. Like dominoes in reverse, one hand after the other shot up into the air, signaling they were done.

"If I'd known a visitor would get you all to work this hard, I would have brought one in a lot sooner," she said, laughing as she collected their papers. She waved Nate up to the front of the room. "Class, this is Master Sergeant Nathaniel Dole. He grew up in Mercy and even went to this school. He's a Marine and he's visiting our class this week, as part of our reading project on heroes."

There were several exclamations of "Cool!" from the back of the room, a couple of yawns and several whispers between the children.

"I'm sure you all have questions for Sergeant Dole. We'll do a brief question-and-answer period today and maybe another one tomorrow. Now, who has a question?"

A dozen hands reached upward, fingers wiggling. Jenny laughed and gave Nate's shoulder a pat. "You're on," she whispered.

Nate got to his feet and eyed the crowd. "What do I do?" he whispered to her."Just be honest. If there's one thing a kid can spot from fifty paces, it's an adult telling a lie. No gory stories, of course, but you can tell them the truth. The goal here is to get them more interested in heroes so they'll want to read about them, too."

Nate shook his head. She had him confused with the man he used to be. "I'm not the right man for that."

"You're perfect." Jenny gave Nate a long, slow smile that ricocheted through him with the force of a hurricane wind. "The one thing you always did well was be a Marine."

If she only knew, he thought, *how right she was.*

He wasn't a Marine anymore, not the kind he'd dreamed of being. And thanks to the bullet that had torn through his knee, he never would be again.

Jenny walked over to her desk, leaving Nate to face the class alone. He pointed first to a little girl with blond hair who seemed to have a continual sniffle. "What's your question?"She dabbed at her nose with a crumpled tissue. "What's a Marine do?"He drew himself up and gave her a nod. "Good question. The grunts are the first ones into the hot spots. For instance, we'd take a beachhead with an amphibious assault and cordon off an LZ, then..." His voice trailed off as he noticed the furrowed brows surrounding him. "Uh, we go in first when there's a war and make a safe place for planes to land the other troops." He pointed next to a small boy with glasses.

"What happened to your leg? How come you got to have a cane?"

"I, ah, had some knee surgery." Not exactly a lie. Not quite the truth, either, but there were some things he wasn't ready to talk about, Jenny's advice about being honest be damned.

"Where's your gun?" Jimmy interrupted, before he could be called on.

"I don't carry it when I'm not on duty." He pointed to a girl in the back row who had her hair in twin pigtails. His mother, he remembered, had always done his sister's hair like that.

For a second, he felt a pang at not having seen Katie since he came home. He missed her and his brothers—Jack, Luke, Mark. All were married now, settled down with families—nieces and nephews he barely knew because he'd been gone from Mercy more often than not.

He shook his head and, with skills honed over years of being apart from his family, Nate brushed the thought away. His mother had been calling and asking him over, but he'd made one excuse after another. He'd see his sister and brothers when he was ready. When he could somehow explain the man he'd become.

He was far from being able to do that right now.

"I'm sorry, I didn't hear your question," he said to the little girl.

"If you're a Marine, how come you're not dressed like one?" she asked. "How come you're not wearing your uniform?"

Nate's grip on the cane tightened. The muscles in his jaw formed into immovable lumps, as if someone had injected them with concrete.

The question wasn't a hard one. But it required an answer more complicated than he could give to a group of nine-year-olds at eight-thirty in the morning.

"I just decided to wear something else today," he said finally.

"Can you wear your uniform tomorrow?" Jimmy asked. "I bet it's really cool. Do you have a lot of medals and stuff?"

He'd *had* medals. Past tense. He thought of the dark-blue coat, once hung with ribbons and golden pins whispering of past deeds.

But now...

Now he didn't wear it anymore. It had been far too painful a reminder, so he'd stuffed it into the dark recesses of his closet. A few months ago, that uniform had been his life. He didn't have the athletic prowess of Mark, the brains of Luke, the business acumen of Katie or the focus of Jack. Nate thrived on action, adventure. And the only thing he seemed to be good at, since the Christmas he got his first G.I. Joe, was battling the bad guys—and winning.

Now that he wasn't wearing the clothes of a Marine, he felt lost, as if he wasn't sure what uniform he was supposed to wear anymore.

"Can you wear your Marine clothes tomorrow? I bet it's really awesome," another boy said.

"No." Nate's voice came out tight and strangled. He cleared his throat and tried again. "No, I can't wear it."

"Why not?"

"Yeah, why not?"

He cast a help-me look at Jenny. She grinned at him and stepped forward. "That's enough questions for today," she said. "It's eight-forty-two. Time to get started on our vocabulary words. Now, everybody copy down..."

While she talked, Nate scooted around the desks and made his way to the back of the room. He took out his phone and read the message that had arrived late yesterday. Whether he liked it or not, he had to stay in Jenny's class for the entire week.

After Jenny had left, he'd called his V.A. doctor, thinking the physician would tell Nate he had a good reason to go on staying at home and off his knee. But no, the doctor had disagreed, and when the story of Jenny's visit had slipped out, he'd ordered Nate to a week in Jenny's class as "therapy" for his knee. Whether this was going to be good for him or not remained to be seen.

Looking at the wide-eyed, eager faces around him, he realized Jenny had been right.

These kids were going to eat him alive.

Chapter 3

"I think I should alert the Pentagon," Nate said to Jenny after morning recess a couple of hours later.

She laughed, the sound of it as light and airy as clouds skipping across the sky. He had always loved the sound of her laughter. There had been a lot of things he'd realized he'd missed when he came back home, but none caused the wrench of longing in his gut the way Jenny's laughter did.

"Why do you say that?"

"You've got this classroom running better than a lot of platoons. I've never seen such organization, especially with kids."

She pulled open the door to her classroom and waved the children inside. Nate stayed on the opposite side of the stoop, providing crowd control. "You should see me the first day. It's all chaos until I get to know the kids and they get to know me."

"I bet you have a schedule and a routine all set before the first bell rings on opening day. If I remember right, you weren't the type to like chaos for very long."

The last child skipped across the threshold, followed by Nate. Jenny swung the door shut and latched it firmly. "No, I wasn't." Her voice had dropped into a softer, almost melancholy range.

Jenny's childhood, he knew, had been a topsy-turvy one. She'd never talked about it much, but it had been clear her flighty mother and absent father had made her young life unpredictable. Throughout their courtship, she'd called Nate her "rock," the one support system she could count on. With him, Jenny had seemed to let loose, live more for the moment, as if she trusted him to be there when she needed to come back to reality.

Inevitably, though, she'd always rein herself back in, focusing on work or homework or whatever else was more important then, as if she'd suddenly realized the consequences of being too spontaneous. They'd had fun when they'd dated, when Jenny had let down her hair and really let him into her heart and her world.

He remembered the fights, the days when it seemed there was no way to repair the damage between himself and Jenny, but he also remembered so much more. Laughter over nothing at all. Hugs on the porch. Kisses sneaked behind the shed. Teasing, torturous touches in the lake during summer camp.

"Jenny, I—"

She turned to him, her emerald eyes wide. Waiting. "Yes?"

Save for a slight maturity in her face and a lightening in her hair, Jenny Wright was the same woman he remembered. Her laughter, her smile, her eyes. All of it exactly the same, as if the past ten years had passed in a blink.

But *he* was different. And he'd be fooling himself if he thought she'd want anything but the old Nate, the strong, can-do-anything man he'd been. That was the man she had loved, not the shell of a used-up soldier he'd become. "Never mind."

"Don't do that. You were about to say something. Tell me."

He looked past her, into the bright and sunny classroom that so captured Jenny's personality in the vibrant wall hangings and the sunflowers decorating the bulletin boards. "I...I think Jimmy is trying to feed Lindsay a worm."

"Oh God, not again," she muttered and spun away.

Within thirty seconds, she had the offensive invertebrate back outside, Lindsay calmed, and Jimmy seated at a desk in the hall. "Exile worked well with Napoleon," Jenny explained, joining Nate at the back of the room. "And it works well with Jimmy Brooks, too."

"You're a genius."

"Nah, I just have a system that works for me. All teachers do." She glanced at her watch, then stepped away from him, clapped her hands and two dozen heads popped to attention. "Story time, children. Everyone grab a mat and take a seat on the floor. Today, we'll read together instead of having a silent reading period."

A few minutes of scrambling, and then the class had assembled in a circle on the floor around a small rocking chair. Jenny grabbed a book off the shelf and pressed it into Nate's hands. "Here you go."

"What do you want me to do with this?""Wear it." She grinned. "No. Read to them."

"Me?"

"That's what you're here for." She leaned closer and the scent of sandalwood wafted up to greet him. In the bottom of his footlocker was a box of letters that held that very scent, faint now after all these years, but still discernible if he placed them very, very close to his face.

How many times had he done that in those lonely years in the Marines? Those days after he'd lost her, when the only thing he'd had was a few sheets of sandalwood-scented stationary? Too many times, he knew.

He jerked himself back to the present when he saw her staring at him. "What'd you say?"

"I said, go read to them before they start a riot in the circle." She gestured to the group of kids, already starting to argue and tease each other.

He grinned. "Your wish is my command."

Jenny smiled back. "Now why can't all men say that more often?"

"Because we rarely mean it." He caught her chuckle as he made his way through the crowd of children, who parted like the Red Sea to make room for him and his cane to wriggle through. Once he was settled in the chair, he cracked open the story and began to read.

At first, his voice droned in a monotone, the cadenced speech pattern he'd developed after so many years in the military. But then, as the pages passed and the story began to grow more interesting, Nate slipped into the voices of the characters, adding inflections to the old man, high pitches to the shrieking neighbor woman and a deep baritone for the firefighter who all starred in the tale.

The children stopped squirming and talking. They perched their elbows on their knees and leaned forward, ears pitched toward the sound of his voice. When he reached the last page, several of them let out cries of disappointment.

"Let's thank Mr. Dole for his spirited reading debut," Jenny said, stepping into the circle.

The applause that encircled him could have been coming from Carnegie Hall. Nate shut the book. "It was fun."

"I told you so," she whispered, taking the novel from him and replacing it on the shelf. "You always were a ham."

The children got to their feet, replacing their carpeted mats in the pile and heading back to their seats. Jenny grabbed a stack of worksheets off her desk and handed them out, directing the class to write a short paragraph on the story and draw a picture of their favorite character.

Nate came up beside her. "I was not a ham," he said. Jenny laid the extra sheets on her desk and quirked a brow at him. "Who starred in every production put on by the Mercy Elementary Players?"

He chuckled. "I don't think playing the lead in *You're a Good Man, Charlie Brown* qualifies me for Oscar status."

"You loved it. Admit it. I'm surprised you didn't go into acting."

He let out a snort. "There's plenty of that in the Marines, believe me. Pretend the drill instructor doesn't make you so mad you want to scream until your voice gives out. Pretend the food in the mess hall doesn't taste like something left over from the Dark Ages. Pretend you don't miss the people back home so much you can barely sleep at night."

She toyed with the pencils in a white *Hug a Teacher* mug on her desk. "Did you?"

"Did I what?"

"Miss...people?"

"Yeah," he said quietly. "A lot of them."

"Miss Wright?" A little boy in the second-to-last row raised his hand.

She got to her feet and left her desk, as if she were grateful for the change of subject. "Yes, Lionel?"

"How do you spell *grenade launcher*?"

"Why? There weren't any weapons in the story."

"I know. I'm writing about Sergeant Dole instead. He's cool. I even got a picture of him killing the—"

"Lionel, that wasn't your assignment."

"Yeah, but I'm writing a story." He raised his paper as proof. All of the lines were filled in with neat, tight script. "And didn't you always say it's not so important what we read and write about, but that we're reading and writing?"

"Well, yes, but—"

"This is what I want to write about." He turned and replaced his paper on his desk, pencil at the ready. "So can you tell me how to spell *grenade launcher*?""Some interesting reading material for today?"

Nate saw Jenny pivot toward the woman who'd entered the room. "Dr. Davis!" she said. "I didn't hear you come in."

"Apparently not." She looked down her glasses, surveyed the classroom, then crooked a finger in Jenny's direction. Jenny crossed the room and met the principal at the door.

"What were you reading to these children today?" Dr. Davis asked.

"This is heroes' week. Our first book was about a firefighter who rescued a family." Jenny withdrew the novel from the shelf and handed it to the principal. The two of them moved into the hall, leaving the door ajar.

Dr. Davis flipped through the pages and harrumphed. "Then why are the children writing stories about war weapons?"

"They're not—"

"Jenny is an excellent teacher," Nate interjected in a soft tone, joining them. "She gets these students motivated and hasn't taught them anything inappropriate. The grenade-launcher thing came about because the kids heard I was in the Marines and one boy decided to write a story about me instead of the assignment."

"I was about to explain the right way to do their worksheet," Jenny said.

"I hope you don't think it would be fun" —Dr. Davis directed a pointed glance at Jenny— "to share war escapades with these impressionable minds."

"No, ma'am, I did not," Nate replied. "Miss Wright, in fact, kept everything away from that focus."

"Well," Dr. Davis said after a moment. "That's a relief." She handed the book back to Jenny, then left.

Jenny poked her head back into the room. "Class, continue working on your assignment, doing it the way I told you to." She gave Lionel a pointed glance. "I need to talk to Master Sergeant Dole in the hall."A few voices uttered the fatal, "Uh-oh" as Jenny shut the door a little more to block prying eyes and ears.

She crossed her arms over her chest. "I don't need you to fight my battles for me."

"Against Dr. Dragon Lady?" he said. "I think you could use all the allies you can get."

Another teacher came striding down the hall. Jenny lowered her voice. "Nate, don't come marching in here and try to fix my life like it's old times. I don't need you to take charge anymore. I'm a big girl now."

"I wasn't trying to do that."

"Oh yeah?"

He took a step closer to her, invading her space, putting a chink in the wall of invulnerability she had built up in the years since they'd broken up. "Yeah."

With that one word, the air between them hushed. For a moment, she was lost in the depths of his eyes, her heart racing like a hummingbird. He grinned at her, the same easy grin that had always made her melt. The smile reached his eyes, softening the hard lines put there by his years in the military. For a moment, he became the Nate she remembered. The Nate she couldn't say no to.

The Nate she'd—

Jenny heard the click-click of heels against linoleum and looked away. Dr. Davis was coming back around the corner, heading down the hallway toward her classroom.

Oh, no.

She considered grabbing Nate and ducking back into the room before the principal reached them—until she glimpsed a familiar pair of overalls coming toward her from the opposite direction.

Oh, God. The *Animals Where You Want 'Em* guy. He'd probably come to collect on his payment after all.

But no, he had something with him. Something smaller than a pig. And furrier, too. In fact, it looked a lot like—

A goat.

"Is that what I think it is?" Nate asked, his whisper warm against her ear.

"I really, really hope not," Jenny said.

Dr. Davis's heels clicked toward them from one end of the hall, the goat's four hooves clacked from the opposite direction. It was like watching an approaching tidal wave and being powerless to stop it before it took out the defenseless coastal bungalow.

"Hide me," Jenny said to Nate, ducking behind his broad back.

"Hide you? From what?"

"From the goat that's about to eat my career."

Chapter 4

"Sir! You can't bring that, that *thing* in here," Dr. Davis called. "Get it out of my school immediately."

"No, ma'am, no can do. It's too late." Ed Spangler stopped, gesturing behind him, grinning like a gold medalist in the Olympics. "We're already going to be famous."

If ever there was a time for the floor to open up and devour her, this was it. The photographer from the *Mercy Daily News* stood behind Ed, camera at the ready.

"What?" Dr. Davis sputtered. "You can't...you won't...*you wouldn't.*"

Ed turned to Jenny, who'd realized she couldn't hide any more from her fate. "Miss Wright, when you kissed my Reginald, it turned my business upside down and inside out. I haven't gotten so many calls since my cow Eloise ran down the center of Main Street with Larry Bertram's bull in hot pursuit, if you get my drift."

Dr. Davis blanched. Beside her, Jenny saw Nate suppressing a chuckle.

"This here is Miss BoJangles, my Tennessee Fainting Goat. She's harmless and cute as a button, but she has a bit of stage fright. If you could kiss her, too, for the papers, it might just turn her career around." He gave Nate a jab with his elbow. "Not to mention put *Animals Where You Want 'Em* on the map."

"I can't go around kissing every animal on your farm," Jenny said.

"Sure you can. Besides, this one's a real cutie." Ed gave the tan-and-white goat a little push so she was only a few inches from Jenny.

The children had crowded around the door of the classroom, poking their heads out and watching the commotion. "Kiss her, Miss Wright!"

That was the last thing she needed—commentary from the third-grade peanut gallery.

"Remove this goat," Dr. Davis said. "It's disrupting my school."

"I'd read five books to see Dr. Davis kiss a goat," Jimmy Brooks said to Lionel, his voice low but not so low that the adults didn't overhear him, too.

Alex snorted. "I'd read seven. Ten if we could get that cow in here."

Jenny shot a glare at the boys. She'd be lucky if she'd be able to find a job giving Yahtzee lessons at the community center when this was over.

Dr. Davis backed up a step. "Get that animal out of my school. Now!"

"Hey, keep it down." The man waved a shushing hand at them. "She faints when she gets scared."

Jenny's career was self-destructing right there in the hallway. On one side were the students, cheering her on to kiss the goat. On another, the photographer, ready to capture the moment and blast it all over the front page. Completing the unemployment line triangle was Dr. Davis, her face turning more crimson with every passing second.

And then there was Nate, who'd come up beside her, silently offering his support. He was a breath away from her shoulder, his presence both a comfort and a distraction. For a second, it felt like old times—her and Nate against the world.

"If it was me, and I was up against this enemy," he whispered with a tease in her ear, "I'd turn the situation to my advantage."

She turned to look at him. "How?"

"Use the power of the press," Nate said. Their gazes connected. A light bulb went off in her brain. She gave him a smile of gratitude, which he returned with one that sent a shiver of hot adrenaline through her.

Focus on the problem, not on Nate, even if Nate was part of the problem—at least the problem causing all the turmoil in her gut.

"I'll kiss the goat," Jenny announced. "But only if you also run a story on Dr. Davis and her *great* support of the teachers at this school." She stepped to the right, looped her arm into the principal's, and smiled big.

The photographer raised his lens and snapped the picture before Dr. Davis could protest. "Can you say that again, so I can get a quote for the caption?" He withdrew a pad and pen from his chest pocket.

"Certainly." Jenny repeated her statement and spelled their names. "Dr. Davis has implemented a wonderful program to help boost our school's reading scores," she added.

The principal's eyebrows arched in surprise. For the first time since Jenny had met her, Dr. Davis seemed to be at a loss for words.

Jenny had won that skirmish. Nate gave her a grin of triumph and it felt as if the hall had done a 360-degree turn around her. "You forgot something," he whispered.

"What?"

"You owe someone a kiss."

For a second, she thought he meant him. The anticipation of pressing her mouth against his for the first time in almost a decade roared through her veins.

Despite it all, she *had* missed him. His eyes. His smile. His—

"Miss BoJangles is waiting for her shot at stardom," Nate said.

The goat. He'd meant the silly goat. "Oh. Oh yeah." Jenny swallowed and bent down to the omnivore, pretending she wasn't disappointed at all. "You ready, Miss BoJangles?" The goat let out a "baa" and skittered back a couple of steps.

"She's nervous," Ed explained. "It's her first kiss."

"Mine too. With a goat anyway." Her first kiss at all in a long, long while. Besides the pig, she amended. Maybe that's why she'd been reacting to Nate's presence like a bee around a new flower. Yeah, that was all it was.

Jenny bent down, leaned forward. The photographer trained his lens on them.

"Kiss the goat! Kiss the goat!" the kids chanted again.

The goat's eyes widened.

"Yeah, kiss her," Nate whispered in her ear, and when he did, Jenny knew she was kidding herself if she thought the next few days were going to be a breeze. With Nate around, she was in trouble. Big trouble. She'd be better off spending the week on Ed's farm with Reginald.

At that instant, the lunchtime bell rang. All the classroom doors were flung open at once, spilling lines of children into the hall in a flood of noisy shouts and chatter, exploding in volume when they noticed the farm animal in their midst.

The goat started, then collapsed on the floor, rolling to her back, her four legs jutting straight up like fuzzy toothpicks.

"Oh, damn. She's gone and fainted." Ed let out a gust. "*Now* how am I going to get my picture?"

When the final bell rang at the end of the day, grade 3-B dispersed like birds heading south for winter. They were gone in seconds, sweeping out of the room in a flurry of backpacks and shouted goodbyes. Nate took a seat on the edge of a desk and let out a sigh. "Is it like that every day?"

Jenny laughed. "Pretty much. You should be proud of yourself, though."

"Why's that?"

"You survived your first day of third grade." She grinned. The sunlight streaming in the broad windows on the far side of the room glinted off her golden hair like a halo. She reached up and twisted it into a ponytail, securing the hairdo with a rubber band she snagged off her desk. In half a second, Jenny seemed to transform from organized professional into—

The girl he used to know. And love. A long time ago.

Whoa. That was treading on territory best left untraveled.

"Yeah, I survived," Nate said. He'd also survived his first day being back with Jenny. He didn't know which had been harder—the exhausting children or the continual push-pull in his chest.

"It does get easier," she said.

"Does it?" Nate slipped off the desk and crossed to her.

"Yep. I promise. When I was a student teacher, I went home many days and said I was going to quit the next morning. Then some kid would be there waiting for me when I got into work and he'd smile at me, or she'd bring me a picture she drew at home. And I'd stay." Jenny's smile turned wistful and she took a long look around her room. "Seven years later, and I'm still here."

"You love what you do. That makes it easier."

"It does." She straightened, drawing her attention back to him. "I bet you miss the Marines. I know you loved the military."

More were the words left unsaid. He didn't speak them, didn't negate them. That was the past, and that was where it was going to stay.

"I miss it," was all he said.

"Well," she said, moving to her desk and stuffing a pile of papers into a tote bag. "You're not much of a conversationalist today."

"Sorry." He grinned. "I am a guy, you know. My ancestors were lucky to progress beyond grunts and raised fists."

She laughed. "I'm not so sure the four-word sentences are a big improvement." Jenny swung the tote over her shoulder and grabbed her spring jacket off the back of her chair.

"Where are you going?"

"Home. That's generally what I do at the end of the day."

"Don't."

"Don't go home? I did just spend more than eight hours here. Remember, they don't pay overtime to teachers." She chuckled. "I've got papers to grade, a quiz on Lewis and Clark to write up, a health *and* a science lesson to develop —"

"Forget it." He put up a hand to head off her protests. "Not forever. Just for today. Come with me. Go to dinner. Walk in the park."

She blinked. "Are you serious?"

Was he? Hadn't he five seconds ago vowed to stay uninvolved?

He looked again at the bag in her hands, the coat on her arm, and in that second knew that if she walked out the door and left him, it would be too easy to slip back into the man who'd spent his days warming the sofa cushions.

"Yeah, I'm serious."

"I have a lot to do. The class..." She shook her head and bit her lip. "No. I'm not going to finish that sentence. You're right. I never take time off. I never go out to dinner.

You've made me an offer I can't—and won't—refuse. So, I'll go with you, on one condition."

"What's that?"

"You help me come up with a killer idea for health for tomorrow and a science project that will wow the kids on Friday and I'll be yours the rest of the day."

"Now that's an offer *I* can't refuse," Nate said, following her out of the classroom. "I take it anything that blows up, stinks, or attracts wild animals is out?"

She chuckled as she shut off the lights and locked the door. "Yeah, I'd say so."

"Pity." They began walking together toward the exit of the building, their steps falling into a matched pattern, as if they did this every day. The image of them chatting and leaving the same place—then returning together in the morning—flitted through his mind.

Nope. Not going to go there. This was a temporary assignment. Nothing more. "Remember Miss Marchand's biology class?" he said, if only to bring up the least sexy thing he could think of.

"I remember studying my brains out every night, trying to pass."

"And studying with me because I was better at it than you."

She cast him a sideways glance, an eyebrow arched. "You weren't all that focused on biology when we studied together, if I remember right."

"That's because I had the hottest girl in Mercy High as my study partner."

"I can't blame you for a lack of concentration, then." She gave him a smile he could have considered flirtatious.

"And studying you could be considered biology."

She laughed. "Not the flora and fauna kind."

"Oh, I thought about flora."

"You thought about taking me up to Makeout Hill with a blanket and a Maroon 5 CD."

"Hey, that was communing with nature." He grinned. "And you."

"Not exactly the kind of nature Miss Marchand had in mind for our homework assignments."

"You're right about that."

In a few steps and a handful of sentences, they'd fallen into the repartee they'd shared before, as natural as putting on a pair of shoes he'd had in the back of his closet. It felt good. But also scary. As if the shoes weren't quite the right ones anymore, and yet he still didn't want to give them up.

They weren't a couple anymore. And he didn't have any business trying to take them along that road.

"You know, Miss Marchand still goes around town bragging about 'those Dole boys' and how you, Jack, Mark and Luke were the only ones ever to ace her class." Jenny hit the bright sunshine of the parking lot and turned her face upward to greet the light. As long as he'd known her, Jenny had been a woman who always took a moment to greet the outdoors when she reached it. He, on the other hand, had always been too busy, in too much of a hurry to do more than hop on the next helicopter, flying off on the next mission.

Besides, enjoying sunshine and smelling the roses wasn't exactly cool in the Marines.

Nate laughed. "I doubt that. Poor Katie. She tried hard, but biology wasn't her forte."

"You'd never know it to look at your sister today." Jenny gave him a grin as they crossed the still-full lot. Apparently the teachers at Mercy Elementary were used to putting in a few hours after the children went home. Across the fields behind them, older children were at soccer practice, running up and down between the goals after the elusive black-and-white ball. "Her twins are three now and I think she and Matt are thinking about having another, if they haven't already started trying."

He thought back to what the last letter from home had said about Katie. "My mother said Katie vowed after the twins she'd never have another kid again."

"Apparently Matt can be pretty persuasive." Jenny smiled. "And those twins, once they got past the terrible twos, are the cutest things on earth. Who wouldn't want to have more like that?"

"Not me." He put up his hands. "I'm not kid material, especially after today."

"I disagree. You did great today. The kids really enjoyed having you there. You'd be even better with your own, I'm sure."

"I handle M-16s for a living, Jenny. Not baby wipes and diaper-rash creams."

"Same difference. Just different battles." She turned toward him again and grinned.

When she smiled at him like that, he thought anything was possible. Even that.

He cleared his throat and worked on making his way over the rough asphalt with his cane. He ignored the throbbing in his knee that told him he'd be better off sitting down instead of moving. "That's what my brothers say. Mark and Claire have a baby now, and I hear Luke and Anita are having fun raising their new son even though Emily's officially a teenager."

"You hear?"

Damn. Jenny didn't miss a thing. How had he let that slip by? "I ah, haven't talked to Luke recently." Or Mark or Jack or Katie or even his parents. But he didn't add those details.

"But haven't you been in town for a while?"

"I've been busy. Stuff for my knee." He waved the cane for evidence.

She gave him a dubious look but didn't ask any more. "I'm looking forward to the walk. The weather's nice. I don't get outside for more than a couple of recesses a day and I really miss the outdoors."

"You sound like a hermit."

She laughed. "Far from it. Just your typical busy teacher. Too much to do. Not enough hours. If I'm playing hooky, I might as well do it right." She unlocked the door of an older red Chevy Malibu and dropped her tote bag onto the passenger's seat, then shut the door and locked it again. "There, I'm officially free. For a few hours at least."

"What about Lewis and Clark?"

She waved a hand. "Ah, they're dead. They don't mind waiting for me."

He laughed. He couldn't remember the last time he had laughed this much in one day. It had to have been years ago. Certainly not in the past few months. Not in the weeks since his knee had been blown apart by enemy fire and he'd been left half the man he used to be.

"Oh wait," Jenny said. "I forgot. Your knee. Have you changed your mind about walking? Would you rather drive?"

The pain he'd felt a minute ago didn't seem so bad anymore. Not with her beside him, her face filled with concern. "Actually, my doctor would give you a standing ovation for helping me work it. I haven't been the most cooperative rehab patient."

"You? I find that hard to believe." She chuckled.

"You know me. I don't take direction well."

"You redefine being in charge, Nate."

He echoed her laughter. "Nothing like a day in a third-grade classroom to remind me how little I control."

They turned out of the school drive and took a right onto Clark Street. "Aw, you get used to it. Run a tight ship and things stay pretty much in control."

"Save for the occasional worm in someone's hair." The sun was warm, the weather in the high sixties, a bit unseasonably warm for Indiana in late March. But Nate wasn't about to complain.

"Yeah, except for that. I try to avoid that kind of chaos."

"With more than two dozen nine-year-olds? Pretty impossible, if you ask me."

She shrugged. "Not if you have a good plan."

They passed a line of houses, neat and trim bungalow styles put here when Mercy was first formed. A few neighbors raised a hand in greeting as they walked by. "Always the same Jenny, aren't you? Organized, efficient. Chaos-free?"

"And what's wrong with that?"

"Nothing." They'd reached the corner of Cherry Street. Nate raised his arm to point out Katie's apartment, then realized Katie hadn't lived there in almost four years. She was married now. Living in the house Matt had built on the old Emery Farm property.

To Nate, time seemed to stop whenever he left Mercy for Panama, Columbia, Kuwait—wherever the government needed him. With a pang, he realized things had moved on and changed, all when he hadn't been looking.

Jenny had changed, too. She'd had a life. Without him. One that no longer even needed him to take care of her, as she'd made quite clear to him today. Maybe he was crazy for thinking that she could be his again.

They strolled along the next block, then turned left onto Main Street. "Not a lot of choices here for dinner, same as always," Jenny said. "Maybe we should have driven. We could have gone to that bed and breakfast that's out on the outskirts of town or headed into Lawford. For a real selection."

He grinned. "I forgot how small Mercy was."

"Hey, nine thousand people and growing. It's not that small."

"It's bigger than many of the places I've been stationed in. And the food's always been good, midwestern cooking."

He paused, leaning slightly against a telephone pole so Jenny wouldn't know his knee had started to flare up again. "My kind of place."

"It never was before."

He cleared his throat and looked away, down the short strip of downtown Mercy. "I meant for now."

"A pit stop for a little refueling before you go back to whatever war it is you're fighting these days, huh?"

He heard the familiar fight in her words. He could tell her he was out of the Marines for good and take that fight away. But that would mean opening up a can of worms that he had no intention of dealing with. Not now. "Yeah."

She paused a moment, as if assessing whether she should ask him anything more. Then she shook her head, readjusted her purse on her shoulder and gestured toward Marge's Diner. "There's our best choice for dinner, other than for the Corner Pocket bar and the Pizza Palace."

"They still only deliver on Tuesdays?"

"They added Saturdays, now that the owner hired a helper with a license." Jenny grinned. "Gotta love small-town life. No conveniences."

"And no hassles from big cities."

"There is that." She smiled. Clearly, Jenny still loved the town of Mercy as much as she ever had. He wondered what it was like to love something that much. To be that attached to a place.

"If you're hungry now," she added, "we could eat first, then head over to the park with dessert."

"Marge's is fine. And I'm always ready to eat." Already though, he was regretting the decision. There was one thing a small town was good at—making someone get involved. The intimacy, the familiarity. It all came back and wrapped around him like vines drawing him closer to the one jungle he'd avoided.

"I love this restaurant, even though it's just a simple little diner," she said as they approached the small diner, its bright-blue awning hanging over the sidewalk in welcome. "My parents, grandparents and I used to eat here all the time when I was a kid. It was a lot easier than cooking at home, my mom always said."

How many times had Nate taken Jenny here when they'd been dating? How many meals and sundaes had they shared in the four years they'd been together? She hadn't mentioned any of that.

She'd forgotten. Or wanted to forget.

Nate held the door for her as she entered. "How are your parents and grandparents doing?"

"My mom moved to Arizona last year after her new husband retired. I think it might be their last move, but you know how she is. My mother can't stand to stay in the same place for more than five seconds. It's a wonder I lived in Mercy as long as I did when I was a kid."

"Didn't your folks buy three or four different houses, just in the time I was dating you?""Five. My mother was never known for being a stable person." Jenny shook her head, as if she didn't want to revisit those years. "As for my grandparents, my grandfather moved to an apartment in Mercy a couple years ago, but he's a lot more reclusive since my grandmother passed away and he sold their Lawford house. My dad was his only son and when he died eight years ago, then my grandmother passed away six years later, my grandfather sort of went into a shell. Now, he kind of sticks to himself. Doesn't want to get out like he used to. He's got a dog though, and the Lawford vet said he should get out and walk him."

"Because the dog's putting on some pounds?"

"No, because Spike's been feeling a little down. Or at least, that's what the vet told him." Jenny smiled. "I think Dr. McAllister saw Grandpa was feeling down, more than the dog. Gave him a canine prescription that was actually better for the master than the pet."

"And has he done it?"

A waitress came up and greeted them almost immediately. She recognized Jenny by name and gave Nate a hello. She raised an eyebrow at Jenny's male companion before seating them at a booth along the side wall that faced the street. The waitress—her name tag said she was Jodie—left them with menus, returning a second later with full glasses of ice water.

"Not yet," Jenny said. "But I'm going to go over there later this week and get him out and about one way or the other."

"Always determined, aren't you?"

"I learned that from the best, didn't I? You were the most determined man I ever knew." She slipped the slice of lemon off the side of her water glass, squeezed a couple of drops into the beverage, then dropped the lemon into her drink and stirred it with her straw. "Always knew what you wanted and went after it."

Everything but her, in the end. How could he explain how important the Marines had been—hell, still was? How it made him feel, how it filled some hole in him that nothing else did?

"Nate Dole! Is that you?" Dave Brooks hurried over to their table. Without waiting for an invitation, he swung an empty chair from a nearby table over to their booth and plunked himself down. "How are you, buddy? I haven't seen you in what, ten, eleven years?"

Nate nodded and gave his old high-school friend a smile and clap on the shoulder. Still the same irrepressible grin on Dave's face, albeit under a chubbier face and thinner hairline. "It's been a while."

"So, you two back together? Or just catching up?" He arched his brows and gestured between them. "You two were always such an item. Surprised you didn't marry her while you had the chance. Now she's the most eligible bachelorette in Mercy."

"Under the age of seventy," Jenny added.

"Not to mention the prettiest." Dave gave her a grin.

Something Nate refused to name burned inside his gut. Dave was grinning at Jenny with familiarity, bred, Nate knew, of living in the same town all their lives. Years ago, the three of them had been friends. But now—was there something more?

"Nate and I are just working together this week," she said. "He's helping out in my classroom."

"You are? Hey, that means you've got my boy, Jimmy," he said to Nate.

"You've got a son?" Nate drew back in surprise. "You, of all people?"

"Yep. And a four-year-old daughter. Probably the last guy you expected to see as a dad. I figure my days as a party animal make me a stricter dad, though. I know how to outsmart the kids." He winked.

"Are you married, too?"

"I was. Five years to Kimberly Jenkins. But...things didn't work out. We got divorced four and a half years ago"

"Sorry to hear that."

"Yeah, what are you going to do? Now that I'm single again, picking's are slim around Mercy." He grinned again at Jenny. "I've been asking this one out for years, but she always turns me down."

"You know Lily over at the Corner Pocket has something for you, Dave." Jenny sent a thumb in the direction of the bar and pool hall, diagonally across the street from Marge's.

The other man's face turned a slight shade of red. "She's a good woman. Expects a lot out of me."

"As she should," Nate quipped. "You always needed to be kept in line."

"Hey, not as much as you, military boy. You always were the wild one."

"Not anymore. Those days are over."

Dave gave him a light jab. "Got old on me, did you?"

"Hey, I'm only twenty-nine. Not exactly ancient."

"Bumping up against thirty. That hill's getting closer." Dave grinned.

"Before you both start making me feel like I should go sign up for Social Security," Jenny said, "why don't we change the subject? I'm the same age as the two of you."

"Aw, you don't look a day over twenty-one," Dave replied. "Still the prettiest girl in Mercy."

Dave had said that twice now. Nate had to restrain himself to keep from beating his former best friend into a pulp on the blue-and-white gingham tablecloth.

"So, how's my boy doing?" Dave asked. "He giving you any trouble?"

"He's all right," Jenny said. "Nothing to worry about."

"If you don't count the worm he tried to feed to Lindsay today," Nate added.

"*Again*?" Dave let out a gust. "I swear, that boy is going to turn me gray. It's just been so hard on him since the divorce. With Kim having primary custody, I don't get to see him as much as I would like."

Jenny laid a comforting hand on Dave's. Nate tried his damnedest not to care. "He's probably just acting out. It'll get easier."

"Yeah. I'm sure it will. I'll talk to him."

"He's reading," Jenny said. "And enthusiastic. Those are great things. A worm here or there is nothing much."

Dave brightened and got to his feet, returning the chair to its proper place. "You've got too soft a heart, Jenny. If I'd seen Jimmy do that, he'd be watching *Fear Factor* reruns for a week to see what can happen when you play with worms."

"You are one unconventional father," Jenny said, laughing. "I can see where Jimmy gets his creativity from."

Yeah, not to mention his creativity with words around women, Nate wanted to add.

"Well, it was nice to see you again, Nate. Look me up while you're in town. We'll go shoot some pool." Dave gave him a handshake. With a final wave, Dave left.

Jenny dipped her head to study her menu. "Imagine him saying that about us being together again."

"Yeah, that's a crazy idea."

"Insane."

"So," Nate said, toying with his straw. "You seeing anyone?"

"We are *not* having this conversation."

"Why not?"

She lowered the menu and met his gaze head-on. "Because I've been down that road with you once before, Nate. I know all the bumps and all the scenic views. I also know the cliff waiting for me at the end."

"You're exaggerating."

"Am I? Oh, I forgot. You weren't here after we broke up. You didn't see how it affected me. You weren't here when my father died. You weren't here at all. That was half the problem, Nate. I was dating a ghost."

"I tried, Jenny."

She bit her lip and laid her hands flat on the menu. "We're working together this week. That's all. Then you can go back to shooting guns and taking out bad guys. And I'm going to go back to teaching kids to read. We're on different planets, Nate. Always have been. Let's just leave the past where it is, agree that we have a few good memories between us and make it through this week."

It seemed as if everything in Marge's Diner had come to a halt. Jenny's words hung there in the air between them, waiting for Nate to accept them. That's what he should do.

But following orders, especially when he had a good instinct about something, had never been his strong suit. Nate was the risk taker, the first one into the battle, the one the CO pulled his hair out over, then ended up pinning a medal on when the smoke cleared.

"I have a science project for you," Nate said. The words left his mouth before he could take them back. "You and me. Again."

Chapter 5

Jenny had never eaten a piece of chicken so fast in her life. Once Nate dropped the relationship bomb on the table, she knew the dinner had been a mistake. What had she been thinking? That he'd asked her out for a friendly little conversation?

The worst part was that she'd considered his proposal for half a minute. Maybe even a full minute. Then she'd come to her senses, turned him down flat and ordered a dish of chicken parmigiana. As if everything should go right back to normal with a little mozzarella cheese and tomato sauce on top.

"What about launching rockets?" Nate said after a long moment of uncomfortable silence passed between them.

She looked into his chocolate eyes and thought he'd already done that—with his words and his mere presence. She didn't need any more of those. Not today. "Rockets?"

"For your science lesson. Me and the guys, we used to do it for kicks when things got slow on the base."

"I don't think Dr. Davis would want us lighting fires on the front lawn."

"Oh, you don't need any matches or anything. Just a film canister, an Alka Seltzer tablet and some water."

"Really? And it makes a rocket?"

"Yep. Nice demonstration of the laws of motion, too."

Jenny cupped her chin in her hands. "The kids would love it, but we're studying animal behavior in science and how the human body works in health this month. I'm not quite sure rockets fit in there."

Nate chewed, thought for a minute. "Then let's Heimlich."

"Heimlich?""Yeah. It's something everyone should know. Plus, you have that fake torso in your room. We could use that for a great health demonstration."

She sipped at her water, avoiding his gaze and the hypnotic effect the memory of those eyes could have on her. She was here to focus on her classroom. On Nate helping in her classroom. Nothing else. "That could work."

"Good."

She pushed her empty plate to the side. If Nate wanted to make her life and her days more distracting, she was going to do a little of that to him, too. Turnabout was fair— and necessary if she was going to keep her mind on work over the next few days. "And since you know it so well, you can teach it."

"Me? But—"

"You are trained and certified in it, right?""Yeah, of course."

"Then you're perfect. The kids will get to see a hero being a hero."

A shadow passed over his face and then, a second later, it was gone. He didn't say anything further, just attacked his roast beef as if it was the last meal he was ever going to eat.

"I still need a science project for Friday," Jenny said, introducing any topic other than them getting back together.

Nate pushed his plate to the side. "The kids have already responded well to animals. Why not—"

She put up her hands. "No way. I'm not bringing in Reginald or Miss BoJangles again."

"There might be something else you can do with animals that would be fun and less...large," Nate said.

Jenny shook her head. "I've learned my lesson there. Animals are way too unpredictable. It's like begging for pandemonium."

"A little crazy isn't bad, Jenny."She bit her lip and caught his gaze. "Sometimes a little is too much."

Jodie came by and started to ask about dessert. She took one look at their faces, then cut off the sentence, dropped off the bill and, with a sympathetic smile at Jenny, backed away.

Small-town life. Neighbors who understood every nuance, who knew when to offer a hand and when it was best to keep quiet. Jenny loved that sense of community, that blanket that had folded around her for most of her life.

Nate tossed two twenties on the bill before she could even reach for her purse. "Nate, this isn't a date. Let me pay my half."

"Just because I pick up the tab doesn't make it a date," he said. "And even if it did, is that so bad?"

She took in a breath and shook her head. "Nate..."

"Yeah, I know. I'm stubborn that way." He grinned.

She didn't return the smile. Instead, she rose, grabbing her purse from the booth and leaving a twenty on the table out of principle—and to send a message to him and to herself that dating was out of the question. One heartbreak in a lifetime was enough. Jodie was getting a very nice tip. "I'll see you in the morning."

"You don't want to go for a walk in the park? It was part of my promised evening."

She knew where that would lead. She'd already stretched her resolve to its breaking point, sitting three feet across from him, trying not to think about what it would be like to have his lips on hers again, to feel those strong, capable arms around her. "Sorry, no. Lewis and Clark are waiting for me."

He opened his mouth to say something, thought better of it, and nodded. "Tomorrow morning it is then. Me, you and Mr. Body."

Jenny turned and left Marge's Diner before her resolve could overpower her feet and make her turn back.

Nate saw Jenny go and knew he should let her leave. It would be best—for both of them.

But damned if the sight of her leaving didn't undo all his best intentions and have him up and out of the seat, hurrying after her as best he could with the silly cane and his stupid, recalcitrant knee.

He reached the sidewalk just a few seconds after she did. "Jenny!"

She turned around and stopped on the sidewalk. Good thing because he sure as heck wasn't up to running after her. Six months ago, he could have taken on the Boston Marathon without a lot of trouble. Today, a toddler could beat him in a sack race.

"Don't leave yet. Let's talk."

Her mouth curved into a smile that seemed more sad than anything else. "We did, Nate. You know my answer. It's not going to change." She took a few steps forward, meeting him where he stood. "We had a nice thing a long time ago. Let's just leave it there. A memory."

No, he wanted to scream. He didn't want the memory. He wanted the real thing. He wanted Jenny, back in his arms, back in his bed, back in his life.

But to get that, he knew what he needed to do. He had to say the five words that he had yet to get past his voice box. *I'm not a Marine anymore.*

Every inch of him still felt like one. The thought of adventure still quickened in his veins. How could he explain that to her? And how could he expect her to invite him back into her life when he didn't want the small-town, confining life she'd chosen?

Just then, Miss Marchand came down the sidewalk, right toward Jenny and by extension, Nate. Her little dog trotted at her side, on the end of a fancy leash with rhinestones running the length of it. "Why, Jenny Wright and Nate Dole," she said when she spied them. "Fancy seeing you two here. And together."

"We're not—" Jenny began.

"Nice to see you, Miss Marchand," Nate interrupted. Whether he could have Jenny or not, he was tired of hearing her tell everyone they weren't together. That particular nail had been driven home enough today. It was a continual reminder that he couldn't have what he wanted. "It's been a long time since I last saw you."

Miss Marchand looked the same as always. An imposing woman despite her age, Miss Marchand's bearing stood in sharp contrast to her loose-fitting floral dress and short curly gray hair. A plump woman, she looked as if she could be someone's grandmother, though as far as Nate knew, she'd never married. Probably because Miss Marchand expected a great deal out of everyone she met.

Miss Marchand pointed a finger at him. "You, young man, don't come home often enough. Worry your poor mother half to death, traipsing all over the world."

"I'm home now, for a while." For as long as he could stand Mercy and figure out what the hell kind of career possibilities there were for a former war machine with one good working leg.

"Well, good." Miss Marchand looked to Jenny, then to Nate. "You know, you're the only Dole child who is unmarried. Seems I haven't set my sights on you yet."

"Set your sights?" He looked at this former biology teacher, who had to be close to eighty by now. He hoped she wasn't thinking what she seemed to be implying. Undoubtedly, Miss Marchand could run faster than he could; she'd nab him before he could get away.

"I had a hand in all your brothers' and your sister's happy endings, don't you know? I'm not butting my nose in or anything, but I do like to call a spade out when I see one." She smiled at Jenny. "Or a heart or a diamond, whatever the case may be."

Miss Marchand couldn't have dropped a bigger hint-hint about marriage if she tried. Beside him, Nate saw Jenny blanch, then swallow and recover her composure.

"Miss Marchand, you must be playing a lot of euchre lately," Jenny said, her face bright and clearly determined to change the subject. "How are you and Miss Tanner doing in the Mercy Euchre Club? Beating everyone?"

"Don't you try and change the subject now. I'm an old woman, but not a stupid one." She bent down toward her little dog. "Isn't that right, Sugarplum?"

The dachshund gave a little yip in response.

Miss Marchand returned her attention to Nate. "I hope while you're home, young man, you revisit some of your favorite haunts *and* bring back some of those old memories." She cast a hinting glance Jenny's way, before bidding them a good night and continuing on her way with her dachshund trotting alongside.

Seemed half the town wanted him and Jenny back together. That was the trouble with small towns. They liked to butt in on personal business and make it their own. If people thought they could fashion a happy marriage out of two loose ends, they would.

Of course, they only knew half the story. They hadn't been there for the break-up; they didn't know what had happened to Nate in the past few months. As far as Nate knew, Jenny could even be dating someone.

But she hadn't protested Miss Marchand's obvious romantic machinations. If he were smart, he'd take that as a good sign. Of what?

Of a future between them?

Hell, if he were honest with himself, he knew that if it were possible, he'd have Jenny back in his life in an instant. Wanting her had never been the problem.

Keeping her—and meshing their opposite worlds—had.

"I think I need to find Miss Marchand a new hobby," Jenny said after the woman had gone. "She's been running around town with Miss Tanner like Mercy's version of a one-on-one matchmaking service."

The two of them started back toward the school parking lot. "Maybe the Misses have something there. I hear Miss Tanner had a hand in Mark and Claire's relationship, from what Mark told me."

"What she needs is someone matchmaking in *her* life. Then she'll leave other people's alone."

"Is it so bad?" Nate asked. "Her wanting to see you happily married and with a few kids?"

She turned toward him, that emerald gaze connecting with his, her eyes full of honesty and seeking the same in return. "There's nothing wrong with that. The only problem, as I see it, is Miss Marchand's choice. You were never really much for that kind of thing, Nate. White picket fences keep you hemmed in, remember?"

He'd said those words to her once, a long time ago. He winced to think of them now. But they were true. The thought of being in one place forever—particularly this small place—made him claustrophobic. It was why he'd joined the Marines, traveled the world, never had more than a few weeks or months in any one place. "Yeah, that's me. Made for the open range."

"Well, it works out in the end, then. Since we're not dating, you have all the space you want with me. *Except* when you're in my classroom." She grinned, clearly making an attempt at changing the tone from serious to light-hearted. "Then you're all mine from eight-thirty to three every day."

Her smile, that beautiful angelic smile he'd never been able to resist, brought a mirroring one to his own face and pushed the darker thoughts out of his mind. "Do with me what you will, Miss Wright, but just don't make me eat worms."

She wagged a finger at him, a tease in her eyes. "Behave yourself, Nate Dole, and we'll get along just fine."

On the surface, Nate knew it looked like everything was just fine between them again. Yet, something unfinished lingered in the air, telling him he might not want the white-picket-fence life, but he wasn't over wanting Jenny.

Not by a long shot.

Jenny arrived a half hour earlier than normal on Tuesday morning, more to get her bearings before Nate came in than anything else. She'd barely slept the night before and ended up blazing through the rest of her week's work in the wee hours of the morning.

The good news was that she was ahead for the first time in weeks. The bad news? She had nothing to occupy herself after school today. And tomorrow. And all the tomorrows after that when Nate's re-entry into her life would still be lingering in her heart.

"Miss Wright?"

Jenny looked up from the pile of papers on her desk. "Jimmy. What are you doing here so early?"

"My mom dropped me off again. She said you wouldn't mind."

Jenny thought of what might have happened had she not come in early this morning. The building had been pretty empty when she arrived, and Jimmy would have waited in the hall. Alone. She wondered, not for the first time, what had happened in Dave and Kim's marriage.

Not to mention what on earth Kim was thinking lately.

"Did your mom have to go to work early?"

Jimmy made a sour look. "She's meeting someone. Some guy. She says she loves him. Wants to make him my new dad."

Jenny's heart ached for the little boy in front of her, the cowlick that made his hair forever fall into a scoop over his eyes, the big blue eyes that had seen and been through so much in nine years.

Jimmy started to fidget, as if the scrutiny was too much.

"You want to help me put out the morning work?" she asked.

"Sure!" He zipped off, dumped his bookbag and coat in the coat closet, then ran back to her desk. Jenny handed him a stack of spelling worksheets and he took off, weaving in and out of the desks and dropping the papers like little bombs on each desk.

Dr. Davis poked her head in the room. "Miss Wright, may I see you? Now?"

"Certainly." Jenny turned to the whirling dervish scooting around her room. "Jimmy, you can start your paper when you're done handing the others out."

Jenny joined the principal in the quiet hallway. Dr. Davis swallowed. She played with the glasses on the chain around her neck. "You don't have any animals on your agenda today, do you?"

"Me? No. Just an ordinary day in third grade."

"Well, your version of ordinary and mine are quite different," Dr. Davis said. "Be that as it may, I need you to help me today."

"Help you?" Two times in the space of a week, the principal had come to her looking for help. There definitely had to be something in the air. Maybe Mercy needed to check its smog level because Dr. Davis wasn't thinking straight.

"One of the members of the state accreditation board, Howard Mr. Perkins, is coming by today to observe your classroom. Apparently he saw this." Dr. Davis held up that morning's *Mercy Daily News*. Splashed across the front page were two pictures. One of Jenny about to kiss the fainting goat, the other of she and Dr. Davis standing together in the hall with the farmer from *Animals Where You Want 'Em* off to the side. "He's...concerned."

Oh Lord. Not again. Damn that farmer and his penchant for publicity. "Dr. Davis. I had no idea that guy was going to come in here with that goat. I—"

"It doesn't matter. If they think we're running a zoo out of this school," she swung her glasses on the chain again, "I don't know what they'll do." Dr. Davis drew in a breath and seemed to refocus herself. "Please run your classroom efficiently and professionally today. And for God's sake, whatever you do, don't go unconventional on me."

Dr. Davis turned on her heel and walked away, her back stiff and her concerns clear in the heavy set of her shoulders.

Jenny returned to the classroom and began to put a plan into action. Nothing would get off course today. Nothing would run late. If anything went wrong, it would undoubtedly mean her job.

And that was a risk—just like the risk of getting close to Nate again—that she wasn't going to take.

Chapter 6

Nate headed into Mercy Elementary School at the exact same time as he had the day before, surprising himself that he'd actually made it here. Today, he'd opted to walk the five or so blocks from his house to the school as penance for his indecision this morning.

Ever since enemy fire had taken out both his knee and his career at the same time, Nate had found it easier to avoid than confront. When he'd been a Marine, he'd been the exact opposite, but now, without his uniform on, it was as if he'd lost the part of himself that knew how to battle.

He'd wavered for twenty minutes this morning, standing there in his cluttered kitchen, holding a cup of coffee and thinking how much easier it would be just to go back to the couch and not face Jenny, the classroom or, hell, the world again.

But a week with Jenny would do him good, his doctor had said. Well, it might, but it also opened up a barrel of problems bigger than he'd anticipated.

Enough of the self-pity. Enough of the woe-is-me-with-the-bad-knee crap. It was time for him to get over it, get out and do something about the situation he found himself in.

He wasn't going back to the Marines. But he still needed to eat and live, so he better damned well find something to do with himself—and soon. First thing on his list was Jenny's class, whether she wanted him there or not.

In the end, he went. And his sofa sat empty for a second day.

"Mr. Dole! You're here again today?" Alex Herman came running up to him, accompanying him on the walk from the front door down to Jenny's class.

When Nate looked over at the boy, he was struck by the height difference between them. Clearly, he'd been working with adults for too long. The kid looked like a ranch house next to a skyscraper. "Yes, I am. Remember, I'm Miss Wright's helper this week."

"Can you tell us how machine guns work and how you blow up all the bad guys today?"

"Uh, no. That's really not appropriate for a third-grade classroom."

"Oh, okay." Alex walked for a minute, then looked up again at Nate. "You sure?"

Nate chuckled. "Yeah, I'm sure."

He thought of himself at that age, and of his childhood fascination with cops, firemen and G.I. Joes. If he'd met a real Marine at that age, he would have been all over the guy, just as the boys in Jenny's class were, to tell him something —anything—about what it was like. Gory details and all.

"All right." Nate smiled, relenting a little. "If you're good today and do all your work, I'll tell you a few of my stories from the Marines at the end of the day, as long as it's okay with Miss Wright." The cleaner, tamer, G-rated stories at least.

At this point, Nate wasn't even sure if it was okay with Miss Wright that *he* was here, never mind sharing any tales of military life. But he'd cross that bridge when he got to it.

He halted just inside the door of her room. She was bent over her desk, her hair tucked behind her ears again, dressed in a long, light-blue dress that made her seem almost angelic. He'd screwed up yesterday by pushing her too hard, by thinking he could have back the one thing he'd lost.

Whether he'd decided to get off his pity couch or not, that didn't change things between himself and Jenny. She'd made that clear last night and he knew, if he pushed her too hard, he'd only push her away. He'd be best off remembering that and sticking to the task at hand.

He noticed Jimmy at the front of the room, rearranging the books in the reading circle.

"Have I been replaced?" Nate joked, heading into the room. His knee was still throbbing from all the activity yesterday and the walk this morning, but he forced himself not to wince as he made the final steps toward a desk where he could take a seat.

Jenny's head jerked up and she turned toward him. "Nate. You're here."

"As promised."

"I wasn't sure..."

"I keep my promises, Jenny." *Now*, he wanted to add. *Now I keep my promises.* Because he didn't have anything else to do but keep them.

Alex had dropped off his stuff and was already front and center, eager to help, too. Jenny gave him a sheaf of corrected papers to stick into his classmates' folders, then gestured to Nate. "Mr. Dole, can I talk to you for a minute, before the class gets here?"

"Certainly." They left the boys working on their tasks and went out into the hall. Around them, the buzz of morning activity had already started as children made their way down the hall to their homerooms.

"I want to talk to you about today." She tucked her hair behind her ear and took in a breath. He knew, from the movement, that she was nervous. Because of him? Or something else? "There's a member of the accreditation board coming here today to observe my classroom and a few others. I need everything to be perfect."

"As perfect as things can be in third grade."

"That means no funny business." She eyed him.

"You can trust me. Here, at least."

Jenny let out a breath and bit her lip. "That's another thing I wanted to talk to you about. Last night—"

"Don't," he said. "Don't say it again."

"I think it needs to be said, don't you? I can see it in your eyes. You still want to try that experiment of us dating again."

"And what's wrong with that?" He lowered his voice as the hall began to fill with children. "Are you telling me you aren't interested in me anymore? Not at all?"

"No." But she looked away when she said the word.

"Liar."

"Do you remember why we broke up, Nate?" Her voice was low, too, nearly a whisper in the humming, busy hallway. "Because we were from totally different worlds. We wanted completely different things. If you can tell me that's changed, that you want to settle down in Mercy and make this your life, then maybe I'll change my mind."

He leaned against the wall, crossing his arms over his chest and giving his knee a break. "Or maybe you've just made up that little condition because you're afraid."

"Me? Afraid? Of what?"

"Of getting involved. With me. Or anyone else. You're not married. Or divorced. Or dating anyone that I know of. That tells me you've either become a recluse or you're afraid of getting involved."

She frowned. "This is neither the time nor the place to discuss this."

"I agree. So let's pick a time—when we can be alone."

She shook her head. "Persistent, aren't you?"

He grinned. "My mother always said it should have been my middle name."

A trio of girls came chattering past them and into the room. They greeted Jenny and Nate, then headed into the coat closet to hang up their things. "I have to get back to my class," Jenny said, turning to re-enter the room.

"Later, Jenny, we *will* talk about this."

"All I want to concentrate on is getting through today. My class is the most important thing right now."

He wanted to ask why—why she was using that as a wall every time he got close, but he didn't have time. The bell was ringing, and the kids were streaming in. The day was beginning, and he had another six and a half hours with two dozen chaperones before he could have Jenny to himself again.

Two hours later, Nate and Jenny were at the front of the room again, this time accompanied by Mr. Body. As promised, Howard Perkins, the board member from the accreditation committee, had arrived a few minutes earlier and taken a seat in the back of the room. He'd spread out a notebook, readied a mechanical pencil and sat back, waiting for Jenny to conduct her class.

She cast a nervous glance back at Mr. Perkins, then returned her attention to her students. "Today, children, for our health lesson on the human body, we're going to learn about the Heimlich maneuver."

"Heimlich?" Lindsay screwed up her face. "Is that like that Einstein guy you told us about? He was boring. And he had that crazy haircut, too."

Jenny laughed. "No, not like Einstein. The Heimlich maneuver is a lifesaving technique that you do to someone who is choking."

Alex poked his hand into the air and started talking before Jenny acknowledged him. "Like when my sister had a big piece of candy and we had to call the paramedics and they came and—"

"Alex, remember we have to take turns when we want to talk. And wait to be called on before starting." Jenny cast a glance toward the suit in the back of the room. "Let's share at the *end* of the lesson, shall we?" She gestured toward

Nate. "Now, since Mr. Dole is certified in the Heimlich maneuver and CPR as part of his military training, he's going to demonstrate this for us today."

"On who?" Jimmy asked. "On that guy in the back of the room?"

Mr. Perkins popped his head up and for a second, looked worried.

Jenny cleared her throat. "Ah, no. On Mr. Body."

"Mr. Body?" Jimmy gave the plastic anatomy figure a dubious glance. "But he's fake. That's no fun. He can't even really eat. Or choke."

"Our goal here, Jimmy, isn't to have anyone come close to dying."

"Sure would be a lot cooler if you did. We could get that Rescue 911 TV show in here and—"

"Jimmy, get out your health notebook, please."

Jimmy pouted. "Yes, ma'am."

Jenny cast a glance at the clock, then signaled to Nate. "Time to get started. We have just enough time for this before morning recess." Jenny hoisted the plastic torso off the table beside her and placed it on the smaller desk in front of Nate. "Mr. Dole, meet Mr. Body."

Nate put out his hand and pretended to shake the nonexistent hand of the faux man, who had all his organs exposed for demonstration purposes. "Pleasure to meet you. You're looking a little transparent today, sir."

The kids roared with laughter. Jenny gave him a look that begged him not to make the class too fun, lest Mr. Perkins find fun offensive.

"All right, kids." Nate stood and moved behind Mr. Body. "Let's say Mr. Body has just gotten one really big chicken nugget. And he didn't bother to chew it before trying to swallow."

The kids snickered.

"So now that chicken nugget, it's squawking in Mr. Body's esophagus." Nate pointed to the front of Mr. Body's neck. "And now, we have to get it out."

"Or Mr. Body's going to be one dead body," Jimmy piped up.

Nate bit back a grin. "The first thing you need to do is get behind the victim who is choking. Put your right hand underneath their sternum. That's this bone right here." Nate demonstrated. "Then take your left hand and lock it over your right wrist. Then you thrust upward. Like so." Nate gave Mr. Body a lifesaving thrust.

Mr. Body responded by regurgitating more than just an imaginary chicken nugget. Kidneys, liver, heart, lungs— they all went flying across the room in a shower of demonstrable body parts.

The pancreas spiraled up and over the students' heads and conked Mr. Perkins on the right temple. He jerked back, dropped his pencil and blinked in surprise, rubbing at the dent left by the errant organ.

"Guess I won't be on Mr. Body's list of friends to call when he needs a lifeline, huh?" Nate said.

That only made the kids laugh harder. Nate glanced over at Jenny.

She glared back. Apparently she wasn't very thrilled with the idea of a pair of kidneys on her floor.

Across the room, Nate heard the visitor's pencil scratching across his pad. Clearly, he was making a note of the event. The look on his face said he hadn't been too thrilled about Nate's overzealous Heimlich Harry event. The children, however, were still laughing. Nate had a fan club of twenty-five in the room.

And two who would probably be glad to see him gone.

Nate figured he'd start with retrieving Mr. Body's liver. Then he'd set to work on trying to get Jenny's heart back in the right place, too.

By the time the kidneys were back in Mr. Body's pelvis, Jenny could see the writing on the board. Her career was going to go down in a mess of discarded body parts and loose intestines. Howard Perkins had a sour look on his face and a long list of notes on his pad. All bad signs.

She glanced at the clock. "Time for morning recess," she said. "Everyone get on your coats, in table order, and line up to go out."

The children, still laughing at the Heimlich disaster, did as they were told with minimal shoving. Mr. Perkins followed the children outside, taking a seat on one of the benches under an elm tree, the ubiquitous notebook by his side.

"I'm sorry about the disemboweling earlier," Nate said once they were outside. "That's not the normal result of the Heimlich maneuver."

She let out a sigh. "This is not going well. If another thing goes wrong—"

"Jenny, this is third grade. Things go wrong. You can't expect perfection. You know that, I'm sure."

She wheeled around to face him. "On any other day, fine. But today, there's a lot at stake. My job, the school—"

"You worry too much. This was a small thing. It wasn't the end of the world. Mr. Perkins isn't going to recommend pulling accreditation just because Mr. Body upchucked his organs."

She bit her lip, and he knew she wanted to disagree but wouldn't because the kids were all around them and Mr. Perkins was watching from his perch across the way.

"Why do you have to keep such a tight leash on everything, Jenny?"

The tension between them sat in stark contrast to the bright, laughing world of the playground. "Since when did it become okay for you to come back into my world and start questioning my life?"

He paused a moment, taking in the halo of hair around her face. "Tell me this...when have I ever been out of your world?"

In her eyes, in the hitch in her breath, he saw and heard the truth. Never. She hadn't forgotten the years they'd spent together, the kisses they'd shared. The dreams they'd whispered to each other in the back seat of his Grand Am, parked behind the old Emery Farm property.

She hadn't forgotten and God forgive him, neither had he.

"I-I-I better go stop Jimmy. Seems he's got his hands on some bugs." In a flash, Jenny was gone, across the playground and about as far away from him as she could get in the schoolyard.

From where he was, Nate saw Jimmy presenting his insect treasure to Lindsay at the same time Alex came up and thrust himself between the two. The two boys exchanged a few words, with each casting glances at the pretty brunette.

Then, before Jenny reached them, the first punch was thrown.

Jenny broke into a run. Nate did, too, not the best run but one nonetheless and he skidded to a stop beside the fighting boys a second after she did.

"Stop it!" Jenny said, trying to pull the boys off one another. They ignored her, continuing their battle. Jimmy swung wildly at Alex, his face streaked with tears, hitting at anything in his path.

Nate knew the powerhouse of double nine-year-old male energy was too much for Jenny. He inserted himself into the scuffle and pulled the boys apart before one of them hurt the other really badly or worse, hit Jenny. "Hey, hey. Let's not fight."

"He started it," they both huffed out, trying to catch their breath and still look like the victor.

"What was this about?" Jenny said, hands on her hips. "You know fighting is against the rules."

"I wanted to show Lindsay the bug."

"And I wanted to show Lindsay my new sneakers. You got in the way." Alex sent Jimmy an angry look.

"Well, Lindsay is already off playing with Josey. Apparently you two fighting made her lose interest in the bug *and* the sneakers," Jenny said. "Now there's nothing to fight over. And I want both of you to serve detention tomorrow."

"But, Miss Wright!"

"No buts. You know the rules."

Alex nodded, accepting his punishment, and went off in the direction of the swings.

Jimmy kept the chip on his shoulder and scowled. "I bet Mr. Dole would fight for a girl he liked. He wouldn't let her go with some other guy." He glanced up at Nate. "Wouldn't you fight? Isn't that what Marines do?"

Nate swallowed. "Well, yeah, we do, Jimmy, but there are rules for Marines, too."

"Rules are stupid," Jimmy muttered. "All they do is get you in trouble."

Nate exchanged a glance with Jenny. He had to bite back his laugh, but he didn't see an answering sense of humor in Jenny. He saw too much of himself in Jimmy, and he was willing to bet Jenny did, too. That was probably why she didn't think it was funny.

Across the playground Hannah fell off a swing and started to cry. Jenny's face shifted into concern. "Go," Nate said. "I'll handle this."

"Are you sure?"

"Yeah. We speak the same language, Jimmy and me."

Worry about that particular alliance crossed her features, but Hannah's potential injuries won out and Jenny dashed over to the little girl.

Nate waved toward a big rock that sat to the left of the playground equipment, shaded by a big maple tree. "Let's go over here and talk for a few minutes."

Jimmy nodded and the two of them took a seat on the hard, flat surface. Around them, the playground was a noisy whirlwind of activity and shouts as the kids started up an impromptu kickball game, made good use of the playground equipment or just played a rousing game of tag.

"You know, Jimmy, when I was a kid," Nate said, "I was a lot like you."

"You were?"

"Yeah. I wanted to be the hero. I wanted to win all the battles, take on everyone who thought they were bigger than me."

"Did you? And did you win?"

"I took most of them on, but then Ricky Lincoln came along."

"Who was he?"

"Someone who taught me a very important lesson." Nate draped his arms over his knees and for a second, turned his face up to the sun and enjoyed the moment in the spring air. Just as Jenny would have. A feeling of peace stole over him, something he hadn't felt in a long, long time.

After a minute, Nate returned his attention to the little boy beside him. "When I was ten, I wanted a new bike more than anything in the world. I *had* a bike, but it was a hand-me-down from my older brother. What I really wanted was a bike of my own. Money was tight for my mom and dad because there were five of us, so my dad and I cut a deal. I'd save up half the money and he'd kick in the rest."

"You had to work for something you wanted?" Jimmy shook his head. "Man. My mom always buys me whatever I ask for."

"I'll tell you something, Jimmy, when you work for something of your own, you feel really proud. I earned that money and I bought that bike and whenever I rode it, I felt like a superhero."

"Really?"

"Yep. Because *I* bought and paid for it. It made me feel like I could do anything."

"Huh." Nate could see Jimmy turning that over in his mind. "Was that it? New bike, happy ending?"

"Not exactly. First day I was out in the neighborhood, riding my new bike around, and who came up but Ricky Lincoln. He was bigger than me. And stronger. And he wanted that bike."

"Why?"

"Because I had a new one and he didn't."

Jimmy's eyes were wide with interest. He was hooked on Nate's story, as caught up in the telling as a reader of a great book. He had scooted closer, his body turned to face Nate's. "So what happened?"

"He and I got into a fight. I was beating him, even though he was bigger. I was a pretty tough kid. Guess I watched too many action movies when I was little." He grinned, saw the blank look on Jimmy's face and added a bit of explanation. "He was like John Cena."

"Oh, yeah. He's cool."

"Anyway, Ricky started to cry. That had never happened before when I'd been in a fight. Granted, I hadn't been in a lot of them as a kid, but never had I seen anybody cry. I didn't know what to do, so I stopped fighting. I just kind of stared at him."

"Did he beat you up after that?"

"No. He kind of...gave up." Nate remembered how Ricky had seemed to shrink into himself, like he'd left a part of his strength on the ground with the fallen tears. "I felt bad. Really bad. So I asked him what was wrong. If I'd hurt him or something."

"And what'd he say?"

"It took him a while, because he was this big tough guy and telling the truth wasn't something Ricky did often. But after a while, he told me he wanted my bike because he didn't have one at all. In fact, he'd never even ridden a bike. Ever."

"Ever in his whole life?"

"Yeah. His parents were really poor and couldn't afford one either. But Ricky, he was the strong guy around school, and he wasn't going to let anyone know that. So he decided to try to get one by using the only thing he had—his fists."

"And when it didn't work, he gave up?"

"Yeah, but giving up kind of changed something in him, too. Made him more like me, I guess." Nate drew in a breath, his mind running back over those images from almost two decades before. "I told him how I'd saved up for mine by doing odd jobs and mowing lawns and stuff like that. And I offered to help him do the same."

"Why?" Jimmy's eyes grew wide. "I mean, he just wanted to beat your face in five minutes before that."

"Because I knew how he felt. I knew what it was like to want something that you couldn't have." Nate noticed Jenny had finished with Hannah and was standing off to the side, listening in on their conversation, a bemused—and slightly surprised—smile on her face. "And that summer, I taught Ricky how to ride a bike—my bike—until he had enough money to buy his own."

"You did? But weren't you worried he'd steal it?"

"Sometimes, Jimmy, you have to trust people. Even if they've done bad things before, sometimes they can change."

Jimmy shook his head. "I don't know if I could do that."

"Sure you can. You have a built-in truth-o-meter, you know."

Jimmy raised a doubtful brow.

"Everything you need to know about what to do and when to do it is in here," Nate said, pressing a hand to his abdomen. "All the right answers are there. In your gut. Listen to it and it will tell you when to trust someone and when not to, when to make up and when to fight."

Jimmy was quiet for a long time, digesting those words. "Maybe I should tell Alex I'm sorry," he said finally, looking across the playground at his former combatant, now toeing at the ground from a seat on a swing.

"Sounds like a good start to me."

Jimmy let out a breath, then heaved himself up to his feet, seeming older than his nine years. "I wish all grown-ups were as smart as you, Mr. Dole." Then he ran off, without explaining what he meant.

Jenny came over and took a seat on the rock beside him, smoothing the skirt of her pale-blue dress beneath her as she did. In the sun, she looked younger, almost like the girl he'd known in high school. When they'd been kids, they'd sat on this exact rock once and debated whether Mallomars were better than Three Musketeers bars. As Nate remembered it, Mallomars won, hands down.

"I never heard you tell that story before," Jenny said.

"It's not one I tell. When I was a kid, keeping Ricky's reputation intact was more important, at least to him." He grinned.

"I remember you guys being friends when we were kids. You were such opposites. It seemed so unusual."

Nate shrugged. "Now you know why."

She cocked her head and studied him. "You surprise me, Nate. I never dreamed there was anything about you I didn't know."

"There's a lot, Jenny. A whole lot." More than he would get into now, on this big rock in the middle of the Mercy Elementary playground. But someday, if she'd give him a chance, he wanted to tell her.

She opened her mouth to ask him something else but was cut off by another third-grade calamity.

"Miss Wright! Cole pushed me!" called one of the kids from the kickball game.

"That's my cue to get back to work." She glanced at her watch. "And it's time to go back in."

He reached for her hand before she could run off. "Wait, just for one second."

She glanced over her shoulder, saw the kids had remedied their own situation, and turned back to him. "Okay. One."

"What I told Jimmy is true. Sometimes you have to trust your instincts with people. No matter who they were before, you can give them a second chance."

Around them, the busy world of third grade went on, filled with shouts and laughter. The birds called to each other from the trees, seemingly annoyed that the tranquility of their homes was being disturbed by young voices. The world went on, oblivious to an old love that one person was trying to rekindle and another kept blowing out.

Jenny clasped her palm over their joined hands, the touch both warm and inviting, as if they'd made a connection. A flare of hope rose in his chest. Then she let go and stepped back, doubt filling her green eyes. "*Have* you changed, Nate? Or are you still going to leave this place in your dust and rush off to the far corners of the world, always the superhero?"

He didn't know the answer to that. He knew he couldn't go back to who he was before. But he didn't know who—or what—he was going to become now. "I don't know, Jenny. I can't make you any guarantees right now."

"Then my gut is saying not to take a chance on something I can't count on." She gave him a quick, sad smile, then left him.

Alone, on a rock. He couldn't have picked a better metaphor for his life right now if he tried.

Well, hell.

Nate got to his feet, grabbed his cane, and decided he'd had just enough of that. The self-pity fest was over. He sure as hell wanted to feel like a superhero again. In his heart...

And in Jenny's eyes.

Chapter 7

Nate had been right. Boy, did Jenny hate to admit it.

Mr. Perkins had actually found a little humor in the pancreas dive-bombing his temple. "Miss Wright, I think your class, though unconventional, has some merit," Howard Perkins said after the morning recess. The children had their heads buried in a math worksheet and Nate was busy setting up for that day's history lesson. Jenny and Mr. Perkins were standing off to the side, reviewing his notes from the Heimlich disaster. "That said," Mr. Perkins continued, "I'm concerned about the recent public events involving yourself and your classroom. That, coupled with the low reading scores, has me concerned that Mercy Elementary is worried too much about having fun and not enough about education."

"I assure you, Mr. Perkins, we are very committed to education. A lot of the fun things we've done have been incentives for the kids."

"A Tennessee Fainting Goat as an incentive?"

"That was an... accident. The goat won't be returning."

That seemed to reassure him. He gave her a nod and pushed his glasses up on his nose. "Glad to hear it. Though I do hope you can focus on more serious matters from here on out." He walked back to his chosen seat, again opening the notebook and clicking a new lead into his pencil.

Nate raised a brow at Jenny. She gave him a shrug that said she wasn't sure if things were going well...or worse. He sent her a surreptitious thumbs-up, then crossed to Mr. Perkins.

Oh no, Jenny thought. Here came Nate again to the rescue. She did not need him interfering, not when she'd just straightened everything out.

"Mr. Perkins, why don't you try something with the children today?" Nate said, placing a hand on the man's back and easing him up and out of his chair. "I'm sure they'd love to have another participating guest."

"Mr. Dole," Jenny said, laying the hint heavy in her voice, "I'm sure Mr. Perkins doesn't want—or need—to be involved right now. He's happy observing."

"Miss Wright is correct," the other man said, pushing his spectacles up the bridge of his nose. "I couldn't possibly—"

"Sure you could. The kids are just about to start their history lesson for today."

"What are you doing?" Jenny mouthed to Nate, giving him a pointed look that told him she didn't want him butting into her classroom again. Short of dragging him out of the room like an errant puppy, though, there was no real way to stop him. She had a feeling serving Nate with a detention wouldn't be much of a deterrent.

Nate gave Jenny a grin and a confident look that told her to trust him. That was the whole problem. Trusting Nate.

And yet, he had been a good addition to the classroom thus far. He'd worked wonders with Jimmy earlier. He'd enthralled the kids with his reading and his presence. Thus far, he hadn't done anything that made the situation in her classroom—or the pressures on the school to please the accreditation board—worse.

Save for the flying pancreas incident.

"Well, I always did like history," Mr. Perkins said, rubbing his chin. "What are they studying?"

Interest piqued in Mr. Perkins's eyes. For the first time that day, he cracked a smile. Maybe Nate's idea wasn't so crazy after all.

"Pompeii," Jenny said, stepping forward and joining the duo as they made their way to the front of the room. "It's part of a series we've been doing on Europe. Today, we're talking about the volcano that wiped out that city."

"Really? I like volcanoes. In fact, my undergraduate degree is in geological studies." Mr. Perkins shoved his glasses up again.

"Really?" Nate said. "That would you make the perfect leader for our volcano eruption."

"Eruption? Like...a re-enactment?"Jenny gestured toward a small volcano the children had made from papier-maché. Beneath it, they'd built a mini city from toothpicks and recycled milk cartons from lunch.

"Just like the real thing," Nate said, leading the other man toward the display. "Here, you won't need this." He laid Mr. Perkins's pad and pencil on Jenny's desk.

"What's the plan here? Blow up Mr. Perkins?" Jenny whispered, stepping back to Nate's side.

"I hadn't considered that." He laughed. "Actually, my idea is to teach your criticizer what it's like to be a teacher. And get him away from that little notebook of his for a while."

"Have I told you today how brilliant you are?"

"Not lately, but you're welcome to let loose any time you feel like it."

She gave him a little jab in the shoulder, then crossed to Mr. Perkins, who was standing over the Pompeii exhibit, ready to launch death and destruction on her cue. "The volcano has a two-liter bottle inside it. You can use a funnel to pour in the ingredients—"

"Miss Wright, I know how to make my own volcano. I do have a degree in geological studies." Mr. Perkins drew his shoulders back and thrust his chest forward, clearly now in his element. "I can mix the ingredients in the proper ratio and explain the physics behind the eruption to the children."

"It's just...you really need to be precise. Too much of one thing and—"

Mr. Perkins turned to her, confidence on his face. "I can handle it."

Dread sank to the pit of Jenny's stomach. Why had she agreed to this plan? If anything went wrong—

Jenny backed away to stand by Nate, both of them far enough from the volcano to save them, should Mr. Perkins get too overzealous in his recreation of the Pompeii disaster. The children, separated by an empty row from Mr. Perkins, had squirmed in their seats while the adults settled the matter and now sprang to attention to see what their previously silent guest had to say.

"First, let me begin with a history of the volcano, and the one in Pompeii in particular..." Mr. Perkins launched into a twenty-minute lecture on lava and magma. By the time he got to the actual eruption, the excitement of speaking on his favorite topic had him chomping at the baking soda, ready to wipe out the toothpick Pompeii.

"Be careful with the—" Jenny began.

But it was too late. Mr. Perkins, in his zeal, had quickly funneled in a mixture of vinegar, food coloring and a few drops of dish detergent, then begun spooning in the baking soda without regard to the chemical results.

Mini Mount Vesuvius took no prisoners in Jenny Wright's classroom. The faux lava bubbled up with a gushing force, spewing out of the newspaper and glue form, churning down the sides in cascading pink bubbles, and falling to the floor in a spreading puddle of destruction.

"Cool!" the class shouted.

Jenny gasped and dove for the paper towels. Nate bit back a chuckle and rushed for paper reinforcements, too. Mr. Perkins, eyes wide, watched the spewing pretend lava and reiterated facts from 79 A.D. "Imagine it, children. The people were going about their daily lives when this monster hit. Pliny, the historian of that time, wrote that the earth shook, and the sea swept backward, crashing back in on them with a tidal wave. It was incredible."

"You can say that again," Jenny said, keeping a smile on her face as she got up the worst of the gloopy mess with a pile of paper towels. "Class, now that you've seen what a volcano can do and how it wiped out our little city—"

"Not to mention half the desk and the floor," Jimmy added.

"—you can write an essay on what it was like to go through this, and survive it," Jenny continued. Her first priority was to restore order. Then she'd get to the mess— both the lava one and the Mr. Perkins one. "Not everyone died in Pompeii. Many made it to the boats and survived. Now, tell me your story and add in the details of the volcano."

Within seconds, all twenty-five children had paper and pencils before them. There was little sound in the room besides the busy scribbling of words.

Jenny tossed out the paper towels and took a look over her shoulder at Nate, who had finished cleaning up his half. He was grinning at her again, damn him.

"Well, that was a great deal of fun, if a bit...messy." Mr. Perkins looked down at his suit, no longer as pressed and neat as it had been that morning.

Nate had been right. Again. Mr. Perkins wasn't mad. He nearly glowed with joy at the experience.

"And the kids learned a lot," Jenny added, handing Mr. Perkins a damp paper towel to wipe of the worst of the lava damage. "You have a wealth of knowledge, Mr. Perkins."

He glanced at the class, still busy writing. "I'm happy to see them take such an interest in the subject."

She knew now what lesson Nate had been trying to impart when he'd turned the tables on the accreditation board member. He'd been giving Mr. Perkins a taste of Jenny medicine—without the kissing pig. She'd do well to take advantage of this and plead her case while she still had him on her side. "So, sometimes unconventional can work for conventional lessons, wouldn't you agree?" she asked.

Mr. Perkins smiled. "You have me there, Miss Wright." He picked up his things from her desk, still swiping at his suit with his free hand. "Well, if you can bring up this school's reading scores using some of these methods, then we'll give your school a second chance. I'm interested to see how all of this fun," he indicated the Pompeii project with a sweep of his hand, "stands up on a test paper."

Then he was gone, taking his notebook and pencil with him.

Nate crossed the room to her, shared triumph in his chocolate gaze. For a second, it felt like old times. Her and Nate against the world.

"We won that battle," Nate said, his voice low in her ear and setting off an eruption of its own. Every time the man was near her, heat coiled between them, awakening the sleeping memories of the times they used to share.

"But not the war," she said, reminding him, and herself, that there were other goals here. She shouldn't think about herself, her heart or the simmering need growing in volume inside her.

"Not yet, Jenny, not yet." His gaze met hers and for a long, long second, she wasn't sure if he was talking about the classroom or them. "But we will. Somehow."

⸺⁓⸺

"I don't know what you did, Miss Wright," Dr. Davis said, approaching Jenny as she and Nate were cleaning up the classroom at the end of the day, "but please do it again tomorrow."

Jenny blinked. Had that been a *compliment* from the principal? "I don't think I did anything different today than on any other day."

"You impressed Howard Perkins. He's going to give a glowing report to the board this afternoon after he returns. That's one in our corner. If I could, I'd give you a raise and a company car for that one." Dr. Davis grinned. Actually grinned.

Had Dr. Davis been inhaling from the school's helium tank? She looked happier than Jenny had ever seen her. "I'm very glad to hear that," Jenny said. "I hope this means good things for Mercy Elementary."

"You and I both, Miss Wright." Dr. Davis gave Nate a nod. "I hear you were also instrumental in making this class great today, Mr. Dole. Mr. Perkins said you were a 'wonderful addition to the classroom environment.' That's a direct quote, by the way."

"Just doing my job," he said.

"Well, I'll see you both in the morning." Then Dr. Davis walked off, humming a jaunty tune under her breath, a light step in her walk that hadn't been there a week ago.

"What was in the school lunch today?" Jenny asked, returning to her desk now that the children were gone and the chairs put up for the night. "I've never seen her this happy."

"Don't knock it. It's a nice change from earlier in the week. The dragon has become a dragonfly, I think."

She grinned. "You are terrible."

"I try."

Jenny paused, the red grading pen in her hand. "I want to thank you for what you did with Perkins today. You..." She drew in a breath instead of finishing the sentence.

"Go ahead. You can say it. I was right."

She pursed her lips. "I hate to admit that, you know."

"Yep. But I love to hear it all the same."

"Okay. I'll say it. You were right. A little help, *once in a while*, isn't bad." Jenny directed her pen at him. "But I don't need you fighting all my battles. I'm quite capable on my own."

"I noticed that." The tease in his eyes disappeared, replaced by something heated. "You've grown up into a hell of a woman, Jenny Wright."

She inhaled, before she forgot to breathe. "And you've grown up, too. Into more of a man than you ever were."

He grinned. "I wasn't sure you'd noticed."

She swallowed. "I noticed, Nate." Every second of the day. In her dreams at night. In her thoughts, anticipating when he'd arrive in the classroom.

Oh yeah, she'd noticed.

When they'd broken up, they'd still essentially been kids at twenty years old. Jenny, a couple years into college, Nate partway through his first tour in the Marines. They'd barely known what they wanted out of life then. But now, they were adults, and knowing what they wanted wasn't the problem. That, Jenny could see in Nate's eyes, and feel in the answer churning within herself.

Having what they wanted, without it hurting themselves or anything else—*that* was the problem.

"We've had such a great day, I say we go out and celebrate," Nate said.

"Celebrate?" That hadn't been where her thoughts were leading. Not unless his idea of a celebration involved lip locking and Makeout Hill."Let's go down to Sam's Sweet Scoop and split a sundae."

He meant ice cream. Not anything else. Jenny dropped her gaze to the work before her. If she were smart, she'd stay here and away from re-involving herself with Nate. They might be grown up now, but that didn't mean he wanted what she did out of life or that any of the problems they'd had nine years ago had disappeared. If anything, the problems had grown up, too. "I shouldn't. I have the math tests to grade and the essays to look over—"

"I'll help you." He grinned. "If you help me polish off a banana split."

She put down her red pen and looked up at him. "You sure know the way to a girl's heart."

"I remember what you used to like. Banana splits were your favorites."

He remembered. What other things did he remember? The way she liked to be kissed? The way she liked him to hold her? Her memories warred with the saner parts of her that told her going out with Nate only opened up an old wound that had never really healed.

"Only the chocolate and marshmallow parts," Jenny said, focusing her mind on ice cream, not the mind-melting thoughts of Nate. "I left the pineapple end for you."

"I think it's a good trade. Sharing an ice cream with you, in exchange for grading a few tests."

"You don't know what you're getting yourself into," she said, holding up the thirty-question math test as proof.

"Oh yes, I do, Jenny." But when his gaze met hers, she had to wonder if even *she* knew what she was getting herself into.

Sam's Sweet Scoop was teeming with after-school activity. The advent of spring had everyone out, ready to start indulging in icy treats a little early. Miss Tanner and Miss Marchand sat at one of the outside tables, ice creams of their own before them and one banana split on the ground for Miss Tanner's enormous Doberman, Sweet Pea.

Nate and Jenny made their way into the small bright shop. Nate held the glass door for her and let her pass through first. She brushed against his chest as she did. The touch of him against her awakened a hundred nerve endings and memories from years ago. Oh, she knew the feel of his chest. Her brain had never forgotten the pattern of those muscles, the feel of the hard ridges.

For just a second, she wanted to step back from her organized, scheduled life, to lean against his chest and let him carry the burden.

She'd done that in the past, and he had let her down by leaving her over and over again, then distancing himself emotionally. So she'd learned to take care of herself, to put everything into straight little organizational lines. Not to depend on a man, especially this man, who jetted off to the next adventure just when she needed him most. She wasn't about to change that now.

"Crowded in here, isn't it?"

So he'd noticed their close quarters, too. "Yes, very." He stood behind her in line, pressed in by the crowd of people anxious for a double-dipped vanilla cone.

"Makes waiting in line more bearable," he said in her ear.

Makes it unbearable, she thought. *Makes it impossible for me to think. To breathe. To remember exactly why I thought getting involved again with Nate was a bad idea.*

"Next!" the kid at the counter called, waving them forward, his white envelope-shaped hat bobbing on his head.

Jenny moved forward with Nate. "A dish of chocolate please," she said.

"Oh come on, live a little," Nate said. "Go for the whole shebang."

"I shouldn't. It's bad for—"

"For what? It's one dessert. Not a lifetime of bad habits." Nate turned to the server. "One banana split, extra toppings, nuts, and whipped cream."

"You got it." The kid turned away and prepared their order, swirling the whipped cream on top like snow on a mountain.

Jenny's mouth began to water. She looked at her lowly dish of chocolate ice cream beside the banana split masterpiece and hated to admit Nate was right. She hadn't had one of those in so long. Probably since she and Nate had last been here together. "All right, you win," she said. "I'll trade you."

"Oh, no doing." He picked up his boat-shaped bowl and held it close to his chest. "But I'll share. And I'll even feed you a couple of bites."

Heat quickened in her gut at that thought. Oh, that would be wrong. Very wrong. But so much more delicious than just the ice cream itself.

Nate paid the server, tucked his cane under one arm and picked up the second dish, too, turning toward the outdoor tables. "Ladies first."

"Let me get one of those for you."

"Let me be a gentleman and spoil you."

When was the last time a man had spoiled her? Heck, when was the last time she'd been out with a man, never mind let one take the lead? Months, she knew.

"Okay, I will. But only because my last date was so horrible, and I think I deserve a little spoiling."

They selected a table by the sidewalk. A bright-red umbrella shaded the round white table, surrounded by a pair of white wicker chairs. Jenny sat and took her bowl of chocolate. Nate pulled his seat close to hers.

"So who was your last date? Dave?"

She laughed. "No, not Dave. I've never gone out with Dave Brooks, no matter how many times he's asked." Was that relief she'd seen in Nate's eyes? Perhaps Nate had been a little jealous of the friendship she'd built up over the years with his old best friend. "My last date was with Gerry Herber, who teaches woodshop at the middle school. He spent the whole night talking about how building a birdhouse teaches teenage boys about life."

Nate chuckled. "That might be a bit of a stretch."

"Oh, he had more theories, like one about how a good hammer can set you on the right path. A bad hammer is bad karma. And choosing the wrong length nail for the job—"

"Will make for twice as much work in the end."

She laughed. "Yeah, something like that."

The spring breezes whispered between them, a hint of a chill still in the air, but not enough that Jenny wanted to go back inside. Birds chirped from nearby trees and people strolled along the sidewalk, clearly enjoying the taste of the next season.

"Are you ready?" Nate asked.

"For what?"

"For your bite of heaven." He held out a spoonful of banana split, chocolate sauce coating the cold vanilla ice cream. It did, indeed, look like heaven on a plastic spoon.

Her gaze went to his eyes. She suspected the bite of heaven wasn't in the dessert at all. Being here with him was a mistake. She was already wrapped up in him again. Thinking about kissing him, touching him...

Loving him. All over again.

Instead of doing any of those crazy things, Jenny opened her mouth and took the bite of sundae. As promised, it tasted amazing. "Sam's Sweet Scoop never disappoints," she said after she swallowed.

"Nice to know some things stay the same," Nate said quietly. He reached for her hand, clasping it in his own. "Jenny, I want to ask you—"

"Why if it isn't Miss Wright! Fancy running into you here!"

Jenny didn't need to turn around to know who was behind her. Ed Spangler. The *Animals Where You Want 'Em* guy. In a public place. With her. Again.

She sent up a quick prayer that he was here without an omnivorous companion and turned around, a smile plastered on her face. "Mr. Spangler. Nice to see you again." *Not.*

"I was here in town, going after Eloise again," Ed explained. "She is one determined heifer when she's got her mind on Larry Bertram's bull." He gestured behind him at the aforementioned Eloise, hitched up in the back of a pickup truck and looking quite unhappy about having to go home without her true love.

"I'll bet she is," Jenny managed. Beside her, she saw Nate smirk.

"I wanted to thank you for how gracious you've been with my animals," Ed said. He removed his hat and clutched it to his overalls. "Not all people like kissing a pig or a goat. But you, you've always been real nice to my animals and real patient with me. I'm afraid my antics might have gotten you in a little trouble with your boss."

"It worked out all right." She hoped. But she wasn't going to tell Ed Spangler that. All she needed was for him to show up in Dr. Davis's office with a baby chick as an apology gift.

"I think what you're doing with those kids is mighty admirable. Getting them to read and everything. And Reginald thinks so, too."

An endorsement from a kissing pig. That should carry her far down the unemployment line. "Thank you."

"Anyway," he added, replacing his hat on his head, "I just wanted to say I'm glad to see a teacher who ain't too fired up about rules and such."

Behind him, Eloise let out a moo.

"Well," Ed said, "I guess that's my cue to go. You have a nice day. And if you ever need another animal, you just call me, Ed Spangler, *Animals Where You Want 'Em*." He grinned. "I got a llama who's mighty friendly. You'd like her."

Then he was gone, riding off in his bright pink pickup truck at a turtle's pace, Eloise bobbing along in the back.

"A llama? Now that's one I hadn't thought of," Nate said.

"Don't. Dr. Davis will have a heart attack if I bring in one more animal."

"Aw, you're no fun. What happened to the Jenny I used to know? The one who broke all the rules and didn't care?" He moved the banana split in front of her and watched as she dug in, ignoring the uneaten dish of plain chocolate. "Remember the time you and I released those tadpoles into the goldfish tank in Miss Marchand's room?"

"And then had to fish them all out by hand?"

"What about the time we covered all the lockers in the high school with green construction paper for St. Patrick's Day?"

She swallowed the bite of ice cream and nodded. "And had to serve three days of detention."

"And when we went skinny-dipping in the pond behind the Emery Farm?"

The air between them stilled. The thread of tension between them, always there from the minute she'd seen him again, suddenly went taut at the memory.

The heat of a blush filled Jenny's cheeks. She remembered that night. Every second of that night. So many times, when she'd been alone, she'd brought back that memory, one of the ones with Nate that had been her happiest. When they'd been most in love and thought nothing could ever break them apart. "You're just lucky we didn't get caught," she said finally.

Nate shook his head. "What happened to you, Jenny? You used to be..."

"Fun? I am fun. Ed Spangler just said so."

"You *are* in your classroom, but it's like you use it all up there. And the rest of your life has no room for fun anymore."

She picked at the banana split but found her appetite for the dessert had waned. "It's easier this way."

"For what?"

"Just easier, Nate. I'm grown up now. I don't do those kinds of things anymore."

"What, no more skinny-dipping?" He seemed to tease her with his smile, but there was more in his words than he was saying.

She felt a prick of regret for those days but pushed it away. The last thing Jenny needed in her life right now was a complication. A six-foot-tall Marine was the biggest—and strongest—complication she knew.

"No. Not anymore." She offered him more of the ice cream, but he shook his head, so she got to her feet and threw out the remains of their treat.

He joined her and they began to walk toward the park, located just across the street. A few couples strolled along the paved pathways of the park, some mothers pushed their babies in strollers, a few kids ran from tree to tree, playing a game. But overall, most of the activity was across the street, leaving them alone.

"Was I that terrible to you?"

"What do you mean?"

"When we broke up. You've changed so much since then. I hate to think I was the cause of that."

She spun toward him. "You know, Nate, not everything is about you and me. Or a relationship we had nine years ago. Maybe I like order in my life for another reason. It keeps me on track. And maybe it has nothing at all to do with you."

"If it has nothing to do with me, then why won't you take a chance and date me again?"

She strolled along the paved pathway, barely seeing the new buds of grass, the fresh tulips blooming along the edges. The scent of new beginnings hung in the air, but not between her and Nate.

"Maybe I'm not interested in you anymore," she said. "Did you ever think of that? Maybe I'm not attracted to you. Maybe I don't think we have anything in common anymore."

"Really?" He took her hand, stopping her in her tracks, and brought it to his lips, but didn't kiss it, just held it there, her delicate fingers in his large palm, a tease and a tempt all at once. She felt like a hummingbird in his grasp, fragile and delicate, yet protected from the strong winds of life. "So if I turned your hand over," and he did just that as he said the words, "and kissed your palm, then kissed a trail back up to those lips that I have missed for nearly a decade, you wouldn't want one bit of that?"

She swallowed. "No."

He tugged her hand, drawing her closer, pulling her into his space. She felt as if she was on his territory now, as if she had lost her footing. "And if I said I was sorry and I'd been stupid for letting you go, would that make any difference at all?"

"No." But her heart told her she was lying. To herself, to him.

He stared at her, long and hard. She felt the sting of tears in the back of her eyes, but she wouldn't let them show. She couldn't get involved with Nate again. She couldn't afford another heartbreak like the one she'd had before.

Jenny knew, deep in her heart, that if she fell for Nate again, this time it would be permanent. No matter how much older she was now, she didn't have the strength to pick up the pieces after Nate left her a second time. And he would.

If there was anything Nate Dole was good at, it was leaving.

"Then fine. I'll leave you alone. We'll stick to classroom business only." He released her hand and stepped away. "Good day, Miss Wright."

Then he turned and left, leaving Jenny alone in the park with plenty to regret and the plaintive, lonely wails of one heartbroken cow in the background.

Chapter 8

Jenny sat in the small, tidy living room of her grandfather's apartment, sipping a cup of tea on Thursday night and told herself men were more aggravation than they were worth. The past two days with Nate in her classroom had been pure torture. He had, as promised, been all business. He'd come in a few minutes before class started, then left as soon as the day was over. When the children were there, he was all smiles and fun, but no more friendly to Jenny than her orthodontist.

She'd come over to her grandfather's house, hoping that seeing him would get her mind off the stubborn Marine in her life. If anything, her recalcitrant grandfather served as an even bigger reminder of Nate.

"Grandpa, going for a walk with Spike will not kill you. Or the dog. It will be good for both of you."

"I'm quite happy in my chair." Richard Wright settled himself further into his recliner, his thumb on the remote. In front of him, Vanna White turned letters with a bright, perfect smile.

"The Mercy Dog Club will be fun. Spike will get to make some friends."

"Jennifer, he's a dog. He doesn't need friends. He has me."

She rose, came around to the front of his chair and put her hands on her hips. "Exactly, Grandpa."

"Are you saying I'm not a good friend for my dog?"

She crossed her arms over her chest. "You think Spike gets a kick out of *Wheel of Fortune*?"

Her grandfather looked down at his Jack Russell terrier, lying against the chair, head on paws, eyes closed. "He can whine the letter *E*, you know. He'd be a great contestant on *Wheel*, if only Pat Sajak would let an animal on once in a while."

"Grandpa!"

"Oh, all right. I'll go. But only if you go with me." His blue eyes twinkled with mischief.

"I am not—"

"You want to make sure I actually go, right? I could change my mind halfway there and turn around. I am an old man, you know. Feeble-minded and forgetful. Could take twenty steps and get myself lost." He barely disguised the grin under his short white beard.

She'd been successfully blackmailed by a man nearly four times her age. "Well then, you're just going to have to wonder all night what Vanna is hiding behind the clue of 'Thing' with the letters T, L, N and E because I'm ready to go right now."

Her grandfather rolled his eyes but popped the recliner back into place and got to his feet. Together, they leashed Spike, who looked at his master with a question in his eyes when the leather lead was snapped onto his collar.

A few minutes later, an overjoyed Spike, a complaining Grandpa, and Jenny were at the park, where another dozen or so dogs and their masters were milling about while a couple of volunteers set up jumping posts and climbing games.

"Spike's not going to like this," her grandfather said.

"Spike would drag you over to the park every day if he could," she said, gesturing toward the dog. "Look at him. He's in terrier heaven."

Spike was, indeed, leaning toward the group. Her grandfather gave Jenny one more look of protest, but Jenny cut it off with a shake of her head and a gentle push in the direction of the Mercy Dog Club.

"I'm cutting you out of my will for this, Jennifer."

"I've already cut you out of mine for being so cantankerous," she said. Then she grinned at him and joined him on the path that led to the other pet owners.

Along the opposite side of the circle, she saw the Misses. Poor Miss Tanner was trying desperately to corral her determined Doberman, Sweet Pea, and keep him on the path. The big black and brown dog had other ideas—like squirrel chasing—and kept tugging Miss Tanner off the pathway and into the woods. Miss Marchand and the dainty Sugarplum strolled around the circle, navigating the crowd and talking with Miss Tanner on the odd moments when the dog allowed her back into the group.

A hole opened up in the crowd, allowing her to see the people on the other side of the Misses. Jenny blinked, then looked again.

Of all the residents of Mercy that Jenny expected to see walking a dog around the town park, Nate Dole wouldn't even have made the list.

But there he was—and he wasn't alone.

He was accompanied by a medium-sized mutt. The dog was a motley mix of terrier and maybe spaniel, its coat a muddle of brown and white shortish, wiry hair. Neither Nate nor the dog moved fast, mainly because of Nate's knee, Jenny figured.

"Isn't that Nate Dole?" her grandfather asked, gesturing across the way.

"Yeah, he's back in town."

"You knew this, and didn't say one word?"

"I didn't think it was important."

Grandpa raised a suspicious brow at her. "Jennifer, I know you too well. The things you don't mention are the ones that are the most important. How long has he been back?"

"I'm not sure. A few days, I guess."

"And have you seen him?"

She let out a sigh. Grandpa would ferret out the truth eventually. Besides, the entire Mercy gossip chain was represented here today and inevitably, someone would start talking about Nate being back and in Jenny's class. "Every day this week. He's helping out in my classroom *only*," she hastened to add, "as a kind of joint project between his mother and Dr. Davis."

"Grace? Why is she involved with something at the school?"

"I think she thought it would do him good to get out of the house, exercise his knee. So, Dr. Davis put him in my classroom."

"Because...you asked for him?"

"No. Not at all. It was a fluke. I didn't mention our history."

Her grandfather cast her a sideways glance, then looked to Nate, fifty yards away. "Seems that history still exists. You going to do anything about it?"

"I don't want to get hurt again, Grandpa." Since the death of her father, she'd become close to her grandfather, with him serving as a surrogate parent. Her mother had never been much for long talks, being an impatient woman more given to spontaneous trips out-of-state than heart-to-hearts with her only child.

Her grandfather laid a gentle hand on her arm and met her gaze with one filled with love and years of wisdom. "You can't live your whole life being afraid of getting hurt, honey. The more you try to control things, the more they escape your grasp."

Something an awful lot like tears stung in Jenny's eyes, but she blinked and the feeling went away. "We're here to walk Spike, not talk about my love life."

Her grandfather gave her a grin. "I am perfectly capable of walking my own dog. I think, my dear, you should go over and talk to Nate. You need that more than hanging out with an old fuddy-duddy like me." Before she could protest, her grandfather marched off, with Spike in tow, leaving her to either stand there, dog-less like the lone cat in a kennel of puppies, or do exactly what her grandfather had said.

That was the problem with older people. They had the upper hand of experience when it came to manipulation.

Jenny crossed to Nate. Only to satisfy her curiosity, she told herself. And because her grandfather was practically dislocating his shoulder giving her a hinting wave from his side of the circle. "Since when did you get a dog?" she asked.

"This afternoon." He grinned. "I stopped by the Lawford Animal Shelter after school and found Harry there, looking for a home."

"Harry?"

"He looked like a Harry to me."

She laughed. "I suppose he does at that. What on earth made you get a dog?"

He shrugged. "I needed some companionship. I'm used to living with a platoon of guys. Being in that house by myself is a bit lonely, you know. Plus, I needed a way to exercise my knee. Treadmills bore the hell out of me, so I thought this would be more fun."

He started to walk around the circular track marked out on the grass with some rope by the volunteers. Harry hobbled along beside him on the opposite side of his cane.

"Is there something wrong with him? He seems to be having trouble walking."

"He was hit by a car a while back. Dr. McAllister said he was hurt pretty bad and his leg never really healed the same. He's got a limp."

"Like you," she said softly.

"Yeah, like me."

Nate had adopted the one dog no one would have wanted. Because he'd been lonely. The shock of that hit Jenny in the stomach. In all the years she'd known Nate, he'd never, ever expressed any kind of inner weakness like that. Now here he was, letting her see inside and telling her he'd felt doubt, loneliness, worry.

He had opened up and let her see inside him. That was not the Nate she expected.

Had he changed?

"A dog is a kind of permanent thing, you know," she said.

"I know."

He didn't elaborate. Curiosity burned on the tip of her tongue. If he had a dog, he couldn't be going back to the Marines. It certainly wasn't something he could take on missions or leave at the base to be baby-sat by a bunch of grunts. She knew Grace Dole already had a couple of spaniels and doubted his mother would want another dog underfoot in her busy household. Finally, she asked the question anyway. "But...what are you going to do with him when you have to go back to the Marines?"

Nate's gaze traveled across the field, lingering on some distant spot in the woods. Behind them, dogs yipped greetings to each other, and owners traded pet pride stories.

"I'm not going back." His voice was low and quiet, almost inaudible in the busy park.

"You're not? But...but...it means everything to you. That's who you are—Nate Dole, the Marine."

He took a long breath, then stopped walking and turned to face her. "Would it make a difference to you if I wasn't a Marine anymore?"

She blinked. "Of course not."

Nate heard the conviction in her voice and knew Jenny was telling the truth. Had he been worrying himself over nothing all this time? Had he not known Jenny the way he thought? Or had he been too caught up in his superhero image to remember that she had known him before he was a Marine? That she knew the Nate he'd always been.

And maybe she didn't need him to be a Marine to be a part of her life.

The thought stunned him, rocked all the convictions he'd been holding onto so tightly and shoved them overboard into new waters. Nate took in another breath and looked into her deep emerald eyes. "Then let's get out of here. I need to tell you something."

They went to Nate's little ranch house, which was only a couple of blocks away from the park. Clouds had moved in, blocking the sun, and adding a chill to the late March air, so they opted to go inside instead of sitting on the porch swing. Nate lit a fire in his fireplace and put on the coffeepot. Stall tactics, he knew, but he needed a few minutes to find the words he wanted to say.

Jenny waited patiently on the sofa, Harry lying by her feet and gnawing on a rawhide bone. She'd offered to help, but Nate had refused. For some reason, he needed to do these silly little tasks on his own, if only to prove to her that he wasn't completely handicapped.

He came back into the living room, two mugs in one hand, the stupid, ridiculous cane in the other. He handed her a cup, then took a seat across from her in a wingback chair he'd inherited from his mother. If it wasn't for his mother, he wouldn't have any furniture at all. That was top on his list. Get himself some real furniture. Something that looked like him, not a mishmash from his mother's house. As much as he loved his mother, he didn't share her love of chintz.

He was glad he'd taken the time that morning to pick up a little, toss the old newspapers into the recycle bin and get his laundry into a basket. He looked less like a slob and more like someone who could have a little company.

Some particular company named Jenny. Maybe, if he could make things right between them, that company would be here every night and every day.

"When I was deployed in January," he began, setting his mug on an end table and ignoring the coffee for now, "our base was involved in a firefight. We didn't sustain a lot of casualties, but I got hit."

She looked at his knee. "In your leg." It wasn't a question.

He nodded. "The bullet did a lot of damage. Too much. My knee is permanently messed up. Doc said I'll always walk with a limp."

"But..." She looked at him and put the pieces together. "That's why you quit, isn't it?"

He rose and crossed to the fireplace, bending to stir at the fire with a poker. The embers flared when he did, flames licking at the kindling. "When I realized I couldn't be any good to the team anymore, I knew it was time to go."

"Nate, I'm sure there are other things you can do in the Marines."

He rose and turned toward her, the heat at his back. "Not me, Jenny. I was too used to being the rescuer, the guy you called in when things went wrong. I couldn't sit by and watch all the action and not go crazy."

"What are you going to do now?"

He shrugged. "Until you came along and got me off the couch, I was having a damned fine pity party."

"You? You were always the strong one."

His gaze went to the window. Outside, Mercy went on as it always had. A neighbor watered his lawn, an elderly woman played catch with her grandson on a pristine front lawn. A loose beagle sniffed at the trash cans put out for tomorrow's pickup. Life as he'd known it, from inside this house. "Even superheroes have a weak spot, Jenny."

Then she rose and did what he hadn't expected. She crossed to him, took his hands with her own and drew him back down to the sofa with her, one step at a time, accepting him as he was and bringing him into the circle of Jenny. There was no rejection in her eyes, no disapproval. Only the same steady emerald gaze he'd known most of his life. Something warm and content settled in his chest.

"I never knew," she said.

"No one knows. You're the first person I told."

"You haven't even told your family?"

"I've done a good job of avoiding them since I got home." He let out a breath. "I'm a Marine, Jenny. That's who I am. Now, to say I'm not one anymore, it's just..." He looked away for a second, collecting his thoughts, then returned to her gaze. "It's like I'm not me anymore."

Jenny smiled and reached up, cupping Nate's face with her hands. "You were always Nate. Not Nate the Marine."

"I think I'm just starting to realize that, after this week."

Her touch on his face was soothing, yet at the same time ignited something within him that he'd tried to tamp down for days because she'd asked him to, making it clear she didn't want to get involved with him again. But if that were so, then why was she here, her eyes looking into his, filled with concern...and maybe something more?

When he caught Jenny's gaze, Nate dared to do something he hadn't done in what felt like a hundred years. Hope.

He leaned toward Jenny, his palm over hers on his face, pulling her hand into his. "I've missed you, Jenny. More than you can ever know."

She began to protest. To hell with it all.

He cut her off with the best way he knew how. By kissing her. She could slap him, damn it, and it would be a well-deserved hit, but if he didn't kiss her now, and answer once and for all whether or not she still cared about him, he'd go crazy.

Because he sure as hell still cared about her.

She didn't slap him. She didn't pull away. Jenny only hesitated for a split second and then seemed to melt into him, as if his movement had broken down some wall between them.

She tasted of honey and cinnamon, like cookies he'd been forbidden to eat and then had handed to him on a delicate china platter. He inhaled the scent of her hair, the warm, fresh sandalwood scent of her skin. He wished he could bottle everything about Jenny and keep it with him for the days when they would inevitably be apart again.

Her mouth opened against his, a tiny moan escaping her lips and as if in concert, they moved closer, arms embracing, torsos meeting.

It had been nine years since he'd kissed Jenny, but it felt like yesterday and a century ago all at the same time. Fireworks exploded within his head. He wanted more; he wanted everything. He wanted her.

His hands tangled in her hair, in that gold silk, remembering all over again how wonderful it was to hold her. Everything about her felt the same, as if no time at all had passed since the last time they'd been together. She fitted against him perfectly, sliding into the space against his chest with ease.

"Oh, Nate, I've missed you, too." Her words whispered out on a breath. She kissed his lips, his cheeks, the bridge of his nose. "All of you."

He echoed her kisses, tasting her cheeks, her lips, the side of her neck. Nibbling along the one place in the curve of her throat where he knew she loved to be kissed.

She let out a gasp and pressed harder against him. His hand slipped up between them, against the soft cotton fabric of her shirt, cupping her breast. She felt like the sweetest memory he'd ever had, the incarnation of all those dreams that had gotten him through so many lonely nights and horribly long days in sweaty jungles and barren deserts.

"Jenny, I—" His words were cut off by the introduction of a wet, determined nose against his arm.

Harry.

Harry, needing something a little more urgent than Nate did right now. Or at least Harry seemed to think it was more urgent.

Nate, however, would beg to differ.

Chapter 9

A few minutes later, Jenny was back in Nate's arms and Harry was back with his rawhide. Nate had herded the poor dog in and out of the house in a flash, probably giving Harry a heart attack in the process of his lawn visit.

"I have a horrible idea," Nate said now. A devilish twinkle lit his brown eyes.

She laughed. "Then I probably don't want to hear it."

He clasped her hands with his. "Let's take Miss Marchand's advice. Revisit a few old haunts. Resurrect a few old memories."

"Which old memories? Specifically?" She narrowed her gaze.

He grinned. "The skinny-dipping one. To be exact."

"Nate! It's the end of March. I know the first day of spring has come and gone, but it's still only about forty degrees out at night. And the water temperature—" She shuddered.

"Not in a lake, silly. Even I'm not that adventurous." He lowered his mouth to her neck and whispered the words against the hollow of her throat. "In a hot tub."

She gasped. "You have got to be kidding me. Where would we find one? I don't own one. You don't own one and I'm not getting all the way naked with you. Besides, neither one of us has on swimsuits." She pulled back and wagged a finger at him. "And just because we're discussing this doesn't mean I'm considering this crazy idea of yours."

"Jenny, Jenny, Jenny, those are mere speed bumps in our plan." His grin widened.

"I thought you told Dave you gave up your partying ways."

"I did. Except when it comes to you."

When he said those words, deep and husky, something within her stirred. The part of her she thought she'd turned off after they'd broken up, the part she'd tried to tamp down with schedules and organization charts and filing cabinets. When they'd dated, life with Nate had been crazy, spontaneous and...

Fun. More fun than anything she could remember. Not the kind of unpredictability of her childhood, but a sort of combined impulsiveness that only the two of them could create together.

With him looking at her like that and his voice in that deep range only Nate seemed to possess, as if he had a radio band linked straight to her heart, she wanted those days back again. Just for tonight.

One time. What could it hurt? A little fun. Then she could go back to living her life by her watch and her calendar.

"Where do you propose we find a hot tub?" she asked. "And what do we do about the swimsuit problem?"

Nate's smile stretched from ear to ear and the heat in his gaze sizzled hotter than an August day. "We'll improvise."

And with that, Jenny knew she was in for a lot of fun—and a lot more than she'd bargained for.

***

"What happens if we get caught?" Jenny asked twenty minutes later. She stood on the concrete slab ringing Luke and Anita's hot tub, her shoes in her hands and her second thoughts doing somersaults in her stomach.

"Since when did you ever worry about that?"

"Since I became a third-grade teacher in this town. I can get caught on the front page of the *News* kissing a pig but stealing some hot tub time would not make for good publicity for my career."

"It's my brother's house, so I doubt he'd call in the local reporters. Plus, he and Anita aren't home. I already checked. Probably attending something tonight at Emily's school. The water is hot and all it needs now is you and me."

"It's cold outside."

He directed a thumb in the direction of the bubbling jets. "But it's warm in there."

"This is insane."

"Yes. It is. I agree with you. We haven't done anything this crazy since we were teenagers." He stepped closer to her, clutching her jacket in his hands and peeling it out of her grasp. "Which is all the more reason why we should do it now."

"I..." She looked at the tub, her sentence trailing off.

"I promise to be a good boy in there. Most of the time." He smirked.

"We still didn't solve the swimsuit issue."

"Hmm. We didn't, did we?" He pushed her jacket off her shoulders and to the ground. With it, her shoes tumbled out of her hands, landing with double clonks on the concrete. "You're wearing a sweater. That won't work in a hot tub."

"No, it won't." The words came out soft and breathless.

"Khaki pants won't cut it either."

"No, uh...they won't." She must have left her brain cells back in the car because looking at him right now, she couldn't form a single coherent thought.

His mouth turned up on one corner. "Then I guess you'll just have to go in your skivvies."

"That's playing with fire."

"I'm a big boy. I can handle it." He tossed his jacket onto a patio chair beside them, then took off his cream-colored polo shirt and added it to the pile. "What I really worry about is whether *you* can control *yourself*."

"No worries here." At least her words sounded sure.

"Really?" He undid his belt buckle, then slipped his dark-blue trousers to the ground and kicked them, along with his shoes, over to the chair. He stood before her in a pair of cranberry silk boxers and nothing else.

Need surged within Jenny. She wanted to touch his skin, to put her hand on either side of the hard planes of his chest, to press herself to his skin and taste what she had lost so many years ago.

The memory of them skinny-dipping in the lake a decade ago came rocketing back. The tease of the water on their skin, the seductive play of the waves, the slippery movement of skin against skin. And then finally, them sharing themselves with each other, ending the long months of waiting, sealing a love they'd thought would last forever.

She'd missed that feeling. She'd missed him. And God help her, but she wanted to feel all of it again, if only for tonight. His skin was prickling in the cold, but he waited, silent, knowing she was making up her mind.

There really wasn't a decision to be made. Her mind had been made up the minute she'd set foot on his porch last Sunday and he'd opened the door to her, surprise and joy in his eyes.

Her hands went to her sweater, and she lifted it up and over her head, tossing it onto the chair. His eyes widened, as they had that first day they'd met again, with the same mixture of surprise and delight.

He watched as Jenny slid off her pants and threw them to the side. She stood there, in only a simple lace-trimmed white bra and panties, a surge of desire running through her when his eyes darkened with an answering need. Then the cold air hit her legs and torso like a slap across the face. "Okay, whose idea was this again?"

"It's a lot better to hot tub *in* the hot tub than stand outside it and freeze to death," Nate said. He put out his hand. "Come on."

She took his hand and followed him up the steps, the full meaning of what they were doing quickening in her veins. This was wrong. But not so wrong they could be sent to jail. It was only...a little illicit. And for a woman who hadn't broken a rule in nearly a decade, that was enough to get her blood rolling.

Maybe it was just the company. She looked at Nate as he eased himself into the water, his face the picture of bliss. She wanted a little of that, too.

In an instant, she was in the water beside him. Warmth seeped into her skin, covering her up to her neck. Nate scooted beside her, wrapping his arm around her bare waist.

A searing flame shot through Jenny at his touch. The fabric of their underclothes seemed to disappear in the water; there seemed to be nothing between them.

"Comfortable?" he asked. His voice sounded low and heavy, as if he'd weighted it with gravel.

"Yes...No. Oh, Nate, this is..."

"Hot?"

"Yeah." Too hot. Too much to handle.

"A bad idea?" he said, as if he'd been reading her mind.

Hearing him actually voice her thoughts made her reconsider her objections. Only because she was so warm and comfortable, of course.

"Well, we are two consenting adults."

"And we're consenting to...?"

"Hot tub," she said. "Nothing more, right?"

He nodded, his arm still around her waist, the heat there hotter than anything she'd felt in a long, long time. "Nothing more than a little spontaneity."

Oh, this was more than spontaneity. This was a prelude to sex, plain and simple. What had she been thinking? Playing with fire only left her burned in the end. And yet, she wanted Nate. She wanted this.

The water bubbled around her, Nate's touch on her waist easy and secure. Everything seemed to wrap her in comfort and sensuality. How long had it been since she'd let down her defenses to just...be?

The answer didn't require more than an instant of thought. A long, long time.

"Do you want to get out?" he asked.

"No. I want—" she began, turning toward him, and then she didn't care anymore what the consequences were or what she was doing. Jenny moved, the water sloshing over the sides of the tub, to sit in front of Nate. She straddled him and pressed her chest to his, every inch of his torso mapped beneath the soaking fabric of her bra. She wrapped her arms around him and then kissed him with all the emotions and the feelings she'd kept pent-up for so many years.

He groaned and opened his mouth to hers, inviting her in. Her hands roamed his back, the water lubricating the journey, sending her fingertips into a sensory overload. Their tongues entwined, memory igniting with new passion.

The alternate feel of the hot below and the cold above only served to intensify everything. Passion for him ignited inside her, an electrical surge demanding more. Demanding it immediately. A nine-year wait to have Nate again had become too damned long. "I want you, Nate," she said. "I want you again. Now. Here."

"*Jenny,*" he growled, her name barely a word coming off his tongue. His hands slipped between them to cup her breasts, thumbs rolling over the nipples, and she arched backward, sensation surging through her like twin lightning bolts.

"Nate, I-I—"

When he drew his hands up to cup her face, disappointment rocketed through her veins at the loss of his touch on other parts of her.

His hands had served a much better purpose elsewhere.

Nate's gaze locked on her eyes. "Oh, Jenny, you have no idea how much I want you now, too. In a blink, I'd make love to you, but—" He paused, and then a smile, the gentlest one she'd ever seen on his face before, crossed his lips. "But I want to do it right this time. Do *everything* right with you this time. And that means no rushing. No acting without thinking first."

Need still pounded in her veins, but she managed to work a mirroring smile onto her face. "We did jump into the hot tub on the spur of the moment."

He grinned. "That we did. But, ah, for something more serious, I want to take it slow." His thumb traced over her lips and Jenny thought there had never been anything sweeter than that simple touch. "Because when—and I mean *when*—we do make love, I want it to last forever."

She blinked and drew back. Had he said what she thought? "Are you talking forever as in some kind of long-weekend thing or...the other kind of forever?"

"In my book, Jenny, there's only one kind of forever." Even in the moonlight, she could see which kind he meant in his dark brown gaze.

Panic rose in her and she opened her mouth to tell him no, that this was too fast, too much, that she didn't have it in her to do this again. Before she could, a pair of headlights illuminated the yard and a voice cut through their hot tub rendezvous.

"Hey, Dad, there's someone in our hot tub!"

Nate let out a curse. "I think we've been caught."

"Our clothes are on the ground. Our underwear is soaking wet." Despite everything, a giggle escaped Jenny at the absurdity of the situation. "How do you propose we get out of this?"

"Same way we got in. Improvise."

⎯⎯ℓℓℓ⎯⎯

Nate knew he was in trouble when he saw the twinkle in Luke's eye. "Skinny-dipping in my hot tub, little brother?"

"We weren't *completely* naked." He had, more or less, been playing by Jenny's rule.

Luke waved his hand in dismissal. "That's a technicality and you know it. If you were with Jenny, then you're forgiven. Any other woman, and I'll be stringing you up on the front porch."

Nate laughed. "Yeah, it was Jenny. And she's dripping wet and freezing in my car right now, waiting for me to make sure everything's kosher between us."

"It is, except for one thing."

"What?"

"You come to Sunday dinner with the family, and we'll forget this whole thing happened. Otherwise, I'll have to tell Mom."

"That's the kind of thing you threaten a kid with."

Luke gestured at the still steaming hot tub. "And *that's* the kind of antic a teenager does. A grown man knows better." Luke winked. "Though Anita and I have been known to act like kids ourselves once in a while."

"You're blackmailing me," Nate said.

"Exactly." Luke grinned. "You know you can't hide from your family forever."

"All right. You win. I'll be there for dinner."

"And bring a date. You know how Mom hates an unbalanced table."

"Have I told you lately that you're a horrible brother?"

"Hey, wait till Mark and Claire get here this weekend from California. Then you'll really be in trouble." Luke gave Nate a clap on the shoulder, then walked back toward his house, laughing.

Anticipation filled Nate's chest as he made his way to his car. Dinner with his family. How long had it been? Too many years, he knew, since he'd had a leave long enough to be home with everyone. With a pang, he realized he'd been crazy to stay away this long, to distance himself over the years.

From them. And from Jenny.

Now all he had to do was convince her to sit across the table from his brother, after just being caught nearly *au naturel* in his backyard. Nate suspected he'd have an easier time getting her entire third-grade class to elect Brussels sprouts as the new state vegetable.

"I don't know about this," Jenny said Friday morning. "It sounded like a good idea on Wednesday, but now I'm thinking it's just too crazy."

"What can go wrong? Look at those innocent little faces. Those sweet, trusting eyes. Those teeny-tiny feet. Surely you can't expect anything dreadful to come from such a package?" Nate said.

"Anything that comes in a cage with twenty-four brothers and sisters and is a member of the rodent family spells trouble," Jenny said, giving the cage of white mice a dubious look. "No matter what kind of science lesson they can impart."

Nate had proposed the idea earlier in the week and even set up the arrangement to borrow twenty-five mice from the Lawford Research Facility. She'd thought having live animal behavior experiments would be great at the time, but now, with the mice here, it sounded like the exact kind of insanity Dr. Davis would send her to the firing squad for.

"Oh cool!" Lindsay exclaimed, running into the classroom, depositing a trail of belongings behind her in her rush. "Mice!"

"They're for the class to study today. And they're not coming out of the cage," Jenny explained. She put her hand over the latch.

"Can't I hold just one?" Lindsay pouted and looked up into Jenny's face, her eyes wide with begging. "Please?"

"No. We're going to watch them navigate mazes, that's all. Then they go back to the research facility."

"Aw, Miss Wright, but he's so cute. I just want to pet his nose. Can I do that, please? Through the cage? With my pinky?"

Jenny didn't bother to point out that the true "him or her" test for a mouse was a little more complicated than a quick exterior visual. Lindsay clasped her hands together and offered up additional pleading.

"All right. Through the cage. One time. And then you have to pick up your things and start your morning work."

Lindsay's one pat turned into a twenty-second affection fest with the plump rodent. She exclaimed over every miniature part of him and tried out all five digits of one hand before deciding her index finger was the best for rubbing him under the chin.

By the time Jenny had shooed Lindsay back to her seat, the other children were in the classroom, crowding around the cage of mice. Nate provided crowd control while Jenny ushered them through in groups of three to see the animals before sending the children off to do their work.

"There, that wasn't so bad," she said once all the children were seated and busy with worksheets.

"I told you. An animal in the classroom doesn't have to be a disaster."

"I think I need to reclassify that statement. A farm animal in the classroom provides a disaster. These ones are quite cute...and a nice incentive for getting work done." As they had on the day Nate arrived, the children rushed through their paper, hands shooting up like rockets to announce when they were done.

"Let's get the mice out of the way first, then you can take them back to the facility," Jenny said. "I don't want to take any chances by keeping them in the classroom too long."

"Sounds good." Nate hoisted the maze the lab had sent over onto a long table at the front of the room and connected it to a door on the side of the cage. "All set."

She liked this, she decided, her and Nate working together. They'd made a good team. He'd been able to anticipate her needs and had often stepped in throughout the week with a calming word or a bit of wisdom when the students had a playground dispute. If she hadn't known better, she would have thought Nate was a negotiator, not a master sergeant.

Today, though, their week was over. She should be glad. The temptation of Nate would be gone in a few hours. Instead, she wished the day wouldn't end, that Fridays had a whole week instead of one shift day. He hadn't said what was going to happen tomorrow or Monday, or what he was going to do once he was through with rehab for his knee.

Would he leave? Move on to another city, another place?

Another woman?

The thought speared through her. After the hot tub incident, she'd made it clear again to Nate that she didn't want a future with him. That she wasn't interested in dating him.

And yet she'd kissed him good night when he'd dropped her off at home and proven she was a heck of a bad liar. If she could tell him these things from long distance, without the mesmerizing power of his eyes and his touch, then she *might* be able to stick to her resolve.

Now, she realized—too late—that she did indeed want him back. The thought of another woman in his arms...

Made her want to curl up and die of heartbreak.

"Jenny? Did you hear me? I said we're all set. And I think the kids are done. Everyone's waiting on you."

"Oh, yeah. Sorry. I was just..."

"Daydreaming?" He grinned.

"Yeah."

"If it was about me, then I'll forgive you." A tease lingered in his eyes.

She cocked her head and considered her reply. She could say no, and make up some flimsy lie about work or something stupid like that. Or she could invite chaos right into her life again and tell the truth.

Before he was gone again and she was left with a lot of regrets and nothing else, she turned and smiled at him. "As a matter of fact, I *was* daydreaming about you. And what the future for us might hold."

Then, with a smug and secret smile on her face, Jenny pivoted away from Nate's shocked face and let the first mouse into the maze.

Jimmy, Lindsay, Cole, Alex and Lincoln, so dubbed after their human "sponsors," raced through the maze. Lindsay came out the clear winner—by a nose and a whisker.

"I want a recount!" Jimmy—the student—shouted.

Jenny laughed. "There are no recounts in mouse races."

"Well, I think my mouse should race again. He was checked by Alex's mouse coming around the third corner."

"Okay, okay. We'll let him go once more with the next four."

"Awesome!" Jimmy leapt to his feet, inserting himself right beside the starting point for the race. "Can I raise the door?"

"No, Jimmy, you can't."

"Please? I'll be really careful, I promise."

"All right, but you have to wait until we close the second door and get the other mice inside or we'll have mouse city in the classroom."

"Okay, I will."

Jenny and Nate reached inside the maze, pulling out the five squirming competitors who'd finished the race, then brought over four of them to the opposite cage door to return them to their wood shavings nest.

Jenny raised the door, holding Jimmy's mouse securely in her opposite hand. Nate reached inside for the mice waiting their turn to navigate the maze and selected four, herding them toward the tunnel entrance with a wave of his hand.

"What do we have here?"

Jenny pivoted toward the voice. Howard Perkins, Dr. Davis and someone Jenny didn't recognize stood in the entrance of her room. "Dr. Davis. Mr. Perkins. You're just in time to see our science lesson."

Dr. Davis paled three shades. "Science lesson? With *live* mice?"

Jenny gave a bright, work-with-me-on-this-one nod. "We're studying animal behavior this week."

"And seeing who's got the fastest mouse this side of the Mississ...Missi...uh, river," Lionel piped up.

"Miss Wright, you always have something fun for me to look forward to," Mr. Perkins said. "If there's anything I enjoy as much as geological studies, it's the study of mammals." He gestured to the man standing beside him. "This is Craig Scott, another member of the accreditation board. I told him what fun we had with your volcano experiment, and he came along to judge things for himself. We thought we might bring some of your inventive teaching methods back to the other schools we work with."

"Let's show him now," Jimmy said, jumping forward and raising the starting gate. At the same time, Lionel shoved his way closer, vying to see the start of the race, and knocked the maze off-center from the cage door, leaving an opening, not a tunnel.

"Wait, don't!" Jenny cried. But it was too late.

Dr. Davis, Howard Perkins and Craig Scott were already on their way into the room—at the same time rodent pandemonium was letting loose in grade 3-B.

Dr. Davis's shriek could be heard in a three-county contiguous area. The sound startled the mice even more, sending the flood of white fur scurrying for shelter with all the speed of a tornado warning.

They scampered off the table, down the legs, across the seats, then dispersed when they hit the floor, streaming in every direction at once.

The children laughed—until they saw the mice headed for their feet. Then they were screaming and leaping onto chairs and desks, calling for Jenny to rescue them from the rodent invasion.

"Sit down, please," Jenny yelled above the fracas. No one heard her. Or no one chose to hear her. The children went on panicking, Dr. Davis had slipped into a catatonic state and Howard Perkins was watching with bemused interest.

"Do you have something to catch them with?" Nate asked. "A net? A bowl? Anything?"

Jenny tried to think but nothing came to mind, not with the noise and the panic level rising every second. She turned and grabbed the first thing she saw—a dustpan.

Nate quirked a brow at her but took the dustpan and set off on a mouse hunt. Jenny dumped out the mini bucket holding her pencils and scissors onto her desk and set off in the opposite direction.

Dr. Davis stared straight ahead, mouth slack. Craig Scott frowned, withdrew a pen from his breast pocket and clicked the point forward.

"This is fascinating," Howard Perkins said to the principal. "Look how they scattered, rather than flocking together. There's safety in numbers but the mice are so confused, they..."

Jenny didn't bother listening. She was after the two she'd seen in the corner by Mr. Body's re-assembled torso. She bent down, slid the purple container across the floor and caught half of the pair. One down. Twenty-four to go.

She covered the top with her hand, ran to the cage, got the mouse back inside, then shut and latched the door. The children had stopped screaming and were now giggling, but still perched out of rodent range.

Dr. Davis recovered her composure and directed an evil eye at Jenny. "Miss Wright, you must do something about these animals. Now."

Jenny blew a stray hair out of her face. "I'm trying."

"Aren't they incredible creatures?" Howard Perkins said. "What a great science lesson."

"I think it's a monumental mistake," Craig Scott said. He now had a notepad out and had already filled a page with notations about the event. "This is exactly what we *don't* want in our classrooms."

"It was an accident," Jenny said, then hurried off to catch more.

"Three more down," Nate said, coming up to her with an empty dustpan. "I just made a deposit in the mouse bank."

"This is no time to make jokes." It was chaos. Pure chaos. The exact thing Jenny had avoided all her life, and now here it was, personified in twenty-five mice, in her classroom.

"Don't worry. We'll catch them all."

"Look at their faces," she said, gesturing toward Dr. Davis and the two men by her side, "and then tell me I shouldn't worry."

"We'll get through this, Jenny. You've got a Marine on your side." He grinned. "That's enough ammunition for this battle."

Despite everything, Jenny laughed. She could only pray Nate was right. She readied her bucket, then motioned to him. "Then get to it, Master Sergeant, and corral those AWOL rodents. That's an order."

"Yes, ma'am." He gave her a mock salute, then set off, dustpan in hand.

Jenny turned toward her class. The children, clearly less afraid and more intrigued now, were starting to clamber down and look for mice themselves. In the corner, Craig Scott continued to make notes, even going so far as to peek inside the cage and tally the recaptured mice.

"Children, please sit down on your desks," Jenny said. "We'll be able to catch the mice more easily if everyone stays calm and in one place."

"What if one bites me?" Lindsay asked.

"They won't bite you. Trust me, they're more afraid of you than you are of them."

Lindsay gave Jenny a dubious look and drew her legs up on top of her desk.

"Miss Wright, I cannot recommend that this school retain its accreditation if these are the kinds of 'learning' experiences you have at Mercy Elementary," Craig Scott said, moving toward her, his pen and notepad ready to add any other infractions. "The volcanic explosion Mr. Perkins told me about might have sounded good at first, but I have rethought it now. And this—this is a deplorable situation."

Jenny decided she'd had enough of this. Enough of trying to live up to an impossible standard when she knew her students were doing well and learning. She was trying her hardest, damn it, and what she needed right now was support, not criticism. "Instead of giving me a lecture about the problem, Mr. Scott, you could be part of the solution." She thrust the purple container into his hands. "Please."

Craig Scott blinked at her. He opened his mouth, shut it again, then pivoted and stalked out of the room, with Dr. Davis and Howard Perkins right behind him, leaving Jenny's mouse catcher and her ruined career behind.

"Go after him," Nate said. "I'll keep your class under control."

Debbie had opened the connecting door and poked her head in. "What's going on in here? I heard a bunch of screaming."

"I'd shut that if I were you," Nate told her. "There are mice on the loose here."

Before she could spell Mickey, Debbie had the connecting door slammed shut and locked.

"Are you sure?" Jenny asked him. "There are a lot of mice to catch and the children—"

"We'll be fine. Go save your job. I'll save the classroom from the mice."

Without thinking twice, she rose on her tiptoes and pressed a quick kiss to Nate's cheek. The students noticed the impromptu gesture and let out a few "whoo-hoos" of appreciation.

Then Jenny spun on her heel, leaving Nate looking as stunned as she felt. She'd only shown him a little gratitude, but given the way her stomach flip-flopped, Jenny realized that had been more than a simple peck on the cheek.

She'd deal with the consequences of *that* later. For now, she had a school and a job to worry about.

In the parking lot, she found Craig Scott, Howard Perkins and Dr. Davis standing in a circle. Dr. Davis's face was pale and drawn, as if she'd aged ten years in the last five minutes.

"I cannot, in good conscience, let a school like this retain its accreditation," Craig Scott was saying. "I'll be speaking to the board immediately about taking action against Mercy Elementary."

"You can't do that," Jenny said, joining the group. "It was just mice."

"Just mice?" He opened his notebook and skimmed a finger along the report inside. "Don't forget, this school also has a history of reading scores and state academic test scores that have dropped each year."

"They won't drop this year," Jenny said. "We're working very hard to encourage reading in our students."

"Too late, Miss Wright." He shut his notebook and headed toward his car. Mr. Perkins stood silent, as if he hadn't decided which side of the fence to sit on yet.

"I won't let you do this," Dr. Davis said. "You will *not* revoke this school's accreditation simply because of one mishap in a third-grade classroom."

Craig Scott pivoted back toward her. "I can. And I will."

"Miss Wright is an excellent teacher. Her class is reading better and more than any third-grade class in the history of this school. *She* is the reason Mercy Elementary is coming around. With her help, we will—and we are—getting back on track."

Scott's lips thinned. He considered Jenny, then Dr. Davis. "Perhaps the problem isn't Miss Wright, but rather you, Dr. Davis?"

Shock washed over the principal's features, then receded. "Maybe it is, Mr. Scott. Maybe I haven't trusted my staff as much as I should have to use their incredible talents to encourage our youngsters to learn." She directed her look at Jenny.

It was an apology, an olive branch for all the years when Dr. Davis had put roadblocks in Jenny's way whenever she'd proposed something new or innovative. Jenny knew she'd be a fool to ignore the gesture. "Dr. Davis is a wonderful principal. We've had some hard years here at Mercy, but we are working together now and we *will* make a difference, Mr. Scott. I assure you. But we can't do that if you won't give us a chance."

He pursed his lips. "Those mice distracted your class today."

"Yes, they did," Jenny said. "They also made the kids laugh and gave them something to talk about for the next three months. And you can bet I won't let this opportunity go by. They'll be writing a short story about a mouse, fictionalizing what just happened. We may have fun, but we'll make it work, too." She gestured toward Mr. Perkins. "That's what we did when the volcano erupted in the classroom, isn't it, Mr. Perkins?"

"The volcano *really* erupted?" Dr. Davis sputtered. To her credit, she bit back her criticism and instead put a tight smile on her face. "How...adventurous."

Mr. Perkins nodded, pushing up his glasses as he did. "I had a regular Mount Vesuvius in there. Took out the toothpick city and my suit. But boy, did those kids write some great essays about the experience. I've never seen such work from third graders. I was impressed."

Craig Scott tapped his toe against the dark black tar of the school parking lot, considering. "You'll have state tests again at the end of the year. If the scores are up—"

"They will be," Jenny and Dr. Davis said at the same time.

"*If* the scores are up, we will allow Mercy Elementary to retain its accreditation." With that, he turned and left.

"You'll do fine," Mr. Perkins said, stepping up to them before joining his fellow board member. "I hear there's a whole section of questions on volcanic activity." He winked, then went on his own way.

After the men were gone, Dr. Davis let out a long breath. "We're not out of the woods yet."

"No, we aren't. But we have a clear way out of the forest." Jenny smiled and turned toward her boss, who had now become her ally, more or less. "And if we lose our way, we'll just call on Ed Spangler. I'm sure he has an animal for any situation."

Dr. Davis's jaw dropped open. She managed to clamp it, and any protests she might have had, shut. Together, the two of them walked back inside the building. Not really friends, but no longer enemies either.

Cost of one kissing pig—a little bad publicity and the re-entry of Nate into her life. Total price undetermined thus far.

Cost of the look on Dr. Davis's face after Jenny mentioned a rerun of *Animals Where You Want 'Em*— priceless.

Chapter 10

Nate had it all under control by the time Jenny returned to the classroom a few minutes later. She entered the room and paused, brows knitted together when she saw the coordinated, well-behaved activity in her classroom. The students, in groups of five, were canvassing the room, empty paper and tissue boxes in hand. "What are you doing?"

"I separated the students into squads. Each one is responsible for finding mice in a different sector of the room."

She laughed. "Only you would turn a mouse hunt into a war plan."

"We managed to corral all of them except for two." He waved toward the cage where the twenty-three others climbed over each other, safe and secure again.

She nodded, clearly impressed with his work. "Let's hope the remaining two aren't a male and a female."

He grinned. "Yeah, that would create a whole other slew of problems."

"Thank you," she said. "I really appreciate your help and your mouse-capturing abilities. We'll catch those other two ourselves later. For all we know, they might be on their way to Disney World by now." She grinned, then called the class back to their seats and handed out a math worksheet. "This is the last task of the day, children, so as soon as you're done, you can have some free time."

Jimmy's head popped up. "Free time? We never get free time. For real?"

"Yes, I said free time."

The kids let out a cheer and dove into their math sheets, hurrying down the list of problems.

"What happened with the board members and Dr. Davis?" Nate asked.

She told him about the events in the parking lot, earning a chuckle from him when she reiterated the line about calling in Ed Spangler. "I'm glad it all worked out in the end," he said.

"Well, we still have a long way to go, but yes, it looks like it will be okay."

"Good."

The sun from the windows reflected off Nate's dark brown hair. His normally short crew cut had grown out now that he'd been out of the military for a while, as if he, too, were growing into someone else.

She wanted to hope he could have changed from Nate the Marine to Nate the ordinary man. In the few days he'd been here, he'd been a different person. And yet, whenever she'd asked him about the future, he'd given her the same answers as he always had: don't count on him because he couldn't predict where he'd be six days or six months down the road.

He could be here tomorrow...or gone tomorrow and once again, she'd be left with a heart filled with painful memories.

Jenny realized she'd been wrong about the hot tub. Getting *into* it hadn't been playing with fire. Falling for Nate again had been.

"Well," she said finally, "the best news is that you're all done here." The children were finishing their worksheets, and Jenny collected them as they popped their hands up to indicate they were done. "It's been wonderful having you here this week, Mr. Dole, and we'll miss you when you're gone."

Nate's jaw hardened. Jenny was putting up that wall again, using the class to distance herself. She knew they couldn't discuss anything while the students were around. So she was getting it out of the way now, while he couldn't argue back.

The last student finished her worksheet and Jenny announced the promised free time. In seconds, the class had selected other activities, from drawing to puzzles. Some just moved to other desks and chatted with friends.

Nate grabbed his cane and made his way over to where Jenny sat, on the shelf by the window, looking over the worksheets and marking them with a red pen.

"What if I don't want to leave?" he asked.

She looked up at him, surprise widening her eyes. "There's nothing left to do, Nate. It's the end of the day on Friday. You've done your week, accomplished what you promised. Next week we move on to a new topic."

"And what about you? You move on to a new topic, too?"

The buzz of chatter continued around them, the children caught up in their spontaneous moment of fun. Outside the open windows, cars pulled up in the circular driveway, waiting for dismissal.

"I go back to my life, Nate. Come in to work every day, grade my papers, plan my classes. Nothing new there."

"It sounds sad. Empty."

"It sounds like a job. My job." She dipped her head, back to those damned worksheets again.

He shook his head. "No, it's not. It's a box. You can have a job, but you can have a life, too, Jenny."

A couple of the kids looked up and over at them. "Two minutes, and then it's time to get ready to go home," Jenny told them. That started the chatter up again as the children made good use of their last one hundred and twenty seconds.

But one child didn't. Jimmy picked up from the drawing he'd been making and headed over to Nate. "Mr. Dole? I wanted to give this to you."

Nate looked down and saw a crayoned picture of himself and Jimmy, sitting on the rock beneath the tree on the playground. Above them, a bright yellow sun shone in one corner and a few V-shaped birds flew across the rest of the blue expanse of sky. But it was the two figures, composed of simple lines and circles, that got him right in the solar plexus. "Hey, what's this?"

"Nothing." Jimmy drew a circle on the tile floor with his toe. "Just a picture I made."

"It's great, Jimmy. I'm going to hang it on my wall."

"I just wanted to thank you for what you said. I told my mom that story and told her I wanted to make some money of my own, working around the house and stuff."

"Chores, huh? I had a lot of those as a kid."

"Anyway, she and I talked a lot last night and I think things are gonna be better. She's not going to get back together with my dad, but she's going to be home more with me." Jimmy shrugged, as if he didn't care, but Nate could see the happiness in the little boy's eyes. "She said we'll work it out. Whatever that means, but it sounds good to me."

Nate smiled and bent down to Jimmy's level. "I'm glad for you, Jimmy. You're a great kid and you deserve great things."

The boy's face reddened. He mumbled something that sounded like thanks and headed back to his seat.

Nate stared at the picture in his hands. He'd affected a life here, in a way that he'd never affected a life when he'd been in the Marines. Sure, he'd defended people, sometimes saved a life, sometimes even taken one if it had been necessary. But never had he ever had such a big return on a simple investment of a few minutes and a few words.

"I told you, they'll get to you," Jenny said quietly. "Before you know it, you'll be collecting retirement from the teachers' fund."

The two-minute warning bell rang, and Jenny hopped off the shelf and moved to help the kids get ready to go home. Five minutes later, the classroom was empty and they were alone.

Jenny didn't return to his side. She crossed to her desk and buried herself in her work. She could do a damned good job of dodging him when she wanted to. "Well, thanks again, Nate."

"That's it? Just a thanks? A card in the mail next week, signed by all the kids?" He moved to her desk and laid his hands on either side of it. "Don't avoid me, Jenny. And don't pretend this week didn't happen."

She glanced up, all emotion gone from her eyes, as if she was determined not to betray anything to him. "Let's head this off before anyone gets hurt, okay?"

"No, it's not okay. I'm tired of you pushing me away. I'm tired of you telling me you don't want to get involved with me when I know damned well that you do." He slipped around to her side and turned her chair so she was facing him, unable to hide the war of emotions in her gaze. "Are you telling me you didn't feel a thing when you kissed me?"

"No, I'm not." She pushed back her chair and got to her feet, turning away from him. She trailed her fingers down the chalk board, tracing patterns on the black surface. "Of course I felt something. I felt *everything*."

"Then why won't you try again, Jenny? I can't leave this room and forget about you. I know better than that now. No matter how hard I tried to forget you over the years, I couldn't. You're a part of me, and I'm a part of you. We've always been that way."

She shook her head. "I can't, Nate."

"Why, damn it?" He let out a gust and circled around so that she had to face him again. "Why?"She jerked her gaze up to his. "You want to know why I don't like chaos, Nate? Because every week with you was chaos. I couldn't predict anything when I was with you. When you'd be home on leave, when you'd have to go back. Where you'd be. Whether you'd live. I couldn't control any of it." Her eyes misted, then filled with tears. "And most of all, I couldn't control you."

"I didn't mean for it to be that way. It's the way the military is. I'm out of that now, though. So there's nothing in our way."

"Yes, there is. It was never the Marines that made you that way. It was you." She toyed with the eraser, then let it alone. "You still can't commit to a place, a life, anything. You don't want to put down roots. Why is that?"

"I got Harry. That's a baby step." He tried out a grin, to ease the tension between them, but she didn't give him the answering smile he was hoping for. Behind them, the parking lot emptied, children returning home with their parents, to their families.

"Nate, I don't have time to wait for you to take the big steps. I'm almost thirty. I spent two years of my life getting over you. I'm not going to spend the next sixty years waiting for you to be the kind of man I always wanted."

"I thought I was that man, a long time ago."

She shook her head. "I hate chaos and you hate predictability. We're polar opposites. I'm a third-grade teacher with twenty-five children depending on me to give them an education and a school counting on me to do that and more. You can't tell me you'd be happy sitting in this room—or any room—day after day, living the same life for years on end."

"You don't know that I couldn't."

"And you don't know that you could." Her smile was bittersweet. "I'd say that's an impasse, Nate. The same one we came to nine years ago. This is where I go right, and you go left." She picked up her tote bag and slipped it onto her shoulder. "So let's just head off the detour onto Heartbreak Lane now and call it quits before either of us gets in too deep."

As she left the room, Nate realized there was one fatal flaw in Jenny's plan. He was already in too deep—deeper than he'd ever been before.

—ele—

"Jennifer, have you heard a single word I said?"

Jenny looked up from the dinner plate in front of her to meet her grandfather's eyes. "Uh...no. Sorry, Grandpa."

"I was talking about the woman I met while I was walking Spike in the park with the Mercy Dog Club. She was the nicest lady. Shares my love of gardening and even has a little dog, like mine. But it's a dachshund, not a terrier."

"You met a woman at the park with a dachshund?"

"Yep. And we're going to dinner on Saturday night."

Jenny put down her water glass and swallowed her sip before she choked on it. "You have a date?"

He nodded, quite pleased with the event. "Yep. With Alice Marchand."

"With Miss *Marchand*?"

"Don't you remember her? She used to teach you kids back when you were in high school. Biology, I think she said."

"Of course I remember her, Grandpa. This is a small town. You never forget anybody."

Especially the people you cared about the most, the little voice inside her head added. Jenny pushed that thought away. She was here to have dinner with her grandfather, not to dwell on the way things had ended with Nate earlier that afternoon.

"I saw you meet a certain man and his mutt at the park," her grandfather said, interrupting her thoughts. He speared a piece of roast beef onto his fork and ate it before continuing. "Did anything come of that?"

Jenny toyed with her broccoli, merging it with the mashed potatoes and creating more of a mess than a meal. It didn't matter. Her appetite had left her ever since Nate had walked into her classroom and turned her world upside down. "No, nothing."

"You're crazy then."

"Crazy?"

"You're young and you have plenty of years left to enjoy someone. Don't be foolish and set that aside because you think you're doing yourself a favor. You're not."

Leave it to her grandfather to be frank. He was the kind of man who always created a stir at the family reunions because he made it a point to tell the cousins what he really thought about their life choices. "You think I should risk it all?" she asked.

"Of course I do." He pushed his empty plate to the side and crossed his arms in front of him. "You used to be quite the risk taker years ago. Then you got old and safe." He grinned, the wrinkles in his face deepening around the edges of his smile.

"Playing it safe has kept me pretty well thus far in life, Grandpa. I have a house of my own, a retirement fund, a good job—"

"And a lonely heart." He reached across the table and clasped her hand. "Trust me. None of those things matter one whit at the end of the day when you say 'good night' and there's no one there to echo the words."

"I know." She blinked away the sting in her eyes. When had she turned into this emotional mess?

Easy. When the one man who had always had a finger on the pulse of her heart walked back into her life and turned a perfect layer cake into a jumbled, crying trifle.

Chapter 11

On Sunday afternoon, Jenny stood outside the white ranch house owned by the Doles and considered leaving. A hundred times over, Jenny had thought twice about the dinner invitation Grace Dole had sent over to her house yesterday. Nate had called and left two messages on her machine, extending the same invitation. Finally, Jenny had relented.

She was tired of being afraid of chaos. Afraid that if she let a little in, it would snowball into a lot. And then, before she knew it, her life would end up the same as it had been when she was a child, one topsy-turvy moment after another.

"You made me walk my dog, the least I can do is make you go inside."

Jenny pivoted. "Grandpa! What are you doing here?"

"Same as you, coming to dinner at the Doles. With my date." He grinned and indicated Miss Marchand. She stood beside Jenny's grandfather, in a pink floral dress, and, of all things, a matching pillbox hat. A little flower was pinned over the left side of her chest. "Grace invited us both."

"Miss Marchand! What a nice surprise," Jenny said, trying to keep the shock from her voice. Seeing Alice Marchand with her grandfather was not the picture of romantic bliss she envisioned when she thought of a love story.

"Even an old lady like me can have a little romance in her life, you know." She gave Jenny a wink.

"Where are Spike and Sugarplum?"

Her grandfather took Miss Marchand's hand in his own and gave her a smile. "We left them at home. So we could have a little time to get to know one another without the dogs interrupting."

"Sugarplum gets a little...territorial," Miss Marchand explained.

"A little?" Grandpa arched a brow. "My Dockers only have half a leg on one side."

"You exaggerate, Richard. She only got you from the ankle down."

"A small price to pay for your attentions, Alice."

Miss Marchand blushed, the crimson traveling all the way from her cheeks down her neck, turning her nearly the same color as her dress.

So, Miss Marchand wasn't immune to a little love in her own life, too. Well, there was indeed another miracle in the world, right here in the little town of Mercy.

"Are we just going to stand out here, Jennifer, or go on in? And find a little romance for you, too?"

"Grandpa!"

"Well?"

She was outnumbered. Miss Marchand, she half suspected, would drag her in anyway, in her ongoing determination to marry off all the unmarried Doles. Jenny took in a breath, then pressed the doorbell. "Hail, Hail, the Gang's All Here" pealed through the house, inciting the spaniels' barks and a flurry of activity inside.

"Jenny!" Grace Dole flung open the door and immediately greeted her with a smile. "So nice to see you again."

Before she could say a word, she was wrapped up into the Dole family—Jack and Sarah, Katie and Matt, Mark and

Claire, Luke and Anita—they all surrounded her as she stepped into the house.

She greeted each in turn, giving Claire, her friend for many years, a strong hug before releasing her. Despite the clamor and the warmth, there was only one face Jenny really cared about seeing.

And then, in the back, away from the group, she saw him. Nate. Standing at the other end of the hall, Harry at his side. Harry let out a little bark of greeting. Nate's face lit up with joy when he caught her eye.

Jenny moved forward, allowing her father and Miss Marchand to take her place in the flurry of greetings. In a dozen steps, she was beside Nate.

"You came."

"Yeah, I did."

"Couldn't resist my mother's cookies? Or me?" He grinned.

"The cookies, of course."

"That's what I figured." He winked. "And what I counted on when my mother conspired with me to invite you."

"Dinner should be on the table in five more minutes, soon as we get these kids corralled," Grace called.

Nate's brothers passed by on their way to the dining room, giving him a few good-natured jabs as they passed. Matt and Katie's twins barreled past next, chasing after one of the dogs, followed by Luke and Anita's toddler, Ben.

"You ready for this chaos?" Nate asked.

"I always liked being with your family. This was the kind of chaos I could understand. With my mother...it wasn't predictable. Most days, we were lucky my mother even remembered it was time for dinner. She was always off on some adventure. Sometimes she'd drag me along, and sometimes—"

"She'd forget you."

The hall, which had seemed so busy before, suddenly felt silent, filled with ghosts from her past. "Yeah."

"Just because you live your life with a little spontaneity, Jenny, doesn't make you into that, you know."

She let out a breath. "A big part of me knows that. I mean, I'm a rational adult. But..."

"You're not taking any chances, just in case?"

"Basically."

"And I can't change your mind?"

"You, Nate?" She smiled and touched his face for the briefest of seconds. "You are the biggest risk of all."

Grace passed by with a platter of food, reminding them dinner was ready. Jenny slipped away before he could say anything else.

Well, he'd be damned if he was going to let her think loving him was a risk she couldn't afford to take.

Nate didn't know when he'd realized he loved Jenny again. It didn't really matter. He'd never stopped loving her, not really. His feelings had lingered in his heart long after the break-up. He'd carried them with him all these years, from country to country, in and out of battle. She'd been the first thing to pop into his mind when he'd been in a firefight, the one thought that would wake him up in the middle of the night, a deep pang of homesickness crowding into the cot beside him.

When she'd walked into his mother's house today, he'd known. If he'd had any doubts at all, they'd disappeared the second his gaze met her emerald eyes.

He'd always loved Jenny, ever since he'd been born, it seemed. And that was how he wanted it to be for the rest of his life.

Nate took the seat across from Jenny at the dining room table, watching her talk with Claire and Mark, and set a plan into motion. If there was anything he was good at, it was strategizing.

First item on the plan—to show Jenny once and for all he could be the man she wanted him to be. Gee, glad he'd picked the hardest task first.

His mother came by and gave his shoulder a squeeze. "Nice to have you at my table again, Nathaniel."

"Nice to be here, Mom."

"How long before you leave again?"

He looked up into Grace Dole's blue eyes and saw sadness there. Had she always looked like that whenever he'd come home? Or had he never taken the time to really look in her eyes and see the toll his military life had taken on the people who loved him?

His father, brothers and sister had fallen silent, listening for his answer. Taking in the faces around him, Nate knew he'd been the stupid one—too wrapped up in rescuing the world to pay attention to what he was doing to everyone else. No more. Those days were over.

"I'm home for good this time," he said.

Stunned silence.

"Forever?" Jack, his oldest brother, said. "Or are you just waiting on new orders?"

"No more orders. No more uniform. Went and got my knee shot up and now I'm taking up space in the unemployment line."

His father leaned back in his chair at the head of the table. "You sure about this, son?"

Nate caught Jenny's gaze from across the way. "As sure as I am that the sun's coming up tomorrow."

She smiled. And that was enough to multiply the hope in his heart ten-fold. Time to introduce a couple of flanking maneuvers.

"So, what are you going to do instead?" his father asked.

"I thought I'd settle down, get married and catch up with the baby-making machine over here," Nate waved at Katie.

"Hey, I take offense to that. Sort of." Katie grinned. "You just have to be smart about it, Nate, and have them two at a time."

"Wait a minute. Am I the only one who just heard Nate say he wants to get married and have kids?" Mark interrupted. He raised his glass of wine. "I say we start offering the toasts now before he changes his mind." Mark, the confirmed bachelor of the family until his marriage last year to a now very pregnant Claire, gave Nate a good-natured wink.

The other Dole men raised their glasses, then swiveled expectant gazes toward Jenny. She sat there, mouth agape, shock clear on her face.

"Uh, Nate, did you ask anyone in particular before you made this announcement?" Luke asked. "It's not the kind of thing you spring on a girl at a family dinner. Particularly a dinner with *this* family."

Jenny swallowed and wished she had a magical potion to make her disappear. This was not, as Luke had said, the right time or place for life-changing questions.

"I haven't asked Jenny. Yet. But I certainly intend to." Nate's gaze met hers and there was no mistaking the question—or the meaning—in his deep brown eyes.

The fourteen adults squeezed around the Dole dining room table were as silent as goldfish. At the other end of the room, the five children seated at the card table chattered like magpies, unaware a monumental decision had been laid among the dishes of baked lasagna and garlic bread.

"Luke's right," Jenny said. "This isn't the kind of thing you spring on someone at dinner." She got to her feet, pushing her chair back as she did. She murmured an apology to Grace. "I think I should go."

"Stay," Grace said. "My son has no manners, but the rest of us are pretty civilized."

"Thank you, but..." She looked around the table, at the family that had once been as close to her as anyone could be, and shook her head. "I need some time to think."

"I told you that you should have had a ring and flowers," Mark said. "Jeez, Nate, didn't all of us guys getting hitched first teach you anything?"

Jenny left the room, the sound of the Dole men's laughter and gentle ribbing at Nate's inopportune proposal ringing in her ears. She ran for the front door and down the steps. Before she could reach the driveway, Nate was there.

"Wait, Jenny, don't go yet."

She spun around. "Why? Do you have another surprise for me? Something else unexpected? First it's a dip in your brother's hot tub, which, I might add, we got caught doing by his thirteen-year-old daughter. Then it's mice in my classroom, which nearly costs the school its accreditation. Now, you want me to marry you because you threw the proposal out as a joke at the family dinner?"

"It wasn't a joke, Jenny."

"Nate, you've been back in my life for five days. No, six, if you count the ten seconds we spent talking on Sunday. We've been apart for more than nine years. And now, you want me to make a decision about the rest of my life between the salad and the entree?"

"Yes, I do. Because I know you never stopped loving me. And I don't want to spend one more day without you."

She turned away, tears hot in her eyes, and shook her head. "Nate, this is the exact kind of crazy thing I avoid. I don't make decisions on the spur of the moment. I don't believe in that *carpe diem* thing. It's a sure way to..."

When she didn't finish the sentence, he circled around to the front of her and tipped her chin upward with his finger. "A sure way to what?"

"Get hurt."

"Oh, Jenny," he said, the words so soft, they nearly broke her heart in two, "I'm not going to hurt you. Not anymore."

"How can you guarantee that? You can't. And you know it. I don't take chances, Nate."

"So what are you going to do? Grow old alone, because the only one you think you can count on is yourself?" "That's my plan. I don't want to be tied down to a man who's going to let me down or hurt me or make my life this crazy, upside down thing."

"I have news for you, Jenny. You can't count on yourself. Because you are going to change and find out that you aren't who you thought all along."

"What do you mean? I know who I am. I know what I want."

"You want this?" He waved his arm, indicating the quiet, suburban streets behind them. "This predictable life, day in and day out? Dinner at Marge's every Friday? Pizza delivered on Tuesday nights? Bingo at the Presbyterian Church and car washes at the Methodist Church, all as regular as rain in April?"

"Yes, I do."

"Bull."

She swallowed. "How can you say that to me? You haven't seen me in nine years. You don't know what I want now."

"I know *you*, Jenny. I know you better than anyone in the entire world."

She looked into his eyes and knew that was true. She'd never opened up to anyone as much as she had in those years with Nate. Her mother had been too flighty to know her only child, her father had been at work more often than he was home. Even her closest friends believed her to be Jenny Wright, prim and proper third-grade teacher. No one had seen the same Jenny that Nate had.

"You know who you *thought* I was."

"What, did you get a personality transplant? Because the girl I knew wanted to do more than just live in this little town. She wanted to travel the world and see the sights. Write about them in essays that she planned to send out to magazines someday." Nate ran a thumb under her eye, wiping away a tear trailing down her cheek. His voice softened. "She wanted more. Much more. What happened to her?"

"She grew up. Got a job. Responsibilities."

"And had her heart broken by a stupid Marine who didn't appreciate what he had."

A second tear escaped and slid down her face. Thick, pent-up emotion clogged her throat. All over again, the ache in her heart throbbed, as if it had happened today, not a decade ago. "Yeah," she said softly.

"Let me tell you about that Marine." Again, he caught the tear with a finger and whisked it away. "I didn't join the military because I wanted to save the world. I joined because I was scared."

"You? You aren't scared of anything."

"Sure I am. Remember me as a kid? I didn't have the brains of Luke or the athletic ability of Mark. Jack always knew he wanted to be a cop from the day he was born, and Katie, well, she had the energy to be anything. I was…the runt of the litter, even though I wasn't the youngest. I wasn't big and strong in school, and I got lucky when Ricky Lincoln made friends with me because it sure protected my butt from the bullies."

"You sure grew up to be…" Her gaze drifted over his muscular frame, the defined shoulders, tapered waist. "Imposing.""Nothing a good weight bench and a lot of determination couldn't do. I became a Marine because it made me feel invincible. Strong enough to take on the world and especially the bad guys. Then, when I couldn't be a Marine anymore, I felt like that kid all over again. Weak, worth nothing more than a piece of paper."

"Oh, Nate, that's not you. You know that, don't you?""I do now." He took her hands, strong wide palms holding her smaller ones with security and honesty. "When Jimmy gave me that drawing, I saw that I didn't have to have my uniform on to make a difference. Being a Marine didn't make me a man and it didn't make me strong. It sounds corny, but I realized all I had to do was be me."

"Corny isn't bad, you know. It fits right in with Mercy."

He chuckled. "That it does."

In unspoken communication, they traversed the driveway and stepped onto the lawn. Soft blades of dark-green growth sprouted anew from the earth. "But why...why did you distance yourself from everyone when you were in the military? It was like the longer you were there, the less you let anyone into your heart."

"Because if there's one thing the military teaches you, it's that people die. And die young. I saw my friends die on the battlefield and learned pretty damned quick that getting close to people did nothing but make me vulnerable, and that's the last thing you want to be when you're fighting an enemy. So I distanced myself, from the men I was with...and the people I loved."

They crossed to an oval concrete bench under an oak tree and took a seat in the shade. A robin hopped down from the tree and picked at the grass, searching for a late-day worm.

"Then I got shot. At first, I felt sorry for myself. All I could think about was how this had ruined my career. Once I got over the pity party, I realized how close I came to dying. A couple of feet higher, and that bullet would have been in my heart, not my knee cap."

Jenny closed her eyes and shuddered. She couldn't imagine losing Nate like that. For just a second, the thought of a flag-draped casket coming back to Mercy instead of him rocketed through her. All the time they'd dated, it had been her worst nightmare. To think of how close he'd come to that scared her, even now. "I'm glad the shooter had bad aim."

"Me too." He smiled. "Now I realize, though, how stupid it was to keep my distance from the people I love. And to keep thinking that not putting down roots would keep me from getting too attached. Well, I have news for you, Jenny. I want to get attached. I want roots. I want *you*." He took her hand, his thumb circling the back. "I could die tomorrow or, you could be stuck with me for sixty more years. Either way, I don't want to let five more minutes go by without telling you how I feel. I won't let you go again, Jenny, and live those sixty years alone and full of regret."

She got to her feet and ran a hand through her hair. "That's what you say today, Nate. How can I know you'll mean it tomorrow?"He rose to stand behind her and wrapped his arms around her waist. "Sometimes, Jenny, you have to take a leap of faith and know there's someone you love waiting at the bottom to catch you.""It's a pretty big leap you're asking of me."

"Be adventurous," he whispered, his breath warm against her ear, awakening every nerve in her body, "and love me as much as I love you."

She pivoted to face him. For a long time, Jenny studied his face. In her gut, she heard the answer she'd been seeking. Just as Nate had promised Jimmy, all the answers were already there. Joy that she'd finally found what she'd been seeking, and that she'd allowed herself to trust in it, ran through her. "Only if you promise me one thing."

"Name it."

"There won't be any llamas at our wedding." Then she leaned forward and kissed him, before the look of surprise could disappear from his eyes.

Epilogue

"I can't believe I let you talk me into this," Jenny shouted over the roar of the engines. "I must be crazy."

"Crazy in love." Nate grinned, then leaned over and checked the straps across Jenny's chest. Confident they were secure, he turned to his own and did a double-check there, too. "You said you wanted a little more spontaneity in your life."

"A little. Not a sky-full."

He just grinned more at her. "Wait till you see what I have planned for our honeymoon, baby."

A surge of excitement and fear ran through Jenny. She adjusted her veil, made sure her dress was secure, then took her husband-to-be's hand and stepped forward on the platform. "You know our students will never stop talking about this."

"If they ever pause long enough from naming all those mouse babies." Nate had been hired as a permanent aide in her class while he went back to school to get his teaching degree. Dr. Davis had been thrilled with the improvement in the school and the boost in the state test scores at the end of the school year, which had assured Mercy Elementary's accreditation.

"At least we caught those last two mice finally."

"Unfortunately, *after* they had a little fun in the back of the classroom."

Jenny laughed. It had taken three weeks to find the last two strays, long enough for them to start making themselves at home—and then some. "Good thing it's only third grade. I didn't have to give too many details on where that nest of babies came from."

"Give it time, Jenny, and you'll be explaining more than just that. At least, that's my plan." He gave her another grin, then put a palm over her flat stomach. "Let's see what we can cook up on our honeymoon."

The thought of a baby—her and Nate's baby—soared through her. Claire and Mark had welcomed a daughter into the world last month. Miss Marchand, who'd been a regular visitor to Jenny's grandfather's house, had started dropping hints lately about the last Dole son's failure to procreate. Yet.

If Jenny had anything to do with it, it wouldn't be long before there'd be another nursery to decorate. Nate's live-for-the-moment advice had started to rub off on her—and her biological clock—ever since they'd set a wedding date.

"Have I told you lately that I love you, even though I think you're insane?" she said, smiling at him.

"Long as you marry me right now, that's all I care about."

The minister behind them cleared his throat. Jenny and Nate pivoted, hands clasped, and in a few minutes, had recited the words that joined them for life, for better or worse.

"Ready?" Nate asked her.

"As ready as I'll ever be." She did a 180-degree turn with Nate by her side and faced the roaring sky going by. The farms of the outlying areas of Mercy, more than twelve thousand feet below them, looked like a jigsaw puzzle full of rectangles. A multicolored bouquet of balloons and wedding guests stood beneath a huge "Congratulations" sign and a great big X to mark the spot where the new Mr. and Mrs. Dole were to make their landing.

"Okay, here we go. One. Two. Three!" Nate clutched Jenny's hand and together the two of them leapt off the side of a perfectly good airplane and into the air, spiraling down fast and furious.

She should have been terrified. But with Nate's hand holding hers—and a damned good parachute on her back—Jenny felt more secure than she ever had in her life.

Have you enjoyed the Mercy, Indiana series and the Dole family? Read on for the first chapter of KISSED BY CAT, a fun new rom com set in Mercy!

Kissed by Cat Preview

Being chased down Broward Street by an ugly, hungry Great Dane at one in the morning did not rank on the top ten of Catherine Wyndham's favorite ways to spend an evening. She'd much rather have been curled up in front of a fireplace with a fuzzy blanket, a saucer of warm milk, and a freshly opened can of tuna.

The lumbering beast of a dog opened his jaws and lunged forward. Catherine scampered up someone's back porch, across the railing and into the next yard, leaving the dog barking at nothing but cold November air.

For the ten thousandth time in two hundred years, Catherine regretted ever tangling with that witch. She'd always had a bad habit of helping stray and mistreated animals. She'd picked the wrong black cat one day and had thus been cursed by Hezabeth the witch to live a half-life—which was really no life at all.

Today, though, had been a good day, relatively speaking. Catherine turned the corner, quite pleased with her getaway.

She jerked to a stop. There it was. Their scent. She lowered her head to the ground, concentrating as she tracked. Her instincts perked up, telegraphing a warning signal, but she ignored it.

Five more seconds. Then I can—

And then she was being scooped up by a pair of strong, masculine hands. She shrieked and tried to twist away but the man held tight, depositing her into a small metal cage, with no more effort than he'd use to flick a whip.

She let out a second scream of protest. "I know, I know," he said in a soft, crooning voice. "Right now, you probably hate me, but believe me, it's for your own good."

She glared back, swatted at the bars. Futile gestures. He had the upper hand -- not to mention bigger hands that could transport her anywhere he wanted her to go.

She hated that. Hated being eight inches tall and about as powerful as a gnat wrestling a gorilla.

He *did* have a kind face at least. Better to be kidnapped by a prince than an ogre. She'd been with both in the last two centuries. Handsome didn't always equal nice or bright, but it did provide a better view.

Ugly or cute, none of the men she'd met had been the knight in shining armor that could end the curse put in place by Hezabeth—her revenge against Catherine for setting the witch's cat free.

You love animals so much, how about a taste of life like one? the witch had cackled. Before Catherine could get away, Hezabeth had thrown some powder at her and muttered something in an ancient language. From that day forward, Lady Catherine Wyndham, heir to the Wyndham estates and fortune, daughter of the Earl and Countess of Wyndham, had ceased to exist. And, thanks to Hezabeth's addition of a Catch-22 twist, Catherine had no hope of ever breaking the curse with some storybook ending.

It didn't matter. Finding Prince Charming wasn't at the top of her To Do list. Hadn't been in fifty-odd years. *If* he even existed, the chances of meeting him when she wasn't sporting whiskers were pretty slim.

In the half-light of the car, she could see a day's worth of stubble on the man's chin, softening the hard edges of his jaw. Lines zigzagged down the left side of his face, disappearing beneath his collar.

Scars. From what? From whom?

Her gaze skipped over the marks and connected with his eyes. Large, brown, and almost...soft.

They looked at her with a kindness and compassion she'd rarely seen in two hundred and twenty-five years of life. All those cities, all those people, and not one had seen her as much more than a waste of DNA. But now, in this small town in Indiana, a man with an almost empathetic gaze.

As if he understood.

Impossible. No one knew what she'd gone through. What a nightmare her life had been since Hezabeth had damned Catherine to an existence filled with pain and loneliness, one no sane person would find believable.

She shook herself. She must be due for a distemper shot. She was getting maudlin again.

"You're going to be much happier where you're going." That quiet, singsong voice again. "It's warmer there, too."

Fat chance. Being locked in a cage didn't fit Catherine's definition of happy. She wrinkled her nose and cast him her iciest look.

He chuckled. "You'll thank me after you get a good meal in you." He shut the door to the car, came around to the driver's side, got in, then put the car in gear and started driving. He did a good job ignoring her plaintive wails from the seat beside him.

Nice eyes or not, she didn't want to go wherever he was taking her. She had things to do and this man, with his do-gooder, save-the-world-and-the-whales charity mission, was getting in the way.

Catherine paced the cage, inspecting every inch. Thin metal bars, secure lock. A flat metal base, cool against her feet.

She silently cursed in English, then added a few choice words in French. The orphans had been close by, maybe five minutes from her. She'd been so focused on finding them she'd ignored the warning signals and thus, had ended up in the hands of Dr. Doolittle.

She'd rescued so many animals over the course of her lifetime—kittens, puppies, even a lost turtle once. It had become her mission, she supposed, which was ironic given that all the trouble in her life had started with saving one black cat.

Still, she wanted to find those kittens. If she could reunite them with their mother, she hoped it would give her a little more closure. Make it easier to accept the inevitable end of her life.

And then, just maybe, she'd find a taste of what she was seeking when she came to Indiana in the first place. The ordinary life. No castles. No kings. Just a house with a white picket fence and cookies in the oven.

The problem was getting away before her "rescuer" took her home and made her over into his pretty pet by stringing pink ribbons and a silver bell around her neck.

"Here we are," he said cheerily a minute later, as if he'd just pulled up outside Buckingham Palace. "Your temporary home." She hissed, but he just chuckled again. "Ah, give it a chance, little one." He came around and opened the door. He lifted out the cage, hefted it awkwardly into one arm and carried it toward the building.

Tall and well built, he had the muscles of a man who had worked hard in his life, not one who bench-pressed his way to perfection. The scent of him—a dark, very human scent —teased at her nose. Wood shavings, pine, a bit of sweat. And warmth. Like a blanket she could cuddle into.

She would *not* feel any kind of fondness for this Humanitarian Harry who'd interrupted her quest. Once he put her down, she'd find a way to escape and be on her way before he could say "God Save the Queen."

He opened the door, letting it shut behind them. There was a moment of total darkness as they traveled down a hall and into another room. He flicked a switch, sending the room into light. Catherine blinked until her eyes adjusted. The man laid the cage on a metal table in the center of a small, austere, white room. She peered through the bars, then shrank back. The sheen of stainless steel glinted back at her. Instruments. Medicines. Needles.

Panicking would do nothing but put her at a disadvantage. She held herself steady, focused on escape.

"Let's get you more comfortable, shall we?" He bent and peered into her cage.

Those eyes. Brown like a river of coffee, so kind they seemed to take her into his heart and hold her there, the way she'd always hoped home would be, but never had been, even two hundred years ago.

Catherine leaned forward, nose to the metal bars.

"Ah, there you go." He reached in a finger and stroked the bridge of her nose.

She lashed out, catching him good with one nail before he yelped and pulled back. That would teach him for kidnapping her.

Do it again, Buster, and I'll show you nineteen more like that one.

He chuckled and wagged his injured finger at her as if she'd been an errant child. She hissed and spat and yowled her frustration, but he merely smiled.

"You're really going to make me work to get your affection, aren't you?" He reached for the latch.

Catherine stilled. Finally. A chance to escape. She lowered her body, feigning acquiescence. He unlatched the door and reached inside, two broad warm hands at once encircling her and drawing her out of the cage. His grip was firm, secure.

Unescapable.

Catherine fought against him anyway, but he cradled her close, within the soft comfort of his sweater. A well-worn wool, washed so many times it felt rather like down. He ran a hand along her head, crooning again, saying nothing at all really, but sending a sense of calm rippling through her veins.

Against every instinct she'd honed in the last two centuries, Catherine relaxed, snuggling into that warmth, allowing herself to relax.

Such a long, lonely road I've traveled. How nice it would be to let someone else take care of me. For just one tiny, blissful minute.

And then, she'd go back to her life. To finding the kittens. To worrying about the curse, the deadline looming over her.

A low, quiet, strange rumbling started in her throat. Catherine jerked upright. The sound stopped. The man kept stroking her head and again, she relaxed. A second later, the curious sound started again, vibrating through her as gently as the wash of a tide.

Why was *that* sound coming from her throat? What did it mean? And why did it feel so good?

"There you are, little one," he whispered, touching every nerve with what seemed such intimate knowledge of the best-feeling places, "I knew I could make you purr."

She closed her eyes and forgot momentarily about escape. Absorbing simply this man, his touch, his kindness.

A few more seconds, that's all. Then she'd—

There was a squeak. Catherine opened her eyes only to see a second, bigger cage. He'd betrayed her. She shrieked but couldn't stop him from placing her inside and shutting the door.

"I'll be back, don't worry," he said. "Sleep tight."

Catherine hissed and swatted at his retreating form. A second later, the room was plunged into darkness.

She settled onto the newspaper-covered floor and let out a heavy sigh, ignoring the bowls of food and water beside her. Oh Lord, she was tired, more tired than she could remember feeling before. Maybe because the end was near.

Six more days and her fate would be sealed. For better or worse, this half-existence would be over.

She only had those few days to get a taste of what life might have been like—had she been able to go down a different lane. A life that could have included a husband, children. A home of her own. She'd missed out on all of that, thanks to Hezabeth's rather warped sense of revenge. If only--

Enough self-pity. Catherine got to her feet and paced the length of the metal container, clean newspaper crunching beneath her paws. She was in a bit of a sticky wicket, to say the least.

First on the agenda was escape. She'd deal with figuring out how to get back to the kittens, and the alley where she'd stashed her small reserve of cash for safekeeping, later. She'd had two hundred years to ponder her fate and hadn't reached any answers yet. Better to stay busy with the things she *could* change.

There had to be a way out. Finding a twenty-five-year-old blonde busting out of the locked two-by-three cage where he'd last seen a pale orange tabby would undoubtedly shock Humanitarian Harry into cardiac arrest. As appealing as that idea was, Catherine pushed it aside and went back to trying to figure out how she could pick a lock with four paws and a spattering of whiskers for tools.

The clock on the wall ticked along at a steady pace. Catherine had four hours to find a way out. Four hours until she changed from a cat...and became a woman again.

She had until sunrise to pull off a miracle.

Garrett couldn't sleep. Charlie, his Chocolate Labrador, snored loudly at the end of the bed. In a corner basket, Ferdinand and Isabel, a pair of muddled-blood cats, lay stretched out and quiet. Garrett, the only human in the room, lay on the bed, eyes open, arms crossed behind his head.

He'd come back to the house he shared with his Aunt Mabel at one in the morning. As always, he'd stopped to check on his elderly aunt, turning off the blaring TV and covering her with a blanket before heading to his own room. Up until a couple weeks ago, when Aunt Mabel had come down with a bout of pneumonia and temporarily needed more care, he'd lived in a cottage that sat on the back of her land.

When her home had been part of an estate, the little house had been the gardener's home. Ten years ago, Uncle Leo had converted it into a rental property. But when Leo died, leaving a grieving and frail Mabel alone, Garrett had moved into the cottage. Just at the right time, too, given all that had gone wrong in his life then.

Garrett rolled over and punched his pillow into a new shape, but it didn't make him any sleepier. His thoughts went back to the stray he'd found that night. She was such a tiny thing, all spit and fire. Despite her temper, she was a beautiful cat—short-haired and petite, with a pale orange coat, almost blond in color. He chuckled. Whoever took her home would need a lot of patience and cat treats to win over the grumpy girl.

Exhaustion weighed on him, but not enough to grant him sleep. His mind refused to quit, to give in and stop the reminders.

Garrett hadn't slept for more than two hours at a stretch in three years. Every time he closed his eyes, the nightmares returned, tearing at him, making him relive that horrible night again and again.

To hell with it. He got to his feet. The Monday morning sun would be up in an hour or so and then sleep would be pointless. As he'd done a thousand times before, he decided to go to the office before the rest of the world woke up. There was always work.

Ever since his last assistant had quit, he'd been running himself ragged, trying to keep up with the appointments, the shelter, and the day-to-day of running his practice. Dottie, his receptionist, was a big help, but what he really needed was a second pair of hands to work with the animals. Problem was, he'd been through three assistants in the past six months.

Either he couldn't hire good help, or he didn't have the personality to keep good help. He had a feeling it was the latter.

Standing around thinking about the problem wouldn't get it solved. He needed to work on plans for expanding the shelter and hopefully come up with a strategy to convince the Lawford Community Foundation to finance his dream. Their support thus far had been barely tepid, which admittedly was partly his own fault. He wasn't exactly a great communicator. If he was going to make his dream happen, he needed a miracle before Saturday night.

Without looking in the mirror, Garrett showered, shaved, and dressed. He avoided his reflection, slipping into jeans and a light blue button-down shirt, stepping into loafers and combing his hair into the same pattern as he had for almost twenty-eight years. Minutes later, he'd fed his cats and dropped them off at the cottage for the day, then set off for the office. Charlie panted in the seat beside him, eager for work.

First thing, he'd see how that cat was doing. After tangling with her last night, he'd put off an exam until today. No sense igniting her temper more than he already had. Once she was deemed healthy, he could find her a home.

He'd miss her, despite her cranky personality. He missed every animal that left his building. *You can't keep them all,* his mother always told him, *or you'll be running a zoo instead of a veterinarian's office.*

He already had three pets, more than enough for the cottage and for his aunt's home. And here, in the office, there was always a dozen or so waiting for his attention. Between the shelter and his veterinarian practice, hundreds of animals came into his care each year.

He loved them all. Well, except for Miss Tanner's giant Doberman. What he wouldn't give for a little help with Sweet Pea, whose name had nothing to do with her description or her personality. Even Dottie feared the dog, a nearly maniacal barker who ate almost everything in sight. Garrett had to admit he dreaded Miss Tanner and Sweet Pea's annual appointment. Not to mention her continual "emergency" visits with the dog.

Where her Doberman was concerned, Miss Tanner was a canine hypochondriac.

But the rest of the animals had a piece of his heart. Maybe because they never looked at him with a touch of horror in their eyes, never stood there with a question they dared not ask on their lips. They responded only to his touch and his voice, as if they were blind to everything else the world judged about Garrett McAllister.

He pulled up in front of the small white building decorated with a simple sign: "Garrett McAllister, D.V.M.". The sky was beginning to turn from gray to light pink as the sun edged up the horizon.

Charlie settled onto a padded dog bed by the front door. Garrett made his way through the darkened office, knowing the path without the help of a light. He'd worked here most of his life, first with Doc West, then by himself when he bought the practice from Doc three years ago. There'd been a year when he'd lived—and worked—somewhere else, but his life had always been here. These rooms were more like home than his own. More familiar, more comforting. The place where he most belonged.

He unlocked the door to the exam room. Last night, the shelter had been full, so he'd kept the tabby here. What he'd do with her once patients started coming in and out at nine, he didn't know, but he'd figure something out. A freezing rain was predicted for tonight and he had no intentions of letting the cat wander Lawford's streets.

He flicked on the light. She was sitting on her haunches, every sense on alert. Like she'd been expecting him.

"Good morning," he said. "Did you sleep?"

She glared at him in response.

He laughed. "Neither did I." Her food bowl was untouched. "Didn't like the selections on the menu? Let's try some canned food, then." He pivoted, reached for a can on the shelf and opened it into a bowl. The first signs of morning orange sky peeked through the blinds. The tabby let out a howl that sounded almost panicked. "I'm coming, I'm coming," he said, turning back toward her.

She was frantic now, pawing and gnawing at the bars, shrieking in frustration.

"It's okay, little one. It's okay."

She began to toss herself against the door of the cage. Was she in pain? Sick? Garrett rushed to unlatch the lock and thrust his free hand inside to catch her.

With a howl, she leapt past him, missing his grip by millimeters, dashing across the room and out the door he'd left ajar. She was gone in the space of a heartbeat. "You won't get far. Not unless you can open doors, too." Garrett picked up the bowl of food and left the room, following the cat's path. The office was small and most of the doors were shut. He'd find her soon enough.

※

One more second and it all would have been over. Her secret discovered—in one heck of a big way.

Nothing like making a grand entrance.

She darted out of the room, down the hall and through the first open door she saw. Just in time. She could feel it beginning to happen. The tingling, the stretching and expanding of her body from cat to woman.

She braced herself, hugged against the wall, knowing the pain was coming, yet jerking away in shock when it did. It was always like this when the change started. She'd never gotten used to it, even after two hundred years.

"Here kitty, kitty," came the man's voice. She heard him tap against the plastic food bowl. "Shrimp dinner. Come and get it."

By day a woman, by night a cat. The curse can only be broken if you find a man who loves you as both a woman and a cat. Every day, Hezabeth the Witch's screeching voice echoed in Catherine's mind.

Her arms and legs began to lengthen, the fur transforming into pale skin. Catherine closed her eyes and envisioned a quiet meadow, songbirds, blooming flowers, anything but the hideous half-animal/half-human creature she was for the next few seconds.

There was another momentary protest of pain from her body and then, finally, it was over.

Before she opened her eyes, Catherine ran a hand over her face and skin. As the end of the curse drew nearer, she worried one day it would all go horribly wrong, leaving her stuck between the two worlds and looking like some fifty-cent sideshow in the carnival.

Not today, thank God. Everything felt as it should. Human. Womanly. And then, she realized—

Naked.

"Here kitty, kitty." His voice again, closer. A few feet away.

Catherine scrambled to her feet, her eyes still unseeing— the last part of her body to adjust to the switch. In a second, she'd have her vision, but right now she was essentially blind.

How could she be so unprepared? The first time she'd transformed, she'd been caught naked in a marketplace in

London during the bustle before the holidays, with vendors scrambling to set out their wares in the early morning.

When an unclothed woman had suddenly sprung up in the middle of the square, the fishmonger had dropped his mackerel, the butcher nearly chopped off his index finger, and the ladies readying the dress shop for the day had swooned, silly bats fainting like they'd never seen a woman without clothes before.

Ever since, Catherine had made sure she was ready for the change, whether it meant stealing clothes from a washerwoman's line or diving into a charity donation bin.

But this time, she hadn't had a second to grab anything. She stood naked and cold against the wall, her vision now a blur of colors. How would she get past him? How could she explain being here at six in the morning?

Not to mention the nudity thing.

"Kitty?" The door across the hall clicked open, then shut. "Kitty?" Closer, on the other side of the pine door. *This* pine door. And then, the knob turned.

A miracle would take more time than Catherine had.

Continue reading KISSED BY CAT

To everyone out there who loves Olive and Hank just as much as I do.
I love you.
And, while I'm at it, never forget how much of a badass you are. I'm your biggest cheerleader.

"Luke, I swear to fuckin' everything stop messing around and help me. It's Olive's favorite holiday, you know this." Hank stared down at his best friend and firefighter brother, Lucas, with a hard glare.

When Lucas responded with an eye roll, Hank growled from deep within his throat. Lucas might be his best friend, but right now he was about to become his *dead* best friend.

Ignoring Hank, the jerk continued going through the box of decorations that Hank and Olive only put out in December, like he had all the time in the world. "Everyone knows it's Olive's favorite holiday." Lucas picked up a Christmas stocking from the box and examined it. "Even the aliens do."

"Don't I know it." Hank laughed as he cocked his brow at his best friend. "You know we have an alien-themed tree in our bedroom now, don't you? It used to be plaid-themed but somehow morphed into aliens without me even realizing it."

"I'm sure there is tons of anal probing going on up there." Lucas's eyes twinkled as his smile spread from ear to ear.

"Dude!"

"What?" Lucas shrugged, not even remotely trying to hide his smile. "Just sayin'."

Shaking his head, Hank snatched the stocking from Lucas's hand and hung it on the fireplace. "I wonder how the fuck you're my best friend half the time?"

"I thought Dog was your best friend, so hell if I know?"

The corner of Hank's mouth quirked. "You're right, Dog *is* my best friend. So I really don't know why I keep you around."

As if on cue, Dog, their child-sized Maine Coon cat, hissed from the other room, making Hank's face pale as he swallowed. Usually, when it came to Dog, the girl was putty in his hands.

Except when he did things she wasn't fond of.

And right now... Dog was pissed.

Is this how Olive feels most of the time?

Hank normally laughed it off when Dog had an attitude with Olive, but being on the receiving end of the cat's fury was no joke.

Right now Dog wanted to commit murder and Hank was first in line. And all because he put her in a Christmas sweater.

Well, tough shit because Olive thought Dog was downright adorable dressed up in it, so it was staying on whether Dog liked it or not.

Deciding it was best to ignore their cat and whatever plan she'd come up with to get back at him, Hank cleared his throat. "Can we get back on task? We have to get everything together before Olive and Miranda get back from shopping."

This way I can take the sweater off Dog before bloodshed happens...

A dreamy look ran across Lucas's face. "Oh, Manda Panda."

"What about her?"

"Nothing." Lucas grabbed another stocking from the box, examining it, before picking off invisible lint.

"You finally get her to talk to you?"

"She talks to me every day."

Both of Hank's brows shot toward the ceiling. "That so?"

"Yeah, I mean it's normally to yell at me to stop calling or texting her, but she's still talking to me. So, it counts."

"I don't think that actually counts as talking—"

"It does," Lucas cut him off as he smirked. "I'm a master at these things. It counts."

Hank opened his mouth to say something, but then stopped short. "Suddenly I now get what Olive means when she says you're a lot to handle."

"I'm a lot to handle all right. Just ask your sister." He waggled his brows.

"Lucas," Hank warned, his eyes narrowing on him. If he didn't watch it, Hank would gladly punch him in the gut.

Lucas dropped the stocking into the box and held his hands up in surrender. "Kidding. I'm kidding. Miranda won't let me near her with a ten-foot pole. Trust me, I've tried."

"Good."

Although, Lucas puffed out his chest in triumph as he spoke his following words, "One of these days, I'll get her to break."

"Do *not* break my sister or I'll kill you." Hank's lips thinned as he glared daggers at him.

Okay, sure, there was no doubt in Hank's mind his sister and Lucas would be perfect for each other. That being said, if Lucas so much as made his sister shed a tear or was the reason she'd stubbed her toe or anything else for that matter, Hank would be the first to dismantle the man.

Lucas might be his best friend, but Miranda would always come first.

"Pfft."

Hank's right brow arched. "Really?"

When Lucas greeted him with another playful smile, Hank snatched one of their holiday pillows off the couch and chucked it at his head. "You're a piece of work."

Lucas laughed as he dodged the pillow with ease. "True."

Hank rolled his eyes as he decided it was best to leave it alone as he walked back to the fireplace with a shake of his head. "Would you do me a favor and stop your yappin'? If you don't quit screwing around and actually help me, I will kick you in the balls."

"I'd like to see you try." Lucas shifted his body to Hank, a mischievous smile on his face. "Ever since you got married, I don't know if you even have balls anymore. The guys and I have a bet that—"

"For fuck's sake. I can't lose my balls. Are you kidding me right now?" Hank glared at the ceiling as he contemplated murdering him. However, before he could follow through, Hank's eyes caught their festive Santa clock on the wall.

Shit.

They were running out of time. Hank knew Olive would be back from their last-minute holiday shopping extravaganza —as his sister liked to call it—within the hour.

A heavy sigh escaped him as he closed his eyes. He already knew it would be hell on Olive being at the mall with a crap ton of people.

People—Olive's least favorite thing in the world.

After his sister and Olive left that morning, Hank had gotten the bright idea to finish putting out their December decorations in hopes of making Olive's day even just a bit more bearable. Which included the stockings that hung on the fireplace and the tiny tree Olive used to hide in her bedroom growing up.

If it were up to Hank, they'd keep everything out all year, but he understood why Olive insisted on putting them away in January.

Hank had to admit it was nice to put a few decorations out in December. Their house might be a full-time winter wonderland, but Hank couldn't lie. Since they didn't put their stockings out until right before Christmas, it always made it more special.

Kind of like the holiday season was finally there.

Hank wasn't huge on Christmas before Olive, but now... freaking call him Santa Claus. The holidays meant just as much to him as they did Olive.

Seeing her happy made him just as happy. And that's what this time of year did for her.

"Don't get all snippy with me, Tank. You and I both know you'd lose your head if it wasn't attached."

"For your information, I haven't lost anything in..." Hank paused, as he thought for a second. "...at least a week."

"Ha." Lucas flicked his eyes up. "Did you forget about being late two days ago to the station?"

"I wasn't late 'cause I lost something," he stated matter-of-fact, as he glared toward him.

Bastard.

Lucas's brows pulled together. "Sure it wasn't 'cause you lost something?"

"It wasn't. And if you must know, I was late 'cause I was deep inside my wife as we played out a scene in her new book. It was research."

Lucas dropped whatever he was looking at and turned to face Hank with his brow cocked. Then just as fast as the shock appeared on his face, it morphed into doubtfulness. "Why don't I believe you?"

Shit.

Try as he might, Hank couldn't stop his smug grin that formed. "Probably 'cause that's only half the truth. I was already late since we were testing out the logistics of a certain position and then I couldn't find my phone once we got it right."

"I knew it!" Lucas's whole face lit as he threw his fist in the air. "While we're at it, though, what position?" He clapped his hands together, his smile even wider.

"The mind-your-own-fucking-business one."

"You're no fun, Tank. You used to be more fun before you got married." Lucas pulled out his phone. "But you do make me a shit ton of money. Rick and Tim both owe me twenty bucks."

"You have got to be kidding me."

"When have I ever kid about such a thing?" He held his hand over his heart.

"Come to think of it, I should get a piece of your winnings since it's always *me* you're betting on."

"And why would I do that?" Lucas brushed him off. "Now, can we stop this annoying talk? We gotta get this finished before Miranda comes back."

"You mean my *wife* and Miranda."

"Yeah, yeah, her too," Lucas grumbled, as he looked through the box. "I'm still pissed Miranda didn't want me to go with them." Lucas's eyes moved back to Hank. "I begged and I *never* beg."

"You beg all the time." Hank's brow quirked. "It's annoying."

Ignoring him, Lucas continued. "I could be out there with them right now. Holding her bags, maybe pushing her to try on something skimpy."

"That's my sister."

Lucas shrugged with a wicked smile on his face. "I know."

"I will kill you."

"You can try but you'd forget something along the way." Lucas laughed. "I can't believe she's only in town for a little while, and yet, she's out there shopping with *Olive* when she could be here with me."

"Trust me. Olive doesn't want to be out there shopping either. She's gonna need a least a day or two to recover from it."

"That's what I'm saying. Miranda should've asked *me* to go and not Olive. I was the better option."

At this point, Hank almost agreed. Although, Olive would always be the better option between the two of them. He knew this was going to be hell on her once she finally made it home. Hopefully having all their December stuff up would help loosen the annoyance from her a little.

"It took her like what, a month to get over your wedding last year? I think it was only ten people max."

"Something like that," Hank agreed.

"And here I thought you were locked away with your bride doing all the naughty things she writes about in her books, but no. Instead, you were hidden away as she recovered," Lucas scoffed, shaking his head. "You've lost your touch, Tank."

"Believe me, we did all those things and more." The corner of Hank's mouth curved into a wolfish grin. "But yeah. She needed to de-people as she likes to say."

"So you *did* do the whole role-play hose thing from her firefighter book? I knew it!" Lucas pulled out his phone again. "Tim owes me another twenty and Rick ten."

"For fuck's sake, man."

Great, now Hank's eye twitched as a dull throb appeared behind his eye. He really should find a way to cash in on Lucas's earnings. At this point, they'd both be able to retire.

As his annoying best friend messaged their buddies, Hank thought back to last December twenty-fifth. That was the day when Olive and Hank had officially tied the knot in their winter wonderland home.

Lucas was by his side and Olive had Miranda. His dad, Jim, officiated it and his mom, Robin, made the food along with their wedding cake.

Hank's heart warmed. He really lucked out in having the best parents in the world. Especially when you compared them to Olive's. Hell, his mom even made a point to add two small Bigfoot prints on top of the cake to appease Olive's wacky conspiracy theory side.

And then of course, there was Rick and Tim who also attended.

It was small, but nice.

And that's exactly how he wanted their wedding to be.

Just the people that cared about them and the ones they cared about.

Thank fuck they hadn't seen Olive's parents since that day in the hospital. The mere thought of them still pissed Hank off. If it were up to him, he would've personally kicked them out of the room and then beat—

Stop. Don't go back down that road, Hank.

None of that mattered anymore. Olive's parents, if you could call them that, were out of their lives. And on Christmas Day last year, he and Olive got married with the people that meant the most to them by their sides.

Olive was completely healed from her accident by then. And truthfully, having their wedding on Christmas Day made the most sense.

It was the day Olive felt most alive.

And that was the only thing that mattered in the world. Hank now got to spend the rest of his life with his conspiracy-loving, Bigfoot-seeking, alien-obsessed love of his life.

It's why he really wanted to get the rest of their decorations on display. After all, he had a huge surprise for her.

"You didn't," Lucas groaned, halting Hank's thoughts. "Please for the love of everything, tell me you fucking didn't..."

Hank turned his attention to see Lucas pointing at Dog in her Christmas sweater.

Dog looks pissed. Shit.

"What?" Hank played dumb, trying but failing not to look at Lucas or the cat.

"Didn't we go through this when you tried putting her in it last year for the wedding? She bit you. If I recall correctly, you needed stitches."

"Did not."

"Yes, you did. I'm the one that took them out, numb-nuts." Lucas walked over to Hank, grabbing his arms to examine them. "Are you bleeding? I should've noticed already, but with all this fucking red everywhere, at this point, you're probably only a few seconds from bleeding out."

"Fuck you." Hank snatched his arms back. "I'm a big boy. I have the same medical training you do, fuckface. So, I could handle it if I got cut. Besides, Dog didn't get me this time."

"You're lucky."

"Whatever. She's cute in the sweater and Olive loves it." Hank glared at Dog. "So it stays."

Dog's eyes narrowed on Hank as she opened her mouth, showing off her perfectly sharp teeth. "That doesn't work on me like it does Olive."

"You know what, I think you just like pain now," Lucas chimed in, shaking his head with a chuckle.

A wicked smile ran across Hank's face. "Pain can be fun."

"Don't I know it. Every time Miranda turns me down I like it more and more."

"My *sister*..."

"I know." The corners of Lucas's mouth quirked upward.

However, as Hank reached for the nearest object to toss at his best friend's head, his phone pinged.

Damn it. Hank knew he heard it, but fuck him he had no idea where it was. *Shit, why do I always lose everything?*

Quickly he began searching through the boxes he'd pulled out from the attic that morning thinking he might have acci-dentally dropped it in one of them. Doing his best to ignore his laughing friend, he bounced from box to box, hunting for his stupid phone.

"You lost it, didn't you?"

"No," Hank clipped, refusing to look at him.

However at that exact moment, the phone pinged again, pretty much calling him a liar.

Fuckin' A.

"Let me call it." A heavy sigh came from Lucas as he pulled out his phone. "Well, shit." He laughed, holding his phone in the air for Hank to see. "Olive sent me a text. She figured you lost your cell and wanted me to tell you she hates people, this is too much, and you owe her. Oh, oh, and something about Bigfoot cosplay." He looked back at his best friend, arching his brow. "Wanna explain that last one?"

"She didn't say that."

"Fine." Lucas pouted. "She didn't, but she should have. Like I said, you're no fun anymore."

Hank watched as Lucas's fingers flew over the screen of his phone, assuming he was texting Olive back.

For fuck's sake. Am I ever gonna catch a break?

With another ping sound throughout the room, Hank wanted to punch himself. Thankfully though, as his phone went off again, he was able to pinpoint the location.

After a few more seconds, Hank spotted the corner of his cell under a pile of holiday throw blankets. He quickly lunged for it, landing on the couch in the process.

Hell yeah, that was only what a few minutes, right? A personal best. He smiled proudly at himself as he swiped through his phone, going to his messages. Before he could open the app, he received another text from Olive.

OLIVE

> Really?! You had to lose your phone, of all the things? Now, I owe Luke $10. You were supposed to lose your keys, not your phone! Come on, Hank. I'm trying to make us money here.

Hank snapped his eyes to Lucas as he glared at his ex-best friend. "You made a bet with my wife against me?"

When his only response was a shrug, Hank almost punched him.

"Like I said, you make me a lot of money."

It's the holidays, you can't kill your friends during the holidays. That'd be too suspicious.

Taking a deep breath, Hank replied to Olive's message.

HANK

One.

Hank didn't have to wait long before she answered.

OLIVE

Hold on there, mister. I did nothing to get that.

Damn, she was quick when she was angry.

HANK

Two.

Olive's reply came instantly.

OLIVE

Hank!

He was enjoying this far too much now.

HANK

Wanna make it three? That's what you get for betting against your husband with his best friend. And for the Bigfoot thing.

It was probably less than a second before he got her reply.

OLIVE

I didn't bet against you. I bet FOR you. You always lose your keys. And what the hell are you talking about what Bigfoot?

A playful smile ran across Hank's face.

Yeah, he was loving every single second of this.

Damn he loved his life.

Hank roared with laughter as he sent back a kissing emoji face. Once it was sent, he shoved his phone in his back pocket to avoid losing it again.

He couldn't stop the smile on his face as he thought about just how much use they were going to get out of his gift to Olive.

The same gift that involved them completely alone on a holiday getaway.

Damn. Olive was going to love it and so was he.

Yeah, this was going to work out perfectly in his favor. With an extra pep in his step, he tossed another pillow at Lucas's face. "Come on, dickhead, let's get a move on. Olive's only got about an hour in her before she loses it."

"Whatever you say, boss, that means Miranda gets back sooner too. Speaking of that, how long is she gonna be in town? She didn't say when I asked."

Hank held his tongue to stop from saying forever. He promised Olive and his sister he wouldn't be the one to tell Lucas Miranda was moving back home permanently. The marketing job didn't work out. She hated her boss, and her boss hated her.

His sister thought it was her dream job come true. It was anything but. The stress was too much, and she just couldn't do it anymore. So sometime in January, she'd be back home for good.

Which honestly Hank was more than happy about. Yeah, he would get his sister back, but more importantly Olive would be getting her best friend back.

Not that they didn't talk all the time, but still. This was going to be good for everyone. Lord knows his mother wouldn't stop talking about her babies being close to her again.

Blah.

"Not sure," he lied. "Hey, you still good to stay in the house while I take Olive away for our anniversary?"

Hank had it all planned out. They'd spend three days at this little cabin he booked only a few hours from where they lived. He'd arranged everything from the cabin owners putting up holiday lights to him being allowed to bring Dog.

It was going to be their perfect holiday escape and the best part was, they'd still be able to celebrate Christmas with their family the day they got back.

It really was a win-win.

"Duh. It'll be nice to not bunk with a bunch of sausages for a change. If it were up to me, you two would leave now and I'd already be moved in."

"Don't fuck up our house."

"I would never." Lucas shot his hand to his chest in shock. "I'm a little offended you think I would."

Before Hank could reply, Dog hissed from the corner of the room as she focused her death stare on Lucas. "Exactly," Lucas agreed.

$$\overline{}$$

CHAPTER TWO

$$\overline{}$$

"SWEET MOTHER OF BABY PEARL, it wasn't *that* bad, Olive. It was just a little holiday shopping. You're acting like I took you to your execution."

Olive glared at her traitorous best friend from the passenger side of the SUV. "Says you! It might as well have been. It was *horrible*. I should get an award for 'Master Dodger of People or something'." Olive folded her arms over her chest.

"You did disappear quite a lot. Although, hiding in the round rack of clothes was a new one. I only thought kids did that." Miranda's nose scrunched as she glanced at Olive for a brief second before focusing back on the road.

"What did you want from me? There were people *every-where,* and I didn't hide in the clothes. I was pushed in there by some loony-bin person trying to grab the last who-the-fuck-knows off the shelf." Olive shrugged, looking away. "And once I was in there, I figured I might as well stay. It was safer."

"It was also a bitch to find you."

A sly smile crossed Olive's face as she turned back to Miranda. "But you did find me."

"Only after pinpointing your location on my phone. Thank God we set that up after the accident. Remind me to thank my brother for that later."

"You aren't supposed to bring that up anymore." Olive's whole body slumped in the seat as she thought about that day. She still hated talking about it, and well... if she were being honest, driving was still kind of rough for her even after all this time.

Olive's body no longer had bruises and her scars had faded a little, but it was still challenging, especially mentally.

Subconsciously, Olive's eyes moved to her leg. Even though she wore pants she could see the ugly scar that ran down her thigh in her mind. Hank called them her war wounds, and he always made sure to pay extra attention to them. But to Olive, they were still a reminder of the day she almost lost it all.

The love of her life, her best friend, their parents, Robin and Jim—who she called her own—and even their pain in the ass, always mad about something cat.

Olive didn't know how much time would need to pass for her to accept everything that happened, but right now it still messed with her from time to time.

Miranda placed her hand on Olive's knee as they came to a red light. "I know. That's why I'm driving your car. It doesn't matter how long it's been, it's okay to have your feelings. You're allowed to feel however you want."

"I should be able to drive my dang car whenever I need to."

"And you do. But right now, you don't *need* to." Miranda glanced at Olive, her eyes flooding with tears. "I've always got you. So if I need to drive the car, I will. Zero questions asked. You're my sister. I love you."

Miranda focused on her. "You scared the shit out of me that day. The phone call... I don't think I took a breath until I saw Hank in the waiting room. I'm surprised they didn't kick me off the plane." Her eyes went back to the road as the light turned green. "That was a hard day for all of us, but it's okay. You made it. Although, I am not fully convinced you didn't have brain damage since you married my dumbass brother. Anyway, you survived and if driving a car freaks you out, no one gets to say shit about it. You survived, Olive. That's all that matters."

Tears welled in Olive's eyes as she looked at Miranda, placing her hand on top of hers and giving it a light squeeze. "I love you. But can we change the subject, please?"

"Sure." Miranda pulled her hand off Olive's knee as a playful smile crossed her lips. "How long do you think it'll take Lucas to figure out I'm moving back?"

Olive barked out a laugh as she shook her head. "Who knows. I still think you should just tell him. Lord knows I'm so freaking tired of him asking about you. I don't know if he'll even leave our house knowing you're here."

"It's sweet, in a stalker kind of way."

"Sure." Olive looked at her best friend like she was crazy.

"Besides, I'm positive he's lost most of his interest anyway." She huffed out a nervous laugh. "When he saw how much I've changed since coming back for the holidays. I don't know, Olive, he just stared at me like I had three heads."

"What do you mean changed?"

"Filled out." Miranda waved her hand up and down her body causing Olive's brow to arch.

"Are you talking about your drop-dead gorgeous curves? Phuullleeaasse. That man worships the ground you walk on." Olive snorted. "You've got nothing to worry about. Trust me. Although..." She turned to her best friend, her eyes narrow. "I'm still pissed at you. This is twice now shit has gone on behind my back and you never told me. First, it was you moving, and now this. If it was really that bad why didn't you tell me?"

"And you started sleeping with my brother and somehow

forgot to inform me, so I think we're even." Miranda sent her a pointed look.

"Uhhh, well. Umm, you see, it wasn't like that. It was more of a research thing and—"

"Blah blah blah, I'm not listening. This is my brother you're talking about. We're just gonna never talk about the *research* you did. Besides, it wasn't that bad at the marketing firm. It's just..." She paused, taking a deep breath. "I was under a lot of stress and my boss was kinda an ass. When I turned down his date he just... I don't know maybe he was offended and it went downhill from there."

Olive's eyes hardened. "I'm gonna murder him in my next book."

"That's sweet of you."

"I'm serious. This was your dream job and just 'cause some asshat couldn't handle being rejected, he had it out for you. You know what? I think I'm gonna torture and *then* murder him."

"Aww, you really do love me."

"I just hate people," Olive scoffed, crossing her arms over her chest.

"I know."

"And I hate people who are mean to my best friend. So much, that she needed to leave her dream job. Don't get me wrong about you coming home. It's a huge win for me, but I still wanna fly over there and punch him in the throat."

"You wouldn't last five seconds on a plane full of people."

"True," Olive agreed. "But hey, I'd be closer to space. Maybe if I got a window seat I could spot anything out of the norm. Ohhh, I should get a night flight. That way I can search for lights that move in weird ways or stay still in the sky. Actually, you know what? This all sounds pretty good if you ask me. Let me just text Hank." Olive bounced in her seat with excitement, her annoyance of shopping completely thrown out the window.

"Don't you dare. It's done and over with. You're already killing him off in a book. That's good enough for me. Besides by January I'll be back. My notice is in. Everything is signed and completed." Miranda's face scrunched. "Ugh, I'm gonna have to start looking for a place to live and find a new job."

"Hey! A new marketing firm recently opened here." Olive snapped her attention to Miranda, her eyes bright and full of enthusiasm. "That reminds me, Dr. Richman and Holly were talking about it when we took Dog in for her annual last month. Oh my God, Miranda, get this, they have a hairless cat as one of their clients." Olive shuddered. "And I thought Dog was bad. I can't even imagine living with a naked cat."

Miranda burst out laughing. "I'm gonna tell Hank to get you one for Christmas. Man, I'd die to see your reaction."

"You wouldn't."

"I would. And thanks, Mom already told me all about the new firm when I flew in. I think their names are Hunter and Abbie. Apparently, Mom's friends with Abbie's mom, and when I told her I was moving back she told me all about it. They're giving WCM Enterprises a run for their money in the marketing department. Maybe if I can get a job with them, I can convince the owners to introduce you to their cat."

"Hell no! First, they'd be stupid to not hire you. And second, you better not. I love Dog. Don't get me wrong, but she's enough cat for me. Besides, you can stay with me and Hank. You're always welcome to live with us. It'll be like old times. You can have the room next to my office."

Miranda shook her head. "I love you but I'd rather not. It's bad enough I'm staying with you right now. I do *not* want to hear my best friend doing my brother. *Ever.*" She shook her head harder. "Eww."

"Don't lie. You just don't want to be around Dog."

"I'm not, but you do have a point. She is kinda mean at times."

"Kinda. Pfft. That's an understatement." Olive rolled her eyes. "She thinks she's my protector now. Ever since the accident I can't tell if she's trying to save me or if she's just plotting for her to kill me on her own terms. I think Dog's just pissed she didn't get to almost kill me herself."

"Probably a little of both."

"You're right." Olive chuckled, as she saw her home come into view out of the window.

"Damn it, why the hell is Lucas here?" Miranda grumbled as she pulled into Olive's driveway.

"Beats me. Wherever Hank is, Luke is. Honestly, I'm surprised Rick and Tim aren't here too. They must be on shift at the station."

"This is true. They're usually a package deal the four of them."

"And thank the Universe, we're home." Olive sighed as she relaxed into her seat. "Luke I can deal with. But if I had to be around another horde of shoppers today, I'd lose it. I'm all for hordes of zombies but in a hurry last-minute Christmas shoppers—nope. I'd rather gouge out my eyes, thank you very much."

"There you go again with your zombies and stuff. What does my brother see in you?"

Olive's eyes lit as she sent Miranda a toothy grin. "Who knows."

They both burst into laughter as they got out of the car and made their way to the front door. The moment they opened it though, Olive's heart soared. There in front of her was almost all of their remaining holiday decorations in their place.

As her eyes skimmed the room, she saw their stockings hung by the fireplace. There was hers, Hank's, and then the one they got for Dog last year.

However, there was another stocking right next to Dog's, which surprised her.

"I said take it down."

"No, my stocking is going up there just like yours."

"And it will, I promise. Luke, I swear to God I will drop kick you. I want Olive to see—"

"You want me to see what?"

Hank froze the exact moment he'd gotten Lucas in a headlock after hearing Olive's voice. As his eyes widened, Hank released him, throwing his hands in the air like he didn't do it. "Olive Oil, you're back."

"I am."

A huge smile spread across Hank's face as he advanced toward her, not caring about the other people in the room. Once he was there, Hank pulled Olive into his arms, kissing her like he did the moment she woke up from her coma. After a few seconds, he pulled back resting his forehead on hers. "You were gone long, but not long enough. We aren't done." Hank snapped his attention to Lucas with narrowed eyes. "Thanks to him."

"It looks pretty good to me." Olive glanced around the room, her smile growing even wider as she fell more in love with her home.

It also helped Lucas was pouting by the fireplace.

Olive really did love her year-long winter wonderland more than ever. Hank gave her this so she'd feel free.

And, she did.

Every second, of every day, she finally felt free.

Hank did that for her.

And during the holidays, when their stockings and a few other things were put out, Olive couldn't ask for a better place to call home. "It really looks great."

"It will once Luke takes his damn stocking down. I said you can put it up *after* Olive gets a good look at everything," Hank growled directly at Lucas who instantly glared back at him.

Boys... She didn't know whether to laugh or shake her

head. At least they weren't on the floor fighting. If they hadn't walked in when they did, Olive was sure they would've been.

"Ahh, let him leave it. It looks good there." Olive winked at Hank's best friend. "He'll just keep putting it back anyway."

"See, your wife gets me. You would think *you'd* get me after all these years, but no." He turned to Olive. "Thank you." After Lucas finished fixing his stocking to make it perfect, he puffed out his chest and focused his attention on the other person in the room. "Hey there, Miranda Panda. Did you have fun shopping? Did you miss me?"

"I did have fun shopping, especially since you weren't there."

"Right through the heart, baby." He held his hand over his chest. "You wound me."

"And yet you keep coming back."

"They do say I'm a glutton for punishment."

"You're a glutton for something all right."

Lucas's eyes heated as he looked Miranda up and down before Hank punched him in the shoulder. "My *sister*."

"I know." The corner of Lucas's mouth turned upward as he winked at Miranda. "You have excellent genes in your family. Olive would have to agree, wouldn't you, sweetheart?"

"Don't call her sweetheart," Hank growled as he punched him in the arm again.

"He does have a point there, Hank. Your sister is a stunner and you aren't so bad to look at either."

Both of Hank's brows shot to the ceiling. "Not so bad to look at?"

Olive shrugged. "I call 'em as I see 'em."

"Oh, really? Wanna make the count fifteen then?"

Olive's eyes rounded for a split second before she glared at her husband. *I'll kill you.*

"I told you, your wife gets me better than you." Lucas

puffed his chest again. "Remind me to tell Momma Parker she's doing the Lord's work."

Hank snapped his attention to his friend. "Olive would be the first to sacrifice you to some alien overlord. Don't forget that." Hank narrowed his eyes at him, which only caused Lucas to shrug.

"It could be fun. Who knows, maybe I'll like it."

"Hey." Olive snapped her hands to her hips. "Don't make fun of me."

Hank walked back to his wife, pulling her into his arms. "I would never, Olive Oil." He kissed the top of her head.

"Yes, you would."

"He would," Lucas agreed. "Trust me, I know this for a fact."

Hank shot daggers toward him. "Don't believe Luke, babe. I wouldn't trust him or his word."

Lucas glared back at him. "You trust me enough to watch your house while you're away."

"We aren't going away." Olive's eyes widened as a familiar panic crept into her chest.

Away? Away where? Will there be people? Will I have to interact with others? Oh God, we better not be going away.

"It was gonna be a surprise, you asshole." Hank tossed the nearest object he could find directly at Lucas. "For fuck's sake, man.

"What? I thought you forgot." Lucas shrugged. "I mean you do lose everything. Your brain is all over the place all the time. So, I figured you needed a segue."

"What's he talking about?" Olive darted her eyes to Hank as worry filled her.

A heavy sigh escaped him as Hank glared one last time at his best friend before turning back to Olive. "I wanted to surprise you."

"I'm surprised all right, I'm just not sure if it's good or bad yet."

"Hopefully, good." With another growl directed at Lucas, Hank focused on Olive. "I was gonna tell you tonight once we were alone. I booked us a cabin getaway to celebrate our first anniversary together." He held up his hands stopping her from speaking. "It's in the middle of nowhere, there will be zero people."

"I like that."

"And since it's a private cabin, we get to bring Dog."

Okay, the cat might be a pain in her ass but knowing she'd get to go with them made Olive feel better. "Keep going."

"I know last year was rough since we had everyone in the house for the wedding."

"It was less than ten people!"

Olive snapped her face to Miranda, sending a death glare her way.

"That's what I said!" Lucas agreed with the traitor.

"Ten is a lot." Olive focused on her annoying best friend. "Plus, look at all the people you forced me around today. Thank the Universe I was pushed into the clothes rack. It was a great hiding spot."

Hank growled deep in his throat as his eyebrow quirked. "Someone pushed you?"

Miranda held up her hands at Hank. "Don't let her fool you. She was probably just lightly touched and used that as an excuse to hide."

"It worked, didn't it."

Miranda rolled her eyes, crisscrossing her arms over her chest. "Until I had to find you."

"You lost her?"

At the panic in Hank's voice Olive didn't know whether it was endearing he cared that much or frustrating since she was a grown woman and didn't need everyone to watch out for her.

"She hid. I found her, didn't I?"

Hank glared at his sister before turning his sights onto his wife. "Olive..." Hank warned.

"What?"

"Sixteen."

"Are you kidding me?!"

"Wanna make it seventeen?"

"I will climb up there and punch you in the face. I was safe. I hid from all the crazy last-minute shoppers. You should be proud of me."

"You let Miranda out of your sight."

"I'm a big girl. I can handle myself just fine."

Hank arched his brow, staring her down. "Didn't say you couldn't, but after the accident, I will *never* let anything happen to you. I thought I could trust my sister—"

"She's home, isn't she?" Miranda snapped.

Ignoring her, Hank kept his focus on Olive. "I won't go through that again. It was torture waiting to see *if* you were gonna wake up."

"He does have a point," Lucas chimed in. "Can't blame him for wanting you safe. You weren't there when we pulled up and saw it was *your* car upside down. Okay, wait, you were there but you know what I mean."

"Why is everyone bringing that up today?!"

Hank placed his hand under her chin so she'd look into his eyes. "Because we love you and never want anything to ever happen to you again."

"I'll be fine *and* am fine, I promise."

"I know." He kissed her again. "You put up with a lot of our crap. That's why this year I wanted to take you away. Zero people. Just you, me, and Dog in a cabin. And when we get back we'll celebrate Christmas with the guys and the family, but just for our anniversary it'll be us."

As Olive looked at her husband, she felt all his love pour out of him for her. He really did complete her in ways she never thought possible.

Before Hank, Olive didn't believe in love.

After Hank, she realized love was real, she just needed the right person to show her.

And Hank showed her.

"Sounds like a dream come true," she replied, melting into Hank's side. "But why does Luke need to stay here if we're only gonna be gone a few days?"

"My lease is up on my apartment. I'm at the station most of the time, so I haven't had a chance to find a new one yet. I'll be on shift, but it'll be nice to come to a place that feels like home after a long day."

Olive's heart melted at his words. She didn't know much about Lucas's family other than he didn't see them or speak about them. And man, did she understand that. Sometimes you couldn't help the family you were born into. Olive more than anyone got that.

That's one of the reasons she never put up a fight when Lucas or heck, any of the guys hung around her winter wonderland.

Sometimes your chosen family was more of a family than your blood family would ever be. Olive was lucky Robin and Jim accepted her with open arms since day one.

Lucas plopped himself onto their couch and kicked his feet up on the table. "Besides, it'll be nice to have this whole place as my bachelor pad."

"Hey, wait a second!" Olive jumped out of Hank's arms. "Nope, no way in hell." She shook her head. "We can't let him stay here on his own. He'll throw some party and destroy everything. No, absolutely not."

"Wait, I was just your favorite. How can you turn on me so quickly?" Lucas placed his hand over his chest again, like he'd been shot. "That hurts."

"Have you met you? You've probably already got Rick and Tim on standby for when we leave."

"Ouch."

Olive swung her body to Miranda. "You're staying here too."

"I already am. Did you forget?" She backed away from the room slowly with her hands up. "You know what, I'm gonna go stay with mom. I'm not staying here with *him*."

"You have to," Olive pleaded. "All your stuff is here anyway and you'll be the only one to keep Lucas in line. Please, I'm begging you. He's got the mind of a toddler."

"Says the woman who believes in aliens and Bigfoot."

Olive snapped her attention to the man on her couch acting like he already owned the place. "I will punch you in the throat." Olive swung back to Hank. "I love that you got us a cabin we can spend our anniversary and Christmas at. I'm still trying to process everything. But if someone's gonna watch our house while we're away and you pick *him*, I get to have Miranda here too. She was already staying with us to begin with." Olive's mind raced with images of Lucas throwing some ridiculous party and destroying half her home, making her blood pressure skyrocket.

Miranda crossed her arms over her chest. "I'm right here you know."

Olive ignored her as she continued. "How could you forget she was staying with us?"

As Hank's eyes moved past her to look at his sister, Olive saw something flash across his face. Try as she might though, she couldn't figure out what it was.

"Sorry about that. It must've slipped my mind. I am known for being forgetful after all." Hank shrugged, way too calmly.

"But you don't forget stuff like this," Miranda spat as she glared at him. "I don't know how you could've forgotten. Mom's still pissed I'm here instead of with her and Dad."

"She's only okay with you staying with us 'cause you're mo—"

"I'll do it!" Miranda screamed, cutting Hank off before she darted her eyes at Lucas. "I won't like it, but I'll do it."

"Well, Manda Panda, it just so happens *I'm* going to really love it." Lucas's brows wiggled before he winked her way.

Ignoring the fight she knew was about to happen, Olive's eyes moved to her husband who sheepishly looked away. She wasn't positive, but for some reason she had a sneaking suspicion Hank knew exactly what he was doing when he asked Lucas to stay while Miranda was already there.

You just don't forget that.

Sure Hank lost everything, but he was brilliant. So him forgetting something like his sister staying with them made no sense. There was definitely more going on than he let on.

Seriously, Miranda had been in their house for the last two days already.

Before Olive could question him, something moved in the corner, catching her eye.

Oh, God...

"Uhh, why is Dog in a Christmas sweater?"

All eyes in the room shot to the cat in the doorway.

"And more importantly, why does it look like all of us are on the menu?"

CHAPTER THREE

"Why the heck are we leaving before the butt crack of dawn?" Olive groaned as she tossed her bag into the trunk of their SUV. It'd been a few days since Hank surprised her with, what she was now deeming her perfect retreat from the world. However, before Olive's hand even left the bag she was tossing into the back, she heard a deep growl come from her husband.

"Why are you so stubborn?" Then to make his point, Hank snatched the bag Olive tossed into the back, took it out, and put it back in, staring her down the whole time.

"Are you serious?" Olive's hand shot to her hip as her lips thinned. "I can put stuff in the trunk without you having to go all caveman on me." When she reached to grab the bag again, she stopped when Hank's eyes hardened even further on her.

For freak's sake. If she didn't like it when he got all growly, she'd punch him in the gut.

Olive rolled her eyes. Don't get her wrong, Olive loved Hank's take-charge attitude, but there were still times he annoyed the absolute crap out of her. Like right now, or like the time he rearranged her books on the bookshelf to mess with her.

Taking a page right out of Hank's book, Olive growled. Come to think of it, she'd never gotten him back for that. Something Olive had sworn she'd get revenge on.

As she looked him up and down, she huffed out a sigh as she gave up. Besides, it was way too freaking early and no one had time for grumpy bullheaded Hank.

Not even her.

Olive moved her hand to her side away from the bag, however she didn't miss the satisfied smirk on Hank's face thinking he won.

He didn't.

She was just gonna file this away for later. It'd already been a pain in the ass getting Dog together, and she really didn't have it in her to deal with Hank as well.

No one would after that she-devil.

There were more important things to address other than him being well... him. "You still haven't answered my question. Why in the hell are we leaving at twelve-thirty in the morning? Who does that? It's still dark out. We should be sleeping or I should be writing. There shouldn't be outside time happening."

"We do," Hank stated matter-of-fact. He grabbed Dog's food and all the other items they were bringing for her and placed them in the trunk with the bag she'd tried to add, all the while giving Olive a side-eye. "And you aren't working. You promised. You're taking the whole month of December off. This isn't like before when you only had Miranda or the times you lied and stayed at home rather than celebrating with our family." His nostrils flared as he stared down at her.

What? Hold up there, buddy! Her lips pursed.

Yeah, there were a few times she might have told a lie or two about going to see her family, rather than spend the holidays with the Parkers. They never made her feel like a third wheel but she always felt bad for encroaching on their family time. It was hard to get used to going from being the biggest disappointment and pretty much no family to having a family that loved and cared for her.

Olive did the best she could, when the people that were supposed to love her, didn't. You can't blame her for being cautious. The Universe knew she spent enough time at the Parkers to begin with.

"You'll never work on a holiday again and you sure as fuck won't ever be alone."

"Hank..."

"Don't *Hank* me." He crossed his arms over his chest as he winked at her. "And the *only* work you'll be doing on our anniversary trip, will be in the research department." His eyes filled with lust, causing a slight blush to creep onto Olive's cheeks.

"I love after all this time I can still get you to blush." He leaned forward, brushing his lips against her ear. "Only now, I know it goes all over your body."

"Can you guys keep it down out there. Some of us are trying to sleep!" Lucas yelled through a window he'd opened in the guest bedroom.

"Ugh." Olive frowned at her husband, as her brow cocked. "Why did we agree to let him stay here?"

"I have no idea," Hank grumbled, flipping Lucas off. "Shut your face, you're gonna wake Miranda up."

"Too late." The window on the other side of the front of their house flew open to reveal a very sleepy Miranda pop her head out.

"Sorry."

"Whoa, Momma, don't you look all sexy and soft in your sleep ruffled state," Lucas purred as he leaned out his window toward Miranda's.

"Eat shit." Miranda promptly flipped him the bird before twisting back to Olive and Hank. "I can't believe you're actually leaving me here with this buffoon. You owe me. I could peacefully be sleeping away at Mom and Dad's right now. But no, I'm here with *him*."

Olive glanced at Hank, worrying her lip. "On second thought, maybe leaving them both here alone wasn't a good idea at all."

Instantly, the corner of Hank's mouth turned up as his eyes brightened. "It's a great idea. They'll either finally get their shit together or one of them will end up dead."

"Twenty bucks on Lucas."

Hank burst into a hearty laugh as he nodded. "Olive Oil, you took the words right out of my mouth."

"You guys got everything you need?" Miranda asked, ignoring Lucas's attempts to get her attention.

"We're all set," Hank replied with a massive smile on his face. "You two kids have fun."

"You sure about that?" Lucas cut him off. "Do you have your keys?"

"Yes, I have my keys. How else do you think I got the trunk open?"

A playful smile appeared on Olive's face as she looked back at their friend. "It took us twenty minutes to find the keys. That's why we're leaving at twelve-thirty instead of midnight."

Hank swung his attention to Olive. "Really?"

"Tim owes me ten bucks!"

"What?" Olive's eyes sparkled as she ignored Lucas celebrating from behind her. "I was just answering his question."

Hank tsked, shaking his head. "Already racking up those numbers I see." Hank's eyes slowly traced Olive's body up and down before stopping on her face. He smirked before giving her another once-over. "You know, instead of baiting me all you have to do is ask."

Olive's jaw hit the floor as she scrambled. She didn't know whether to punch him or herself because she'd be lying if she said she didn't enjoy their extracurricular research activities.

Dang it! Abort! Abort!

Before Olive could say anything, though, Hank turned back to his sister. "Mom's gonna call to check on you guys. She's also gonna stop by. Try not to kill each other before then, please."

"How could I forget?" Miranda rolled her eyes. "I don't know why she's insisting on setting up your place for Christmas. It's not like it doesn't already look like Christmas threw up in here twenty times over."

"She'll be dropping off the food and some gifts." The annoyance in Hank's voice was audible, even to Olive.

Wait. That reminds me!

Olive pointed her finger at both of them. "Don't you dare open your gifts I put under the tree without us and *no* peeking." She narrowed her focus on Lucas. "If I come back and find your gift tampered with, I will murder you."

Lucas's eyes widened. "Do you think *I'd* really ruin the surprise?" His hand flew to his chest like she'd shot him.

"Yes," Olive and Miranda answered at the same time.

"I'm hurt."

"Just don't do it." Olive tried to harden her expression even further, but knew she'd failed when she saw the smirk on Lucas's face. "We'll be back on the twenty-sixth. We'll celebrate then. You're a grown-ass adult, you can wait."

"The grown adult is probably going too far." Hank laughed. "This is Lucas you're talking about."

"Hey! I can hear you."

"I wasn't trying to keep it quiet."

"Asshole," Lucas mumbled, before shrugging it off. "Whatever. I still don't get how you booked your cabin so you'd have to leave the next day. Isn't that kinda a waste of a trip? Why didn't you make it longer?"

"I did that on purpose." Hank pinched the top of his nose

as he sighed. "I've already told you this. And you say I'm absent-minded. Put my sister anywhere near you and you forget how to spell your damn name."

"Hello! I'm right here!" Miranda snapped.

Ignoring her, Hank continued. "We could have stayed all week, I have the time off from the station, but I knew Olive would want to celebrate with everyone. She might hate most people but for some reason, she loves you assholes."

Olive glanced at Hank, nodding. "It's true."

"See, I know my wife. That's why I arranged it, so we'd be home the next day. That way we can celebrate with our *family*. But, I still get alone time with my wife for our anniversary, if you get my drift. But we'll be here for the family togetherness of the holidays and all that shit."

"Eww." Miranda gagged before jabbing her fingers in her ears. "I'm not listening. I'm just gonna skip most of that and go straight to the family part."

However, instead of Olive focusing on Miranda's outburst, Lucas's face caught her attention. She couldn't stop her heart from clenching. "Which includes you, Luke. You are *our* family. And that means so help me God, if you open your gifts before I get home I will sic Dog on you. And then if she doesn't maul your ass, I'll do it myself."

From the backseat of the SUV Dog hissed.

Lucas looked to Hank as he pointed at Olive. "You good with her mauling my ass? And here I thought you were possessive."

"I am."

Lucas's face broke into a playful grin. "I don't think I've ever felt so loved."

"Don't get used to it," Miranda mumbled, as she focused her attention back on Olive and Hank. "How'd ya get Dog in the carrier without us hearing you?"

"I heard them," Lucas remarked. "However, I chose to stay in my room versus helping them and their demon spawn.

Dog used to be the best at the station. Ever since she got around Olive though, she's become something from another planet." He smirked at Olive. "You do that to Dog?"

"Don't call her that," Hank barked, sending a death glare toward Lucas.

"It's true."

Olive laughed. "He has a point, Hank."

Hank snapped his attention to her. "She's gonna remember you said that, Olive Oil. She can hear you, or did you forget the backdoor is still open?"

"She will," Miranda agreed with a chuckle. "Okay, you guys have fun. We'll see you in a few days."

Deciding not to look over her shoulder at Dog, Olive waved at her best friend. If she didn't see Dog's expression, then all was good in the world. You know that if you don't see it, then it didn't happen kind of thing? "Bye, love you. Don't do anything stupid."

Miranda ignored her as she closed her window, making Olive's jaw drop.

Jerk. She's lucky I love her.

"Do you love me too?" Lucas cooed.

"Sure, bud." Hank waved at him. "Love you, Lucas."

"I was hoping that would come from Olive, but I'll take it from you too. Drive safe and let us know when you get there."

"We'll try. Not sure how much service we'll have."

Instantly, Lucas's face hardened as his eyes went to Hank. "Find service. Make sure we know you're okay."

Olive knew that look. It was the same look Hank had given her far too many times for her to count. The one that screamed *you both mean a lot to me and you better be safe or else.*

And honestly, somewhere along the line, Lucas became her brother and she knew Hank felt the same way. Olive swore her accident affected Lucas just as badly as it did Hank.

Actually, she knew it did.

Olive wasn't a stranger to getting random text messages from Lucas making sure she was okay. At first, she thought it was him trying to get information on Miranda, but Olive soon realized he did it to make sure *she* was the one that was safe.

Olive couldn't imagine what was burned into his brain, along with Hank and the other guys when they pulled up to *her* flipped car...

Olive shuddered as she tried to push the memories away.

Not now...

"I promise." Without even missing a beat, Hank knew exactly what Lucas meant. "Now go back to bed and don't fuck up our house. Or, piss off my sister."

"I'll think about it." With that, Lucas closed the window and turned off the light.

"Oh man, why do I feel like we just let the lion loose?" Olive's eyes darted back and forth between Lucas's and Miranda's windows.

"'Cause we probably did."

"Great," Olive grumbled, as her hands went to her temples to massage them. "I'm never gonna hear the end of this am I?"

"Probably not." Hank chuckled as he closed the back of the hatch while Olive walked around to the passenger side of their SUV. Before going to her seat though, she peeked into the backseat. "Hiya, Dog. Nice kitty." Dog glared at her through the bars of her crate. "What the heck is that look for? We're taking you with us. This is a good thing. You should be happy."

Dog opened her mouth and shook her head from left to right, the streetlights hitting her canines perfectly, making them glisten. "Oh wow, did Doctor Richman clean those chompers when Daddy took you in yesterday to get sleepy meds for the car ride?"

Dog hissed.

"Okay, sore subject. Gotcha. Well, just know we love you and wanted you to be there with us. That's why we're doing this. Please don't add this to your *Reasons to Murder Mom* book when Dad is on a three-day shift at the station."

Hank hopped into the driver's seat with a laugh. "She doesn't have a *Reason to Murder Mom* book when I'm at the station. She's just messing with you. Probably 'cause your comment earlier. I told you she'd remember."

Oh, crap on a cracker. He's right. And they say an elephant never forgets? Those people have never met our Maine Coon cat. Uhh, how can I fix this?

Olive looked back at Dog who once again showed her teeth.

No fixing this, gotcha.

Olive swallowed hard as she watched Dog. "I'm actually pretty sure she does have a *Reasons to Murder Mom* book."

Hank's hand went to his stomach as he burst out into another round of laughter. "She doesn't. Give her some credit." Hank scratched the side of Dog's face the best he could through the bars. "You're our family, Dog, and we plan on always taking you with us. You know, just like a *dog*."

Dog snapped her attention to Hank before letting out a low growl.

"I don't think she likes being referred to as a dog."

"Sure, she does." To prove his point, Hank put his fingers inside the crate, causing Dog to immediately rub against them.

You have got to be kidding me! If I did that, I'd lose a digit. Maybe two.

"Why does she let you get away with everything and yet I can't even walk to the bathroom by myself."

"She's putty in my hands," he remarked. "And as for you, she's making sure you're safe. I don't think she trusts you after the accident."

"That makes two of us."

"Olive..."

"What?"

Hank shook his head. "Never mind. Just get in the car. We're wasting valuable time."

Olive closed the backdoor before migrating to the front seat getting in. And just like she did every other time she got in a car, she buckled her seat belt and pulled on it to make sure it was tight. She was good about that before the accident, but she couldn't help being extra careful after. She knew, hell everyone knew, the seat belt was the only thing that saved her life.

"You okay?" Hank asked, studying her.

"Yeah."

"Good." He leaned over and placed a swift kiss on her lips before turning up the heat in the SUV. "Let's get this party started."

"Sure thing, Hot Stuff."

Hank moaned. "You know I love it when you call me Hot Stuff."

"I do it 'cause you're a fireman." She winked. "You play with fire all day."

Hank abruptly stopped the car and sent her a death glare, making Olive hold her hands in surrender. "Kidding. Sorry. I know fire is not something to play with. You've made that very clear. I was just joking. You don't play with fire. Fire bad. Joke bad. Olive bad."

When Hank continued to stare at her, she kept going. "Although, you gotta admit your line of work has given me extraordinary research opportunities. I mean who knew firefighters knew so much about knots. Guess I got that right in my books." A nervous laugh escaped her. "But fire is off-limits. Got it. Heard loud and clear."

"Fire isn't something to joke about." His face remained hard for a split second before the playful Hank was back.

"But I bet you're glad I know my way around tying knots, now don't cha?"

Olive let out a sigh of relief. Don't get her wrong, Hank was right, but still, he was a pain in the ass when he went off on one of his safety tangents. Deciding it was best to lean into the playful side, she smiled. "I'm not complaining, Hot Stuff."

"You will be the death of me one day." Hank pulled on the front of his jeans giving himself more room.

"I'm positive I can say the same thing." Olive laughed as they drove out of the driveway. It only took them a few moments to settle on the road as they turned out of their neighborhood. "You still haven't answered. Why are we leaving at almost one in the morning?"

"A few reasons," Hank stated matter-of-fact. "One, it's a few days before Christmas, traffic is gonna be a bitch. Plus, I figured the fewer cars on the road the better." The pregnant pause between them was enough for Olive to know what he was referring to.

"I'm better now."

"I know, babe. But I also wanted to be able to spend as much time there alone with you as possible. The dates were weird but I was able to work it out this way. And the last reason..." His whole face lit as he smirked. "You'll find out when we get there."

Olive crossed her arms as she slumped in her seat. "Can't you just tell me now?"

"Absolutely not."

That damn smirk! The same one he always had whenever he played some stupid prank on her or something. The *same* one she wanted to jump across the center console and punch off his face.

Seeing as she was still only half awake, she filed it away for later too. "How far away is this place anyway?"

"About four hours, so not too bad."

"Four hours!" Her mouth fell open as she stared at him. "That's like an eternity."

"If you fall asleep, we'll be there before you know it."

Olive snapped her mouth shut as she gawked at him completely dumbfounded. "And miss the chance of seeing Bigfoot on the side of the road in the woods? I think not!"

CHAPTER FOUR

Thankfully the drive had been smooth for the most part. After about an hour, the sleep medication Doctor Richman prescribed for Dog had finally kicked in.

At least Hank thought it did.

There were a few times he checked the rearview mirror and swore he saw Dog staring back at him. However, anytime he'd turn his head to check, her eyes were closed.

Hank wasn't sure if that was a good thing or a bad thing, but right now he was going with good. She hadn't screamed yet, so he definitely considered the ride a win.

While Hank focused on the road, soft holiday tunes played on the radio. And just like he'd done a thousand times on the drive so far, he glanced over to Olive. Each time was the same. She had her face plastered to the window, searching for anything out of the ordinary.

He couldn't help but chuckle to himself.

Hank foolishly hoped at one point she would've dozed off or attempted to nap for at least some of the trip.

However, that was a huge freaking no.

As soon as they hit the interstate surrounded by forests, Olive was on the hunt.

If it wasn't so crazy, he would've thought it was somewhat endearing. And it was, kind of. Hank loved this side of Olive. True, there were more than enough times he didn't understand it, but he still loved it.

The imagination, the adventure, even the zombies. He loved it all.

"Did you see that?"

If Olive hadn't said those exact words about a hundred and fifty times already, she would've startled him. At this point though, he was expecting it. "See what, Olive? I'm driving."

"Over there." Olive pointed to a dense part in the barren winter forest. "Some of those leaves and branches moved. I think I saw eyes." She smashed her face against the glass trying to get a better view.

Hank rolled his eyes while holding in his laugh. Olive hadn't appreciated the first few times he got a good chuckle out of her Sasquatch hunting. "I'm sure it was a deer."

"This early in the morning, no way." She stared at him appalled he'd even fathom such a thing.

"Okay, it was Bigfoot," he replied, appeasing her, but even he could hear the smile in his voice. "Whatever you say, Olive Oil."

Olive grunted low in her throat as she crossed her arms over her chest. "Don't patronize me."

Hank cocked his brow. "I'm agreeing with you."

"No, you're not. You're trying to placate me."

"Maybe." Hank shrugged. "I have to admit you do look adorable. I bet if I were to put down the window you'd have your head out like a dog, sniffing the air hunting for Sasquatch himself in a second."

"Or herself," she corrected.

Hank snorted out a laugh. "Yes, or herself. How could I have been so foolish?"

Olive curtly nodded at him in agreement. "Exactly. That's more like it."

Hey, at least with Olive by his side it was bound to always be an adventure, even if it was one filled with paranormal investigations.

Hank watched out of the corner of his eye as Olive managed to pull away from the window long enough to look in the backseat.

"She's nice when she's passed out, isn't she? We should make that happen more often." Olive laughed. "I hope you got extra of those pills Doctor Richman prescribed."

The moment Hank was about to open his mouth to respond, Dog hissed.

"Uhh..." Olive's eyes rounded as she pushed herself closer to the door in her seat. "I was kidding. I'd never drug you."

At Olive's movements, Hank barked out a laugh. "I was just about to say I don't think she's sleeping. I honestly don't think she's slept at all. Dog's trying to fake you out. "

"As she always does." Olive shifted back to her original spot, a slight pout on her lips.

"It's a game for Dog. If you didn't react like you do, she wouldn't mess with you at all."

"What do you mean act like I do? I don't do anything." Olive crossed her arms over her stomach and glared at him.

"You just wedged yourself to the door as close as humanly possible. Dog smells your fear." Hank laughed as he put his hand on the top of Olive's knee, giving it a light squeeze before she promptly pushed it off.

"That's 'cause she's scary."

Dog purred from the backseat—clearly pleased with Olive's answer which only made Hank laugh harder. "See. It's a game. She loves you."

"It's a stupid game." Olive glared over her shoulder at Dog. "Jerk."

Hank laughed even harder as he placed his hand back on Olive's knee. "She's gonna remember that."

"I bet she will," Olive grumbled before she turned her head to look out the window, no doubt on the hunt again for anything out of the normal.

With a slight shake of his head, Hank chuckled. No matter what was going on, life with Olive was fantastic. And truthfully, Hank still couldn't believe all they'd been through in their lives. From childhood where he was always teasing her, to realizing how much he was attracted to Olive, moving in, and playing the friendly pranks as he liked to call it.

Oh man, and then when he found out about her writing. Holy shit, it was like his world turned upside down.

Before he moved into Olive's apartment, his goal was to finally make her his. However, he was not expecting her to throw him for a loop with the erotic romance author part.

Shit, that still blew his mind.

His Olive. The shy, quiet girl his younger sister called her best friend turned out to be way more than he thought was possible.

And once he knew her secret, he used it to his full advantage. Starting their research experiment was the best thing that could've ever happened to him.

But then...

Hank swallowed hard as the familiar lump in his throat formed.

That day was still burned into the back of his mind and it came up more times than he'd liked to admit. Especially when they got the call for a car accident at the station. Since that day, every single time the announcement would come over the radio, there was always a part of him which panicked.

Hank was now one thousand percent the fastest to get into his turnout gear, since he knew the second he got into the rig, he'd be able to check his phone to see where Olive was.

And as soon as he knew for sure she was safe at home, he'd finally relax and let his mind focus on whatever scene they were about to pull up on.

Fuck, he still had nightmares and it'd been well over a year, almost two at this point. Hank couldn't help it though, he'd never forget Olive hanging upside-down, blood pouring down her face as she hung there unconscious.

He placed his hand on her knee again needing some sort of connection.

If he'd lost her...

He wouldn't have survived. There was zero doubt in Hank's mind about that.

Stop, Tank. Stop doing this to yourself. She's here. You're here. Everything is as it should be. You're off to your cabin getaway with the love of your life.

Keep focused on the here and now.

Hank took a calming breath as he glanced at Olive from the corner of his eye. She looked as happy as he'd ever seen her as she watched out the window.

Seeing she was okay, Hank took one more deep breath before he put his hand back on the steering wheel to focus. He hated reliving those moments.

He stretched his neck from side to side, trying to relax some of the tension he felt.

Olive was safe, he was safe, and right now they were on their way to a secluded cabin to celebrate their anniversary.

Life was exactly how it was meant to be.

He was with the woman he loved more than anything in the world. And Olive was staring out the window, cooking up some fantasy world in her head filled with Bigfoots, aliens, zombies, and anything else she could think of.

And you know what? He wouldn't have it any other way.

As the holiday music played softly in the vehicle, Hank couldn't help but relax into the drive. He was right. Life couldn't get any better than it could at this moment.

Scratch that, it just got a hell of a lot better.

Hank's heart raced as he drove past the sign marking their upcoming exit.

Hell fucking yes.

It would be less than an hour from now until they were at their cabin.

Their perfect holiday getaway.

Again, hell fucking yes!

With a new burst of exhilaration of what was to come, he only hoped it would be everything Olive could've ever wanted.

To him, he didn't care what it looked like. As long as he was with Olive, nothing could ruin this for him.

It was only a few more miles before Hank took the exit. However, as he veered off, he was surprised to see the offramp nearly pitch-black. And as he turned onto the local road, it was the same thing.

"Whoa, it's dark out here."

"Yeah," Hank replied, keeping his eyes focused on the road. Unfortunately, it was darker than he thought it would be. Sure, it was an off-the-map kind of place, but he imagined there would be more streetlights.

Streetlights were important.

It was a safety thing. Okay, Hank harped on it a little more than he should, but since becoming a firefighter, he'd been called to more accidents than he'd like to admit on roads exactly like this.

"Hey, look we made great time." Olive pointed to the clock on the dash, grabbing Hank's attention.

However, the moment Hank glanced down to see what time it was, a massive flash of light blinded him. The last thing he heard was Olive's scream as he lost control of their vehicle.

CHAPTER FIVE

"Oh my God, what happened?!" Olive's heart slammed against her chest as the car came to a screeching halt on the side of the road. Her eyes scanned the area and stopped on Hank after seeing him gripping the wheel so tight his knuckles were white.

Oh my God!

Her chest heaved as Olive tried to make sense of what was going on. It only took another second before Hank flipped his attention to her.

"Are you okay?" His voice held a panic she'd only heard once before.

Was she okay? Olive honestly had no idea. One second, she was minding her own business looking out the window and then boom.

She felt like she was thrown back to the day the other car ran the red light.

Instantly her whole body broke out into a cold sweat as she began to tremble. *Oh God, no. Not again.*

Olive reached for her seat belt to make sure it was still in place. Finding it was, she then touched the roof of the SUV.

Okay, she wasn't upside down and she was conscious.

These were good things. Although, she was sure her adrenaline was moments from giving her a heart attack.

But she was okay.

Olive glanced at Hank again as he stared at her, his face white with his mouth slightly open.

As her heart pounded out of her chest, Olive pinched her eyes closed and opened them again, trying to get her bearings and find her voice.

Everything around her was dead silent other than the static that came over the radio.

Okay, okay, breathe. You're not upside down, you aren't hurt. Hank seems okay. You guys are both alive and—

"Dog!" Olive jumped around in her seat only to see Dog staring at them completely unfazed.

"Olive, fucking answer me. Are you okay?"

Olive snapped her attention to Hank in an instant.

Hearing the tremble in Hank's voice was worse than waking up in the hospital.

"Yes, I think so," she answered, the quiver in her voice matched his. Oh God, her blood pressure was higher than it should be.

Holy shit. This was it. This was the end. Or maybe we're already dead and we don't know it. She panicked as she tried to catch her breath. "What happened?"

"I don't know. This road is so fucking dark."

Olive tried to make sense of everything as she worked on getting her breathing under control. It all came out of nowhere. The flash of light, the screeching tires. All she did was look at the clock and—

"Oh my God!" Olive screamed, causing Hank to jerk back in his seat as Olive jumped out of the car. "Holy shit. Ho-ly *shit!*"

"Fuck, are you hurt?" Hank bolted out of the driver's seat after her as Olive ran to the front of their SUV.

"Oh shit, oh shit. Oh my God. It happened, it really

happened!" Olive paced back and forth in front of the vehicle, waving her hands in the chilled air.

"Olive, what the hell are you doing? Get back in the
fucking car. Are you fucking kidding me right now? Are you
hurt? What the hell is going on?"

Ignoring him, Olive ran back to the passenger side, stuck
her head into their car and double-checked the clock, only to
let out another scream. "The time on the clock, Hank, it
jumped ahead twenty minutes!" She snapped her eyes to her
husband, who was glaring at her with a mixture of anger and
worry. "Do you understand what this means?"

Before Hank could answer her, Olive leaped out of the car
and ran to the back, searching around their SUV.

"Olive, I swear to God, why the fuck are you running
around the car? What are you looking for? Did you hit your
head, are you hurt? Fucking answer me!"

The moment Hank stood in front of her, Olive cocked
her head to the side, like *he* was the crazy one. "Isn't it
obvious?"

"Oh, fuck. You did hit your head, didn't you? And now
you're crazier than ever. Fuck me."

As Hank reached for Olive, she chose to ignore his ridiculous outburst and fell to her knees to examine the underside
of their vehicle.

"For fuck's sake, Olive, what the hell are you doing now?"
Hank grabbed her arm pulling her out from under their car
standing Olive up. "You're gonna give me an aneurysm."

"Hank, don't you realize what just happened? This is huge.
It's exactly the same as that episode of the *X-Files*."

At her words, Hank froze staring at her like she'd gained a
few heads.

*The jerk. Didn't he get how massive this was? Wait, maybe I do
have an extra head or something.*

Quickly, Olive checked to make sure she had only one
head.

Dang it.

She'd be lying if she said she wasn't disappointed not coming up with a new appendage or something.

Both of Hank's brows were up as he stared at her wide-eyed. "What are you talking about? Jesus, you really did hit your head. I have a first aid kit in the car, but I have no idea where the nearest hospital is. Fuck." Hank opened the trunk throwing their bags around searching for the kit.

"Stop. I'm fine." Olive halted him with her hand. "In the episode, Mulder and Scully were traveling down a dark road and then there was a huge flash of light. They lost *twenty minutes*. Holy freaking guacamole. *Hank, we were just abducted!*"

His eyes widened further than she thought possible as he stared at her. "You've got to be kidding me."

"It's true! Just look at the clock on the dashboard. And didn't you hear all that static?!" Olive ran back to the front of the car, pulling Hank along with her. "See." She pointed to the dash. "It skipped ahead."

Olive dropped Hank's arm and did this weird dance as she hopped around on her toes in pure excitement. "Oh my God, we were the chosen ones!"

After one more quick happy dance, Olive tore off her jacket.

There has to be one!

"What the fuck are you doing now? It's cold out here." Hank snatched her jacket from the ground where she'd tossed it. However, as he pushed it toward Olive to put it back on, she blew him off.

Didn't he get how important this was? She'd just have to explain it to him later because this was huge.

Once Olive's arms were free, she flipped them over a few times as she rubbed them to see or feel if she found anything that could be a tracking device.

"Damn." She slumped when she came up empty. However,

instead of giving up, she bolted over to Hank and pulled up his jacket sleeve to check him.

"For fuck's sake." Hank yanked his arm away as he glared at her. "Olive, you have to be kidding me right now."

Olive stopped what she was doing and gawked at him like *he* was crazy. "You don't kid about such things."

"Damn it, you really did hit your head."

"I did not."

"You must have." Hank looked her up and down a few times before he let out a heavy sigh. "This is the last time we stay up most of the night watching your UFO shows."

Olive's mouth flew open. "This has nothing to do with that. We lost twenty minutes. *Twenty minutes.* That doesn't just happen, Hank. This is a big deal."

"No, we didn't." Hank pushed his phone in her face. "Listen, there wasn't this huge flash of light. We weren't brought up to some alien spacecraft and now we can't remember God knows what they did to us. I'm sorry to burst your bubble, but that didn't happen. A truck came out of nowhere and blinded us on this damn fucking piece of shit road. We lost no time, Olive. No matter how bad you wanted us to be taken away by some little green men, it didn't happen."

"You mean gray, and not all of them are Grays. That's offensive." She crossed her arms over her chest as she glared at his phone.

Damn.

As soon as she saw the time, Olive's heart sank. Hank was right, they didn't lose twenty minutes. At least according to Hank's phone. But then... Why did the clock say they did, and why was there static? None of that made any sense.

Olive looked to the sky disappointed before moving her eyes back to Hank. She must have looked how she felt because Hank pulled her into his arms giving her a kiss on the head as he held her tight.

"I'm sorry you're disappointed we didn't end up on some

spaceship. Maybe when I slammed on the brakes and jerked the car, the clock and radio caused a wire to be jacked up. And the static is probably from the shitty stations around here. I'll check it out as soon as we get home. But, Olive, put your jacket back on and get in the car. It's still pitch black out here and it's cold. Please have mercy on me and, Get. In. The. Fucking. Car."

Olive stepped out of his arms still disappointed. However, when she looked at her husband, she saw so much...

Scared, worried, pissed. It was written all over Hank's face.

To be honest, though, Olive was kinda pissed too. He did just shit all over what could've been the coolest thing to have ever happened to her in her life.

"Fuck it."

Before Olive could respond, Hank did what he always did. He picked her up like she was nothing and tossed her over his shoulder in a fireman's pose.

"Put me down!"

"You don't listen."

"Yes, I do."

"No." Hank smacked her ass. "You don't." He placed her back in the passenger seat before pushing her jacket in her face. "On. Now."

"Why the hell are you so grumpy and pissed? You didn't just have your dreams shattered to pieces. *I did.*"

A growl came from deep inside Hank's throat. "We almost got into an accident, Olive. I'm not angry, I'm fucking scared. I thought I lost you again."

"Oh."

"Now, put on your fucking jacket." Hank slammed her door shut, leaving Olive there letting her brain process his words.

Hank hopped back into the driver's seat, and he took a deep breath before turning to her. "Are you sure you're okay?"

She swallowed hard nodding her head. "I think so."

Once she answered Hank immediately grabbed Olive, hauling her into his lap, kissing her like his life depended on it.

"I thought I'd lost you again. And then you fucking got out of the car. Don't do that to me."

As she was perched on his lap, she realized Hank trembled under her body. And for the first time, it was like the reality of everything finally sunk in.

Oh my God!

Her eyes widened as she let herself finally grasp the situation. Hank held her tighter, molding her body to his. As the adrenaline of them possibly getting abducted left her, she felt her own body shake as her heart pounded against her chest.

They'd almost got into an accident.

And they had Dog with them.

Holy shit.

A lump caught in her throat as she glanced over Hank's shoulder to see Dog still staring at them, like everything was right in the world.

But was it? They almost could have lost it all.

Again.

Olive held onto Hank tighter like he was her lifeline as the gravity of the situation hit.

"We're okay. We're all okay." He soothed her back, but she swore he was speaking to himself rather than her and Dog.

"We are," Olive replied.

Because they were.

They were okay. And to be honest, Olive was proud of herself. Instead of jumping right back to that day and becoming paralyzed, somehow her brain went the complete opposite and she thought they were the chosen ones.

Olive glanced to the dashboard to see the time was still off, but the static had stopped.

Okay, this probably wasn't the best coping mechanism to

employ after potentially getting hit by a car, but it was better than freaking out, right?

Maybe it was the fact Hank was by her side, hell, even Dog. But she didn't jump right into the bad. And Hank and Dog made her feel safe. Even in what could've been a horrible nightmare, Hank was there.

It was always going to be okay. Subconsciously she knew that. Honestly, that's probably the reason why her brain jumped down the route of alien abduction rather than the end.

Hank was her safety net.

With him around, Olive was free to be who she was. The Bigfoot loving, alien chasing, zombie wishing, best damn erotic romance author there was.

Her brain didn't have to go to the worst because she had Hank.

Olive had to be truthful with herself though; jumping to aliens was definitely an unhealthy compartmentalization of the situation.

As her eyes glanced back at the clock one more time, she did have to wonder though...

"I love you," Hank spoke, grabbing her attention. Carefully, and as gently as he could, Hank placed Olive back in the passenger seat. "Seat belt. Now."

"I know, we just went through something traumatic." She glared at him. "So I'm gonna let that slide, but you know damn well I always have my seat belt on."

"I know," he replied with a heavy sigh. "Just humor me right now. Please?"

Hank turned, checking on Dog. "You okay, girl?"

Dog yawned still not phased in the slightest.

Good to know Dog really is the spawn of Satan. Even faced with death, the she-devil is unfazed.

Now that Olive thought about it, though, Dog was a little too calm. Okay yeah, she was on sleep medication, but still...

Dog was a little too okay with everything. "You know what? They probably did take us up, got one look at Dog and said fuck this shit and sent us back," Olive mumbled under her breath which caused Hank to narrow his eyes at her. "What?" she replied.

When his brow cocked at her, she huffed. "Fine, fine. Whatever." Although, she couldn't stop herself from sending a death glare toward Dog in the back. "If you're the reason they didn't keep us, so help me—"

"Olive," Hank warned.

"What?"

Hank pinched the bridge of his nose for a moment before facing her, a plea in his eyes. "We have less than an hour left, can we please just chill with the paranormal shit for a little while?"

Seeing as Hank was still a little shaken, and truthfully Olive was too, she gave in.

Olive knew it was her way of escaping. You can't really think about almost getting into another car crash when your mind is racing with aliens and abductions.

Olive smiled at him, her eyes bright. "Can I at least go back to looking out the window for Bigfoot?"

And just like that, the tension in the car lifted as Hank shook his head while a small chuckle escaped his lips. "Yeah, babe, you can."

"Thank you."

"Just for fuck's sake if anything ever happens again, stay in the fucking car. I don't care if we see Bigfoot doing a hula dance in front of us."

"I can't make any promises."

Hank stared at her, his eyes showing all the concern that still raced through him. "For me, will you? It's dangerous on the road, especially now when there is ice. What if a driver came around the corner and didn't see you?"

Olive softened as she listened to his plea. "I mean, I guess you have a point. I'll try and stay in the car."

"Thank you."

"But just so you know, Bigfoot wouldn't hula dance."

"How do you know that?" Hank cocked his brow. "You've never met Bigfoot. Maybe they do that on their off time."

Huh? Well, crap on a cracker. Hank had her there. No way in hell she'd admit it though. "I just do."

Hank snorted out a laugh. "Whatever you say."

Oh man, this was absolutely going into one of her books.

Olive watched as Hank fiddled with the radio for a moment, getting the holiday station back. Once Christmas music played throughout the car, he pulled onto the road. "What were you looking for under the car?"

"I don't know, Mulder did it on the show. He was looking under the car and stuff, so I figured I needed to do it too."

"We're definitely revoking your UFO shows for a while."

Olive gasped as her jaw dropped. "You wouldn't?"

A pointed look was his reply.

"Maybe they put a tracking device on the car or something?" She shrugged, trying to argue her case.

"I don't think aliens need to use such mundane shit as a tracking device on a car, Olive."

Well, damn. Why is he always the voice of reason?

Stupid Hank.

But he did have a point, no matter how bad she wanted it to be true. "You're probably right." Although, Olive glared back at Dog still not one hundred percent convinced it wasn't Dog's fault they sent them back.

"I know I'm right."

"Whatever."

Doing her best to push everything that happened into a box never to be opened again, Olive went back to staring out the window. She wasn't really focused on finding some crazy paranormal anomaly anymore.

No, she was just glad to be safe and warm with the person she loved the most.

It didn't take long for everything to settle as they drove down the dark, winding road. And before Olive knew it, Hank lowered their holiday tunes on the radio. "And that right there, Olive Oil, is why we had to get here when it was still dark out."

As they turned the corner, Olive was greeted with a beautiful cabin completely decked out in holiday lights that looked like it came straight out of a Christmas movie.

CHAPTER SIX

As Hank drove up the long driveway to the secluded cabin he'd rented, he'd be lying if he said his heart wasn't still pounding against his chest.

Yeah, Hank knew they were safe, but it still freaked him out. Almost getting into a car crash would have messed with anyone. In an instant, he'd thought he lost it all again, and when he realized they were fine, Olive went off on her insane alien story.

Hank understood that was her way of dealing with everything but shit. It'd been almost an hour and he still couldn't fathom how Olive jumped to them being abducted versus what really happened.

And fuck that dark road while he was at it.

However, seeing the pure excitement on Olive's face the moment she saw the cabin was worth everything they'd gone through.

No matter how many times he'd seen her childlike wonder when it came to the holidays, it still warmed him.

Olive's eyes were massive as she took everything in, and to be honest, Hank was pretty impressed as well. The owners of the cabin really took his request to make it seem like the

North Pole to heart. Of course, he paid extra to have it all decked out for Christmas, but this was even more than he was expecting.

Maybe, it was the story he told them about how he almost lost her, or perhaps, it was the fact Olive and Hank had gotten married on Christmas Day. Who knew, but the owners really came through. Nearly every square inch of the cabin was a full-on festive holiday spectacular.

The place really did look like something out of those holiday movies Olive had made Hank watch every year.

And if the outside looked this damn good, he couldn't wait to see what they'd done on the inside.

As he pulled to a stop, he couldn't help the feeling that washed over him. It just felt right, almost homey in some strange way.

Damn, I did good.

The corners of Hank's mouth turned up as he wanted to pat himself on the back. He definitely did the right thing booking the cabin.

Now that he thought about it, hell, he might have to make this a regular occurrence, or better yet, maybe they could buy a cabin of their own.

Something that was just theirs.

It could double as not only a getaway for them but maybe a place Olive could use for writing retreats.

He should start looking into buying them a cab—

"Oh my God, Hank, it's beautiful!" As soon as they parked, Olive flung herself out of the car and ran up the front steps of the cozy cabin.

As Hank watched her bounce on her heels, he couldn't help but laugh at her eagerness.

This was Olive in her element.

This was Olive, the love of his life, completely one hundred percent free.

A ridiculously wide smile spread across his lips as Hank

hopped out of the car and leaned against the side. All the while taking the time to observe Olive in pure joy.

Hank's heart tightened as she turned back to point to something with a yip of excitement and then moved onto something else. Hank couldn't help but notice how her eyes twinkled just like the lights and he loved every freaking second of it.

However, as Hank enjoyed his curvy wife bounce around the porch, Dog meowed from the backseat, drawing his attention toward their cat. "Let Olive have this moment, Dog."

The cat eyed him for a second, before she yawned and laid back down in her crate. "Thank you."

Hank's eyes trailed back to Olive. Her excitement coming off her in waves caused his own joy to rise.

It was as if their almost accident melted away. Fuck him, it was like the original car crash melted away too, even if only for this moment as Hank watched Olive examine their holiday getaway.

Damn, he really was a lucky son of a bitch, and he knew it.

Olive spun on her heel to face him. "What are you doing? Get your ass up here. Come on, Gramps, you're taking too long. I wanna check out the inside!"

"Gramps?" He quirked his brow.

"Don't do that brow thing and just get your ass up here."

Hank chuckled as he pushed himself off the side of their car. "Be right back, Dog. Let me get her inside before she has a meltdown." He closed the door so Dog would still be warm as he pulled up the screenshot he'd taken of the directions to get the key from the box so they could get inside.

More and more he liked the idea of buying a cabin of their own or at least renting this one again. No checking in, no neighbors, no big fancy rooms.

And for Olive, no people.

Just him, Olive, and Dog.

That sounded pretty damn perfect if you asked him.

"I'm coming. And we're gonna talk about the Gramps comment later." Hank bounced up the front steps. "You sure are pushy when you want something."

"Look. They have a tree!" Olive's muffled voice came out as she had her head pressed to the window trying to peer inside, as she ignored his comment. "This place is amazing. I can't wait to see it with the lights on."

"It better be with how much I paid for the holiday extras." He laughed, unlocking the box to retrieve the key.

And as much as Hank loved seeing Olive with her face pushed against the window like a kid staring into a candy shop, he needed to get her inside where it was warm.

Then they could really start their anniversary getaway.

"Be careful there, sweet cheeks, or your face is gonna stick to the window." As Olive opened her mouth to maim him with some insult, he flung the door open and flipped on the light, not only taking her breath away but his as well.

Whoa.

Hank was completely taken aback by how it was decorated. It almost made their own home look like a joke.

Now, this was a holiday house to say the least.

Yeah, Hank was totally buying them a cabin.

"Holy shit."

Hank's thoughts exactly.

There was lit garland everywhere. It wrapped around the banister stairs leading to the loft bedroom, then back around to the living room with a fireplace.

And right in the middle of the room stood what looked like it came directly off the pages of some magazine, was the most stunning Christmas tree he'd ever seen. And the open layout of the place only accentuated its sheer beauty.

Again, ho-ly shit.

That was only half of it, though. As they walked inside the

cabin, there was a small kitchenette to the left. And on a tiny island chopping block in the middle, there was a bottle of wine and a gift basket full to the brim with holiday treats.

Fuck him, there was even a plate that read 'Cookies for Santa.'

"It's—it's, I don't think I even have words," Olive stammered as she surveyed their surroundings. Her wide eyes sparkled with merriment as she took in everything around them.

And honestly, neither of them knew where to look next. But what really kept catching Hank's eyes was the joy on Olive's face. From her twinkling eyes that matched the lights, to her rosy cheeks filled with so much glee, he could almost taste it.

Hank didn't know what he did in this life to have Olive as his, but he would do it over and over again.

And right now, as he watched Olive in amazement, he knew life couldn't get any better.

Wait, that was a lie.

Hank planned on it getting a fuck ton better. As soon as he got their things in, he was going to make great use of his time with her.

After their mishap on the road—and that's exactly what he'd be calling it from now on—Hank was desperate to be close to her.

He needed to feel her body against his.

He needed to prove to himself she was okay.

"You go explore and check out the loft. I'm gonna get Dog. Be right back."

It didn't surprise him in the least when Olive tore off her jacket, tossing it behind her before taking off up the stairs.

Well, isn't she going to be my eager little elf? He shook his head slightly, but he couldn't blame her excitement. If the downstairs was any indication, he could only imagine what it looked like in the loft.

"Oh my God, Hank! There is a tree up here too!"

Hank's eyes brightened hearing her enthusiasm. Deciding it was best to get back to her pronto, he took a step toward the door to get Dog and the rest of their things.

Including a very special bag he'd packed.

Yep, this was the best idea Hank had ever come up with.

Happy Anniversary and Merry Christmas to them.

CHAPTER SEVEN

O**LIVE SWORE** her eyes were bigger than flying saucers as she looked around the room. No matter how hard she tried, she couldn't stop being in awe of the cabin.

This was more than a dream come true.

Sure, sex with her super hunky firefighter husband was great and all, but have you ever walked into a place so decked out it was like stepping onto a movie set? This cabin was more than she ever expected or knew was possible.

Wait, hold on.

Scratch that.

Sex with Hank was kind of out of this world.

So, Olive couldn't really compare him to anything. And if she did, Hank would always come out on top.

Come...See what I did there? She laughed.

The thing was, Hank knew how to please her better than she knew herself. No matter how hard she tried to deny that, and Lord knows she'd never tell him.

But this cabin, *this magical cabin,* was seriously a close second.

Olive's hand skimmed the garland wrapped around the banister as she made her way to the loft.

As soon as the upstairs came into view, Olive's breath hitched.

Not only was she greeted by another stunning tree that looked exactly like something out of a department store, but there was also a tiny fireplace that matched the one downstairs.

The best part was the open floor plan.

When Olive got to the top of the stairs, she could still see the main tree right over the metal railing.

The view of the living room from upstairs was more than breathtaking, it was picturesque. That was the only way she could describe it.

As Olive spun around taking everything in, she made a few mental notes to rearrange some of the decorations at home.

After getting her fill of the loft, Olive turned back to the railing and overlooked the living room. When she heard the door open, her eyes quickly found Hank carrying Dog in before he carefully placed her crate on the floor.

Watching Hank from her perch, Olive's smile widened to the point where her cheeks began to hurt.

Holy Universe, she loved this man.

He gave the best of everything to her. He knew exactly what she wanted without even her knowing it most of the time.

Hank always took care of her. From him bringing her snacks while she was in the middle of an intense writing session, to him just knowing how she felt without her having to say it. He knew when she'd had enough peopling for the day. Heck, he even knew when she wanted cuddles or a zombie movie marathon with just one look from her.

Hank was her perfect match in every way.

Who would have thought? Hank Parker, annoying pain in my ass, who never wore a shirt firefighter, was now my husband.

Olive laughed to herself as she watched him bring in the gifts they'd wrapped for under the tree.

How everything fell into place, still blew her mind. Olive couldn't stand him in the beginning and would've gladly disposed of him then hid the body if Miranda gave the okay.

But now, she couldn't live without Hank.

As much as she didn't want to admit it, Hank was her better half. He made her want to be a better person.

Olive was positive somewhere along the line, Hank acquired some secret manual for her. Probably given to him in exchange for some top-secret alien information that he definitely used to his advantage.

This man loved her with everything inside of himself and more, and well, she could honestly say the same about him.

Her life was better because he was in it.

And here Olive thought Hank was just a really good research partner. She flicked her eyes to the ceiling at herself.

She should've known better.

Once someone like Hank Parker got under your skin, they stayed. And damn was she glad he stayed. "I love you."

"I love you, too, Olive." Hank's whole face lit as he beamed up at her. "I love you more than anything in this world."

"Thank you."

"You don't need to thank me." He peeled his jacket off, throwing it onto the back of the couch.

And damn her.

As Olive watched his muscles move under his sweater, that all too familiar feeling of heat washed over her. She knew exactly what was under his long sleeve sweater. And if she were lucky, she'd be getting an up close and personal view very soon.

Hot Stuff indeed.

Pushing those thoughts aside for a moment, Olive softened, tipping her head slightly to the side. "You're wrong. I do need to thank you. I don't know how I lucked out with you, but I did. I just... thank you. I mean, look at this place for one." Her hand waved around the room. "But not even that. It's just everything. I never knew what love was until you came into my life. Now, I know."

"I'm the lucky one," he replied, his eyes focused on her. "But love isn't a cabin in the woods."

Olive snorted. "No, it's so much more than that." Her lips formed into a soft smile. "I love you, Hank. I love you so much. Thank you for being my person."

"I love you too, Olive." The corner of his mouth perked up as his eyes danced. "I can't wait to tell Miranda you called me your person instead of her."

"You wouldn't."

His smirk turned into a full-blown smile in an instant. "It's the first thing I'm gonna say when I see her."

Olive burst into a fit of laughter as she shook her head. "Well, I guess it's true, but at least soften the blow a little and wait until after we get back. She might take her revenge out on Luke."

Hank winked. "They might've killed each other by now."

"Maybe." Olive's face brightened. However, before Olive could say another word, a hiss came from the crate. "Oh, shit."

Hank darted his attention to Dog who stood on all fours glaring at them.

"Maybe I should've opened the crate door as soon as I brought her in." He looked back to Olive with a grin. "You wanna let her out or shall I?"

"Definitely you."

Olive turned to head downstairs but the moment she took the first step, she stopped. "On second thought, I'm gonna stay up here while you do it."

Hank chuckled as he opened the royal highness's chariot.

Ever so slowly, their child-sized cat strutted out of her confined carrier, sniffing the air.

Instead of freaking out like Olive thought she would, Dog walked around examining her new surroundings.

"That's my girl." Hank scratched along Dog's back and the damn hussy loved every single second of it.

Now, if only Olive could get Dog to love her just as much as she loved Hank.

I guess she loves me in her own way.

Olive watched as Dog left Hank's side before moseying over to the Christmas tree to investigate further. "Do you think she likes it?"

"I don't know," Hank replied. "I think so. I mean she isn't trying to hurt anyone, so I think we're in the clear."

"She's locked me in a bathroom before."

Hank stared at Olive from the ground floor, his brow cocked. "She didn't lock you in the bathroom. You ran there and locked *yourself* in."

"She chased me."

"No, she didn't."

"Yes, she did. You weren't there. You were off eating pizza with the guys after leaving me with your man-eating shark."

"Okay, she chased you." Hank gave up, rolling his eyes while holding his hands in surrender. "And you know she likes it when you call her a shark." He let out another laugh before focusing his attention back to Dog as he shrugged. "She seems to be doing okay."

"I forgot about the shark bit." Olive scrunched her nose. Hopefully, it will give her some brownie points. "But you're right, we're gonna live to see another day. She won't be causing any bloodshed. At least not right now."

Hank barked out a laugh. "I'm gonna grab the rest of our stuff so we can settle in," Hank mentioned, looking up at her one last time, his eyes full of lust. And Olive knew exactly what he was referring to.

Oh, hell yes! Come to Momma.

Heat poured into Olive's lower belly as she watched Hank. It should've be illegal to look as good as Hank did, even when he was bundled up in winter clothes. It was a damn shame she couldn't confess she now used him as the model she used for all her male characters in her books.

Olive might love him, but she wasn't going to give him that ego boost.

Although, she had a sneaking suspicion Hank already knew.

"You do that." She wasn't one to let him have all the fun though. Quickly she added, "Before we left I started writing a scene, and well... I just don't know if it's truly doable or not. I've been meaning to ask for your assistance," she purred as she watched her husband trip over one of the bags he'd brought into the cabin.

Hank let out a deep growl as he snapped his attention back to her. "My body is yours for whatever you want."

Oh man, those words made her shudder. "I plan on it."

"On second thought..." Hank slammed the door shut. "To hell with our bags."

"No, go get them." She laughed. "We'll be too tired later and I wanna get my e-reader."

Hank glared at her for a moment before knitting his brows together. "You're no fun. But fine, I'm only getting the rest of the stuff 'cause I might've packed us a few items to help further your research."

Olive's whole body shivered in anticipation at his words.
Oh, hell yes.

However, it was short-lived as she looked at Hank to see him going through what he'd already brought in.

"What the hell did I do with the keys?"

Olive tried to hold in her laugh as she saw them on the small table at the cabin entrance.

The question was should she tell him, or wait it out...

"Seriously, what the fuck did I do with them? It's not like I didn't just have them," Hank growled, picking up Dog's crate to check under it.

"Twenty bucks says I can find them before you," Olive hollered from her spot in the loft which made Hank dart his eyes to her.

"You wouldn't."

"If I can tell you where the keys are in less than thirty seconds, I get a special reward."

Hank crossed his arms over his chest. "Oh yeah, and what reward would that be?"

She winked. "I'll tell you later."

Hank studied Olive for a brief moment, before a wicked smile appeared on his face. "Oh, baby I'm looking forward to it."

"On the table by the door, *Tank*."

Hank's eyes shot to the area as he groaned. "Damn it." He stomped over to the keys, grabbed them and looked over his shoulder, narrowing his eyes toward her. "Not a word of this to Luke. You hear me?"

"I'll think about it." Olive laughed as Hank rushed out the door as he slammed it behind him.

Olive decided it would be best if she went downstairs to help him. After all, the sooner he got their stuff inside, the sooner she could find out what was in his special bag.

However, as Olive placed her foot on the top step, Dog hissed.

Her eyes instantly darted around the room looking for Dog. When she came up empty, Olive figured the hiss wasn't directed at her.

After letting out a breath she didn't know she was holding, Olive put her second foot on the step. This time, though, Dog growled loud.

Out of nowhere, their cat was at the bottom of the stairs staring up at Olive ready to attack.

"I thought we were friends now. What the heck?" As she took another step Dog let out another low growl.

"Um, nice kitty. You know what? I'm just gonna stay up here."

Dog hissed again.

"Uhh, Hank," Olive cried. "I think we were wrong. I'm not sure Dog likes it here very much...."

Oh, crap on a cracker.

Quickly Olive jumped back up the steps to the landing as Dog let out another growl followed by a hiss.

Okay, then.

That settled it.

Olive would be staying in the loft for the remainder of their trip.

CHAPTER EIGHT

HANK QUICKLY MADE his way back into the cabin with the remainder of their bags in hand. After all, he had his wife to get back to, so there was no time to waste. And he'd be a downright liar if he said he didn't want to be near her after everything that happened earlier.

However, he wasn't expecting to walk inside the cabin to see Olive negotiating with Dog regarding her staying in the loft for the duration of their vacation.

He was gone for what? Thirty seconds, maybe a minute tops?

Time to go play referee.

Hank chuckled as he walked to the bottom of the stairs. "Shoo, go explore the cabin and don't bully Olive. I swear, sometimes you forget she's your mother."

Dog looked at him and then back to Olive, contemplating her decision. When she didn't move, though, Hank shook his head glancing back to his wife. "She's trying to fake you out again. She's not gonna mess with you. Just come down."

"No way. *You* come up. It's safer. I'm not going down there. Did you hear her? I think she wants to eat me for real this time."

Hank's eyes dropped as he devoured every inch of her. "*I want to eat you.*"

The second he saw Olive's face flush with heat, it took everything inside of him not to run to her and do just that. Although he knew if he didn't settle whatever argument Olive and Dog were having, she really would stay in the loft the whole time.

And that just wasn't going to do.

Olive's tongue darted out at his words as she licked her bottom lip. "When you put it that way, how am I supposed to argue with that?"

Fuck me! Olive always knew how to push him to his breaking point without even trying. "Exactly. You can't. Now get your ass down here so I can have my reward."

"I'm the one that earned the reward, not you."

His head tilted to the side as his brow arched. "I'd love to beg to differ. We know that reward is gonna satisfy both of us, and Olive..." Hank's heart slammed against his chest as he licked his lips. "I'm starving."

"Just the reward I was hoping for." She took a step toward him. However, the second Olive placed her foot on the top step, Dog let out another hiss, this time accompanied by a low growl.

Within an instant, Olive jumped back pulling her foot off the stairs, her eyes huge as she looked at him and then back to Dog.

That was weird. Usually, Dog would've backed down by now.

Hank studied his cat for a second before glancing to Olive who backed away further into the loft.

"Wait, no." Hank stopped Olive as he kept his eyes honed in on Dog, who'd now placed her paw on top of the bottom step ready to run up them.

"Shit, she really is gonna murder me."

Olive might be right this time... Although, there was something in Dog's eyes that didn't seem like Olive's blood was on the menu.

"Put your foot back on the top step."

"No."

Hank narrowed his eyes at Olive. "Just do it."

"No."

"Olive."

"Don't Olive me. I'm protecting my life here."

His brows shot up as he stared her down. "That's *my* job."

"Give me a break." Olive rolled her eyes, crossing her arms over her chest. "You know what? This is ridiculous. I'm not gonna be bullied by a cat." To contradict her words though, instead of heading down the stairs Olive turned on her heel to stay in the loft.

"Babe, come back," Hank sighed, still keeping an eye on his cat. "I have a theory. Can you humor me? Just for a second?"

Olive spun back around as she quirked her brow, keeping her arms crossed over her ample chest. "Care to share with the class? Or do you wanna let her murder mittens devour me if I take a step toward you?" Olive placed her foot back on the step only for Dog to do the same, her face focused on Olive's next move.

"Is she doing that weird cat thing where they stalk you before they eat you? It kinda looks that way."

Ignoring his wife, Hank kept his attention on Dog. "Pull your foot back to the landing slowly."

"This is freakin' ridiculous. We do not negotiate with terrorists. I thought we'd gone over this time and time again."

"Pull it back," he growled.

As Olive moved her foot back to the landing with a huff, Dog put her paw back on the floor as well, all the while keeping her eyes glued on Olive the whole time. "Great. Now, we know for sure she's screwing with me. What did that accomplish? Huh? *Huh?* I'll tell you, absolutely nothing other than I'm an easy target and she likes to bully me."

Hank continued to ignore Olive's rambles as he watched Dog. "Put both your feet on the top step."

Olive's eyebrows shot to the ceiling. "Why? So, she can finally attack me?"

Hank watched Dog closely as she laid her paw back on the bottom step ready to strike just as Olive had done the same. However, this really wasn't Dog's usual 'I'm messing with Olive' posture. No, this was different. This was Dog ready to do whatever she needed to do—

Oh, for fuck's sake.

Hank didn't know whether to laugh or sigh as he realized exactly what their child-sized cat was doing or attempting to do. He rolled his eyes. "Dog thinks you're gonna fall down the stairs. She's trying to protect you."

Olive immediately flung her eyes to their cat. "You're kidding me. Really?"

To answer her, Dog began weaving in and out of Hank's legs, purring loudly. "I think that's a yes," he chuckled.

Olive's hands flew to her hips. "Sometimes you love me, sometimes you hate me... and then sometimes you try to control me. I swear to everything out there, Dog, I *am* fine. I haven't used crutches in *forever*. I can walk up and down these stairs and not fall."

Dog meowed.

"Don't talk to me in that tone of voice, young lady."

Hank's hand went to his stomach as he barked out a laugh. "Cut her some slack. She loves you and wants you to be safe."

"I *am* safe."

"Apparently, she doesn't think so."

"Well, she's gonna have to get over herself. Her attempts of cock blocking me since the car accident has reached an all-time high."

"That so?" Hank smirked.

"Don't you play dumb here, buddy." She narrowed her eyes at him. "When Momma wants sexy times, she should get sexy times. I shouldn't have to check with the cat first to make sure it's safe." Olive crossed her arms over her chest. "Why is she like that?"

"Who knows." Paying no attention to Dog, Hank took the steps two at a time as he raced up them. He only stopped for a second as he scooped Olive into his arms and tossed her over his shoulder.

What could he say, the man was on a mission.

"Hank!" Olive screamed. "And you!" she growled, pointing down the stairs at Dog who was now licking her paw as if nothing happened. "You're okay with him doing this, but not me going down the freaking stairs?!"

"Dog knows you're always safe with me." Hank tossed Olive on the bed with ease.

Damn, he loved watching her bounce, every last inch of her, and he knew he'd never get over that feeling. Before she could right herself and lunge for him, Hank took a step back, he knew if he didn't, she'd go after him.

In doing so, though, he got a good look around.

Holy shit.

Olive was right. The loft was just as perfectly decorated as the rest of the house.

Yeah, I'm really going to need to send the owners a thank you card.

As his eyes moved from the fireplace by the bed, back to Olive, he smirked. "I planned on getting a fire started as soon as we got here but—"

"Oh, you definitely got a fire started," she remarked, reaching for her top, before yanking it over her head exposing her lace-covered breasts.

Hank groaned as they swayed with her movements. "Good thing I'm a firefighter then."

"I'd say so." Olive placed her hands behind her back undoing her bra, tossing it to the floor.

It took everything inside of Hank not to lose it right at that second. He loved Olive's chest. Her taut nipples always beckoned him.

Fuck, he would never get over how truly beautiful his wife was. From her lush curves, and the swell of her thighs, to a pussy that would bring him to his knees every single day of the week.

Damn, he was a lucky man.

Immediately, Hank reached to the back of his collar, pulling his top over his head before crawling up the bed to his eager wife. The same wife who licked her lips in anticipation which sent a jolt right to his dick.

Fuck he needed to be inside of her, to feel her skin against his and mold them together. He knew he wanted to be close to her after their almost mishap, but now having her under him, it was more apparent than ever.

"I love you." He kissed the side of her neck as she moved her head to give him better access. "I love every single inch of you." Hank peppered kisses down Olive's neck before reaching her chest. He palmed her with one of his hands as his mouth sought out the other. Once he reached her nipple, he pulled it into his mouth. Olive's back instantly arched giving him more of herself.

She always gave him more.

And he freaking loved it. He was one lucky son of a bitch to have someone so responsive to his touch.

Hank released her with a pop before he brought his lips down to hers, devouring her with a kiss so hungry he didn't know if he'd survive. Olive was right there with him though, as she always was.

Hank felt her hands go to his belt, unbuckling it as she unbuttoned his pants. He moaned into her mouth as Olive's hand reached inside to wrap around him. He couldn't help the hiss that escaped his lips as she pulled his dick out, stroking him up and down once, twice before pulling her hand back.

Olive tore her mouth from his as she licked her palm from bottom to top before going back to his member.

Holy fuck. She's gonna be the death of me.

When Hank looked into her eyes, he saw her lust for him, but it was more than that. He also saw her love.

He saw it all, and he knew his eyes matched hers.

Ohh fuck. He didn't know how much more he could take as Olive stroked him.

Deciding he needed better control, Hank drew back, causing Olive to groan in disappointment.

"Hey, get back here." She crawled onto her knees, reaching for him.

"Not this time, Olive Oil. I believe you were the one who won the award, not me."

Olive's whole face lit as she sat back onto her butt, her toothy grin staring back at him. "Then what are you waiting for?"

That's all he needed to hear. Hank jumped into action. He quickly discarded the rest of his clothes then hooked his thumbs into the top of Olive's pants. And in one swift move, he removed them along with her panties, tossing them aside leaving her completely bare.

"You're fuckin' beautiful," he growled as he placed his knee on the bed, getting closer to her.

"Have you seen you?"

Hank laughed, shaking his head. "Trust me, I pale in comparison to you."

To stop her from arguing, which Hank knew Olive was about to, he placed his hands on her knees pushing them apart giving him the view he loved the most.

His heart pounded against his chest as he lowered himself to her core.

Fuck, he loved this and he'd never get tired of feasting on his wife.

As soon as she realized what he was doing, Olive's breath hitched as she looked down at him with heavy-lidded eyes. That was almost enough to unman him right then and there. Taking a deep breath to control his body, he kissed the scar that ran down her leg before moving closer to her core. Once there, he nibbled on the inside of her right thigh gently.

Olive immediately responded, letting out a gasp of pleasure as her hands fisted the comforter.

He loved when she let loose. But he wanted to see more. He wanted to see her completely free.

Hank moved to her lush core as he placed another kiss on the top of her mound while he focused on her eyes. He loved when she watched him, and truth be told, he loved watching her as he did it.

Her pleasure was just as much his, as it was hers. With their eyes locked he flicked his tongue over her clit, causing Olive to arch her back and let out another moan.

To keep her still, Hank placed his hands on her hips, anchoring her to the bed, as he went in for another taste.

"Oh God, Hank," Olive cried as he licked along her seam, stopping only to pull her nub into his mouth. "Oh, yes, more, please."

Since Hank was never one to deny her, he let go of her hip with one of his hands, bringing two of his fingers to her center, entering her slowly while flicking her clit with his tongue.

Hank knew her body better than he knew his own at this point. It only took him a mere second to find her spot before massaging it. Instantly, Olive's heels dug into the bed as she thrust her core to his mouth.

"Hank," Olive panted as her chest rose and fell faster and faster. "Please, oh God. I'm so close I need—"

He knew exactly what she needed. Hank pulled her full clit into his mouth and sucked hard causing Olive to explode.

Hank's fingers kept pace inside her as she shook and shuddered before coming down from her high. He kept his eyes trained on her, peppering gentle kisses to her mound as Olive worked on getting her breathing under control.

Once she was somewhat okay, Olive glanced between her legs to him, breathing heavily. "Whoa."

His thoughts exactly.

Slowly Hank removed his fingers from her core, bringing them to his mouth as Olive surveyed him with hooded eyes.

As she watched, he made sure to lick them clean, savoring her flavor before he kissed her lush mound once more. "And that, my love, was only just the beginning."

As Olive continued to pant, keeping her eyes focused on him, a goofy smile appeared on her face. "Prove it."

In a flash, Hank's eyes lit as he perused her body. "It'll be my pleasure."

Hank rose to his knees and as he stood over Olive, and stroked his dick while she watched. The little bit of moisture at the tip gave him the slickness he needed.

"Why is that so fuckin' hot when you do that?"

Seeing the lust flare in Olive's eyes made him groan.

Damn, he needed to be inside her. Letting go of himself, he grabbed one of the pillows, placing it under her hips giving him the perfect angle to enter her.

As she got into place, Olive's legs fell to the side, ready for him.

Fuck him, this was almost too much to handle.

As Hank looked down at her, completely wide open for him, he never wanted this moment to end.

"What are you waiting for?" She smirked at him. "At this point, Christmas will be here before you fuck me."

"You little shit." Hank arched his brow. With that, he pushed himself inside, feeling her walls tighten around his dick like a vise. He'd never get over the feeling of being as deep as humanly possible inside of his wife.

"More, Hank, please." Olive's hands trailed down her body reaching for her clit, but he stopped her.

Instead, Hank grabbed both her hands pinning them above her head. "Mine," he growled as he pushed himself harder inside her pussy.

As his hips rocked, Olive thrashed beneath him, meeting him thrust for thrust. "Shit, Olive." He let go of her hands as he wrapped his body around hers.

"Hank, please, more. I need more, I need deeper," she begged.

He pulled out only to push in deeper, finding a new pace that worked for them, but truth be told, he didn't know how much longer he'd be able to last.

As his body hummed, his mouth sought out hers. When he found her lips, he kissed her with so much passion and love he never knew if he'd come up for air again. At this point, he knew he needed more with her, to feel her come apart around him. Knowing what he had to do, his hand moved in between them seeking out her core.

Thank everything he could tell she was ready. As he clenched his teeth trying to hold himself together, he used his fingers to flick her clit, causing Olive to explode around him.

He swallowed her screams with his mouth as he rocked his hips, riding out her passion until he couldn't hold back anymore.

With one last thrust, Hank filled her, emptying every-thing he had inside of himself deep within her core.

Holy shit.

Hank slowly removed himself from her before collapsing on the bed beside her, breathing heavily as he came down from his high.

Again, holy shit. Yep, she is gonna be the death of me.

A few moments of them catching their breath filled the

room before Olive propped herself onto her elbow and looked him in the eyes, a playful smile on her face. "I don't think you need to light the fire anymore." She laughed, giving him a quick kiss.

"Babe, I plan on lighting a shit ton of fires the next two days." His eyes sparkled as a wicked smile appeared on his face. "After all, I am a firefighter."

CHAPTER NINE

Christmas Eve Morning

THE MORNING—FOR the most part—had gone exactly how Olive liked it. Her cheeks flushed as she thought back. She would've slept longer if she hadn't awoken to Hank having his own type of breakfast.

And she was his main course.

Not that she was complaining, she loved waking up that way.

Once they were up and out of bed after being thoroughly satisfied, they'd spent most of their time moseying around just enjoying each other's company.

But right now, Olive had other plans.

After all, it was Christmas Eve and that meant Olive had something essential to accomplish. Just like she did *every* Christmas Eve.

Making cookies for Santa.

Besides, how could she not use the cute 'Cookies for Santa' plate the owners left for them? That would be a travesty. The plate even had reindeer on it. She just wouldn't be able to live with herself if she didn't use the plate to its full potential.

So, baking it was.

Olive had the cookie dough ready and rolled out when Hank walked around the corner into the tiny kitchenette. Immediately, she stopped what she was doing and gawked at him.

Holy guacamole.

How was it possible for him to always look so dang good? You know what, at this point, it was just insulting to the rest of the population.

Olive had to admit though, she took advantage of it now. Before they started their research project his constant shirtless escapades used to annoy her, but now she enjoyed them.

Shirtless Hank was hot.

However, for some reason, Hank in dark jeans and a sweater with the sleeves pulled up to expose a quarter of his forearm... whoa, momma. She needed to fan herself.

Olive didn't realize she had a forearm thing, but it was safe to say she did now.

And the worst part was, the bastard knew it.

She couldn't count the number of times they'd be in an argument or something, and Hank would look her dead in the eyes and slightly push up his sleeve, exposing the goods.

Olive swore one time, she'd actually drooled.

Again... bastard.

She'd be lying if she said her characters in her books now didn't showcase their forearms, making their women lose their minds. Art imitates life after all.

"Hey babe." Hank smirked, catching Olive staring at his arms again. As he quickly made his way over to her, he placed a kiss on her lips. "What cha doing?"

Her jaw hit the floor as her brows pulled together, gaping at him like he'd lost his mind. "Making Christmas cookies for Santa. Duh. You know this. I do it every year."

Hank's eyes lit as the corner of his mouth lifted. "Oh, how could I have been so absent-minded to forget we as grown adults need to make cookies for Santa every year."

"*We* aren't making cookies, I am. Besides, we have to." Olive's hand shot to her hip as she stared him down. "Dog expects us to put out cookies for the big man or she'll think he won't bring her gifts," she stated matter-of-fact. "Dog was super worried he'd miss us since we aren't at home. I had to explain to Dog he'd never forget her."

"Did you now?" Hank cocked his brow as he leaned against the small kitchen island.

"Of course, I did. Couldn't you tell that's the reason she was sulking around the house before we left? She was worried."

"Huh? I thought you'd be the first to remind her she was on the naughty list..."

Olive's whole face scrunched as she thought about it. "Well, I mean... I guess you're kinda right, but everyone gets a second, or in her case one hundred chances this time of year." A playful smile appeared on her lips. "The jury is still out on you. I don't think I have enough pull with ol' Saint Nicholas to get you off the naughty list."

"Maybe I like being on the naughty list," Hank murmured as his eyes heated, giving Olive the once-over.

"Of course you do." She leaned closer to him and whispered, "I'm surprised *I'm* not on his naughty list."

"Oh, you are. I can guarantee you that, Olive Oil."

The audacity!

Olive jumped back in shock as she failed to hide her smile. "We'll just have to see about that tomorrow, now won't we? I've been known to be very persuasive. I don't think he'll ever have me on his naughty list."

Hank snorted. "You keep telling yourself that."

"I will."

"Okay, babe, whatever you say." Olive watched as Hank's eyes drank her in. "Just know I can promise you Santa isn't going to forget Dog or *you*." His eyes heated further and Olive knew precisely what that look meant.

"Hold up there, mister. Don't get me wrong, my love of the holidays exceeds anyone in the world. But I can whole-heartedly say I don't think I'm into the Santa role-play thing."

"Who said it would be role-play?" He arched his brow.

"Hank Parker, you are not in any certain terms Santa Claus."

Hank crossed his arms over his chest. "Olive Parker, who said I'm not? Don't I bring you joy? Make sure you're happy, healthy?" His eyes moved up and down her body slowly. "And when I walk into a room, isn't your first instinct to jump into my lap and tell me all your secrets, especially the naughty ones?"

"Hank!"

"I check all those things off the list, so that makes me Santa."

Both of Olive's hands snapped to her hips as she squared off with her husband. "First off there, bud, you don't tell Santa your secrets, *especially* not dirty ones—"

Hank cut her off. "I think you do. How else could you be an erotic romance author? I'm positive you're getting help from jolly ol' Saint Nick himself." He winked. "And since I'm Santa, I know this for a fact."

"Perv. Stop destroying Santa for me."

Hank laughed as he pushed himself off the island and gave her a quick kiss. "You're fun to rile, what can I say? That's what I ask for every year."

"I asked for Dog to eat your face."

Hank laughed again. "I don't know how many times I have to tell you, Olive. The only pussy ever doing any eating or getting eaten in our house has nothing to do with Dog."

"Ssssttttoppp." Olive picked up her spatula and pointed it at him. After a few second standoff with him not moving, she placed her hands on his chest and pushed him away. "Go out there and play with Dog. You're distracting me from what I'm doing. And with all your talk, I gotta make sure these cookies are extra special. Don't forget, Santa hears you all the time."

"Then he knows exactly what I plan on doing with you on this kitchen island."

As Hank advanced on Olive, she took a step back. "No, you don't. Not right now. Shoo, shoo. I have to get these in the oven. Go play with the cat or something."

"Only pussy I like playing with is yours."

Olive cocked her head, a sly smile on her face. "That was pretty good. I'm gonna use that in my next book."

Hank laughed, his eyes sparkling. "Glad I can be of service to you."

"In more ways than one." She winked before shooing him away again. "Now go. The oven is preheated and ready."

"I know for a fact your oven is always ready."

Where was the lie? It was true, for Hank, she was always ready. Probably because of those damn forearms.

Hank kissed her again on the nose before heading toward the living room with a chuckle.

Olive rolled her eyes at him as she focused on getting her cookies done. Yeah, she knew baking cookies for Santa was a kid thing, but dang it, she loved doing it anyway.

Plus, it was a win-win.

She got cookies out of the deal. Baking cookies for Santa was something she did every year, sometimes it was the only thing she did. Especially when she skipped out on going to the Parkers for Christmas.

She shrugged. *Guess I never need to spend another holiday alone.*

Olive used the cookie cutters she brought with them. One shaped like a Christmas tree and one shaped like a giant cat.

Carefully as she could, she placed the cutouts on the baking sheet. If all went well, they would be out of the oven in less than thirteen minutes and they'd be frosting them within the hour. Lord knew it was cold enough. All she'd have to do was open a window and they'd cool in no time.

Speaking of windows, she couldn't help but glance out the tiny kitchen one above the sink.

Everything had been beyond perfect, the only thing missing was snow. But hey, that was okay. Olive was still more than happy with their cabin getaway.

Snow or no snow.

Although, when she left Santa the cookies, she might also leave a twenty-dollar bill. You know? Sweeten the deal a little.

She laughed to herself as she shook her head. *If the Universe wants us to have snow, we'll have it. No need to bribe the Claus man. But snow would make it the ultimate perfect Christmas.*

Olive put the cookies in the oven before wiping her hands on the dishrag. However, as she moved around the small room cleaning her mess, she swore she heard a faint squeaking sound.

That was weird.

Deciding it was best to ignore it, she continued with her task. After all, this wasn't their home. And it could've been a noise from outside.

Even with the weird noise, Olive loved this cabin. Actually, she loved *everything* about the cabin, from the decorations to how cozy it felt. But she missed her family.

It still blew her mind to admit that, but it was true. Somewhere along the line, she went from really shitty parents and pretty much no family, to having the best family in the world. She loved Robin and Jim like they were her own. And then, of course, she couldn't forget the guys at the station.

She snorted out a laugh.

Olive, the person that would rather be caught dead than interact with *humans,* now couldn't wait to get back home to celebrate with Lucas, Rick, Tim, and everyone else.

Funny how things change.

Once the kitchen was clean, she walked over to Hank

who sat on the couch with his eyes closed relaxing. Olive's eyes moved to Dog standing on her hind legs, smelling the Christmas tree.

Holy alien overloads their cat was weird.

The worst part was, as Dog was on her back legs Olive saw just how tall Dog was.

She shuddered. *Holy crap on a cracker*.

If Dog ever did decide to end their truce, Olive wouldn't stand a chance.

Ignoring the weirdo cat, Olive sat on the couch causing Hank to open his eyes. "Hey babe. You get your cookies in?"

"Yes, no thanks to you." She curled into his side as Hank placed his arm around her shoulders. Olive instantly let her head rest on his chest getting herself comfortable.

"Are we gonna frost them when they're done?" She could hear the smile in his voice. "I hope you brought extra frosting 'cause I know of something else we can frost as well."

Olive rolled her eyes. "You have a one-track mind."

"You love it." He kissed the top of her head. "And you say that like you don't, Miss erotic romance author Quinn Sparks."

She sent him a toothy grin as her eyes gleamed with joy. "The only thing I'll ever admit to is that you're a great inspiration for my books."

Hank puffed out his chest. "Ahh, my life purpose has finally been completed."

Olive laughed as she pushed herself off Hank's chest to look at him. "You're so full of yourself."

In an instant, Hank grabbed Olive's hips pulling her onto his lap so she straddled him. "I'd rather you be full of me."

Olive burst out into a laugh as she rocked her hips against him, feeling his member hardening. What could she say? It was their anniversary after all.

However, Olive stopped the moment she heard the squeak again. Only this time it was louder.

"Did you hear that?"

"Hear what?" Hank's hands went to Olive's hips pushing her core harder against him. "Only thing I plan on hearing is you screaming my name."

It was at that exact moment all hell broke loose.

CHAPTER TEN

"WHAT THE FUCK WAS THAT?" Hank pushed Olive off his lap and onto the couch as he jumped up to investigate whatever the fuck just bolted out of their Christmas tree.

"I don't know!" Olive snapped her feet onto the couch as the thing that just propelled itself from the tree ran across the cabin floor. As it scurried toward the kitchen, it froze for a split second before it took a hard right and ended up heading directly to Olive. "It's gonna eat me!"

Thankfully for her, Dog intervened as she jumped to intercept the creature from making it to Olive. Somehow, she missed. However, Dog's movements were enough to scare the thing into turning again avoiding Olive. "Oh my God! This is it. This is how I die. Not by zombies or aliens, or even Dog but by I don't know what that thing is!"

Great, now Olive thinks she's gonna die and I have no idea what it— Holy fucking shit.

"I think it's a squirrel." Hank took off after his cat, who chased after the small animal as it jumped from the couch to the mantle knocking over a few items along the way.

"A freaking squirrel! Are you kidding me? Has there been a squirrel in the tree this whole time?"

"Looks like it." Hank jumped toward the creature again, only for Dog to trip him up and make him miss his chance to grab it.

And here he thought their getaway was going to be a break for them.

Insanely enough, this was not the first time Hank had to deal with this. For some reason, the station would get a few calls from people in their area around this time of year. And instead of pushing them off to the Fish & Wildlife Department they would always roll out to see if they could help.

Honestly, sometimes it was fun. Who gets to say they got paid to chase around rogue animal creatures? He got to live out his childhood dreams of being an Animal Conservationist, so there weren't many complaints from him.

It's not like they couldn't handle a tiny squirrel, right? How bad could it really get? Although usually, he'd be tag-teaming this type of operation with one of the guys versus his cat. Who instead of catch and release, Hank was positive it would be catch and eat for her. And then of course, there was Olive who was freaking out on the couch.

"Grab it and put it outside!" Olive bounced back and forth, leaping around pointing in all directions as she tried to follow the creature's movements.

"What do you think I'm trying to do invite it for dinner?" Hank stopped in mid-stride and glared at her, waving his hand to the kitchenette.

"Don't talk to me that way. It's your fault the thing is in here anyway."

"How the hell is it my fault?"

"I don't know yet, but I'll figure it out. Look, there it is."

Hank darted his attention to the squirrel who was now on the banister, squeaking as it flicked its head from side to side scared.

Shit.

He didn't want it to be scared. Then again, he'd be scared too if some guy and his monster cat were chasing him.

Thinking fast, Hank grabbed the blanket from the back of the couch to toss over the squirrel and trap it.

He groaned, rolling his eyes. He could already hear the shit talk once the guys found out about all this.

"Get it. He's right there!"

Hank took a giant leap forward as he tossed the blanket on the railing.

"Don't hurt him."

"I'm not trying to."

Damn it! The squirrel was too fast for Hank. Before the blanket could fall it propelled itself into the air headed for the tree again.

Before Hank could stop her, Dog jumped into the air after him, her paw hitting the little guy, causing the squirrel to fall to the floor instead of going back into the tree. "Dog, no!"

Thank everything, the squirrel didn't seem hurt. At least not that Hank could tell. The momentary paw to the side only stunned it for a second before it made its way directly toward Olive.

"Ahhhh. It wants to kill me. I told you! Hank get it."

"It's not trying to kill you!" Hank jumped again, tossing the blanket at the squirrel.

Holy freaking hell. This was not how he envisioned spending Christmas Eve with his wife...

As Hank made another attempt to catch him, the squirrel expertly dodged him as it made its way toward the kitchen.

"Don't hurt him. Don't hurt him," Olive chanted from her spot on the couch. She snapped her attention to Dog who ran after the squirrel as if her life depended on it. "Don't you dare harm even one hair on that guy's head, Dog. You hear me?"

Dog hissed her response while leaping toward the creature.

"I mean it, Dog," Olive shouted, as the squirrel did a one-eighty and headed toward the living room, Hank right on its tail.

"Grab the door, I'm gonna try and chase it out."

"Fuck that. I'm not getting off this couch. You're out of your mind if you think I am!"

Hank glared at her. "It's either open the door, or Dog gets it."

"Hell no."

Hank saw his golden opportunity as the squirrel stopped in the middle of the room, jerking its head back and forth.

"Now!" Hank took a few steps toward the creature, praying it would do what he wanted. The moment he saw the squirrel head in the direction of the door, he changed paths and snatched Dog in mid-air as she went after it.

"Thunder thighs don't fail me now!" Olive leaped off the back of the couch and ran full speed to the entrance.

As she swung it open, the squirrel bounded past her flying right out of the cabin. Olive slammed the door with such a force the walls shook. She then spun back to Hank, clenching her chest with her hand. "Holy shit."

"Holy shit is right." Dog jumped from Hank's arms, immediately running over to the door, patting the frame with her paw as she meowed.

"Hell no! You aren't going out there."

Dog replied with a loud hiss as she stared Hank down. "I mean it, Dog. You aren't going out."

Dog switched her tactics and focused her attention on Olive.

"Don't look at me."

Ignoring her, Dog purred as she rubbed Olive's leg.

"Oh, heck no. What in the zombie apocalypse do you think you're doing? You don't get to love on me in the hopes I do what you want. That's not how any of this works."

Dog hissed, pulling back from Olive, but not before swatting her leg at Olive's calf.

The cat then glanced at the door with a growl before stomping back to the tree to investigate.

"You don't think there's more of them, do you?" Olive's eyes widened as she shifted her attention back to Hank.

"I don't think—"

"Oh my God!" she cut him off. "It was in there when we were having sexy times! Do you think it saw us?"

Hank stared at her dumbfounded for a few seconds before he burst into a laugh. "Only you would go right to that observation."

"I'm serious." Olive's eyes scanned the room looking for any sign there might be more lurking.

Before Hank could reassure Olive there weren't more, Dog made another noise causing Hank to turn around. Their cat sat back on her hind legs and sniffed the tree. After a few seconds, she plopped down with a huff as she headed back to the front door.

"I think we're safe. Pretty sure Dog would have just told us if there were more."

Olive snapped her eyes to their cat, as her hands flung to her hips. "You do not murder helpless little animals. You hear me, young lady? I don't care how mean and scary you are."

"For someone who was terrified, you sure are adamant it wasn't hurt."

"Of course I don't want the thing hurt." Olive jutted her chin to their cat. "I just don't trust her though. Dog chased me into a bathroom. Who knows what she'd do to a little fella like that?"

Olive and Hank both stared at each other for a few seconds before the whole room erupted in laughter.

Only them. Holy freaking moly.

Hank shook his head. "Merry Christmas Eve, Olive."

"Yeah, same to you."

Even though the chaos had calmed down, Hank could still feel some unease. Maybe that's why he wasn't surprised to see

Olive pulling out the kitchen chair before standing on top of it.

Once she was safe on her perch, she breathed out an audible sigh of relief. "Wow."

"Never a dull moment with you, Olive Oil."

"Will you ever stop calling me that?"

"Not on your life." He pointed to her chair. "Care to explain what you're doing?"

"Just being cautious. You never know."

Hank rolled his eyes as he walked over to her and grabbed Olive at the waist before tossing her over his shoulder.

Yep, never a dull moment.

"Put me down you big oaf. We've had enough excitement for today. We don't need to topple over and break a bone."

"You're the one that won't walk back to the couch."

"I'm just being cautious, I already told you that. Freakin' put me down or I'm gonna murder you."

Hank laughed as he gently placed Olive on the couch and plopped down next to her. "Is this gonna go in one of your books?"

Olive's whole face brightened as she pulled her feet onto the couch, refusing to let them dangle. "Abso-fucking-lutely."

Hank burst into a hearty chuckle. However, before he could comment, a faint smell of something burning hit his nose.

Olive must have smelled it too since it was only a split second later she leaped off the couch. "My cookies!"

CHAPTER ELEVEN

Christmas Morning

"IT'S CHRISTMAS!"

Olive shot out of bed the second her eyes opened the following morning. "Hank, Dog, get up!" Moving as fast as she could, she bolted toward the stairs, tripping on her discarded shoes.

However, right before she made it down the first step, Hank groaned, grabbing her attention. As she moved her eyes to him with the intent of urging him to hurry up, she watched Hank push himself onto his elbows and give her a once-over. "Happy *Anniversary*." He chuckled, wiping the sleep out of his eyes.

"Oh, yeah. I forgot." Olive bit her lip as she sheepishly shrugged. "Sorry."

Hank shook his head with another laugh as he pushed himself to sit upright.

Instead of heading down the stairs, she quickly turned on her heels and jumped onto the bed. After climbing onto Hank's lap, she grabbed his shoulders and brought him in for a big smacking kiss that echoed throughout the room. "Happy Anniversary, now get your ass out of bed!"

Before Hank could reply, Olive hopped off him and went

back to her first plan as she ran toward the stairs, only stopping for a second to greet Dog who was laying at the end of Hank's feet. With a quick scratch to her head, she poked Dog's butt. "Merry Christmas."

Now run!

At least Dog was sleepy enough to not go for her finger.

However, once Olive was halfway down the stairs, she heard Hank's deep voice from above her. "Come on, girl. Let's go after your mom. Lord knows what trouble she'll get into if we don't."

"I can hear you!" Olive glared up at him from the bottom step as Hank looked over the railing at her with a smirk on his face.

"I know."

As Olive watched him from the living room, she was taken aback. How was it possible for him to be so damn attractive all the time? Like, give her a freaking break.

Olive cursed herself as her eyes traveled down his bare chest to the top of his flannel pajama pants. Oh damn, she was definitely lucky in the husband department. From where she stood, she had the most perfect view of his yum-yum lines that descended right below the—

"Close your mouth, Olive Oil."

Her eyes snapped to his.

Dang it! Caught again. How many times is this gonna happen?
Bastard.

"Shut your face," Olive mumbled as she flung her hands into the air waving him off. Ignoring his pleased smile, she walked to the kitchenette. "I'm gonna get the coffee going."

"Olive..."

"What?" she replied innocently as she peeked her head out so she could see him.

"Sugar, not salt."

"We'll see."

Hank belly laughed as Olive went back to putting the

coffee on. As she hit start on the machine though, her eyes migrated over to the burnt cookies on the Santa plate. She couldn't help the annoyed groan that escaped her.

Stupid cookies.

As she glared at the burnt disasters, Hank's arms wrapped around her. He placed a kiss on the top of her head. "Merry Christmas, babe."

Olive turned in his arms, wrapping herself around him before reaching up on her toes to give him a kiss. "Why does one of the cookies have a bite taken out of it?"

"Don't ask me." Hank shrugged. "It was probably Santa."

Seeing the slight smile on Hank's lips warmed her heart. In the middle of the night, she'd heard him go downstairs, but she thought it was to get some water. She didn't realize it was to take a bite out of one of her destroyed cookies just to make her feel better.

Olive melted into his arms as she realized just how far she'd come in her life and how lucky she was to have him. Not only did Hank accept her and all her crazy paranormal, zombie-filled conspiracy theories, but he also appreciated and nurtured her love for the holidays.

"I love you." Hank kissed the crown of her head.

"Love you too, you big oaf." The corners of her mouth turned upward as she lovingly looked at him. "But I know why you ran down here after me."

Hank chuckled pulling away to grab a mug. "I had to make sure I got sugar and not salt. You forget, I'm the one that perfected that over the years."

"Trust me, I didn't forget." She flicked her eyes to the ceiling. "Jerk."

"But, you love me."

"This is true."

It only took them a few minutes to grab their coffees before heading into the living room. Dog was already at the base of the tree patiently waiting.

See, it was times like this Olive thought Dog was the most precious creature in the world. Then she'd go and ruin it by calling upon Satan herself and terrorize every living thing around. Okay, it was mainly just Olive she terrorized, but whatever.

"Do you think we should start with her?" Hank gestured to Dog.

"I'm Santa!"

Hank laughed as Olive ran toward the tree nearly skidding to a halt in front of it. What could she say? She'd been eyeing the gifts since they placed them under the tree the day they got there.

"We talked about this, *I'm* Santa, but you can be my Mrs. Claus."

"Shut your face."

Hank barked out another laugh as he sat back on the couch, kicking his feet on top of the coffee table, crossing one leg over the other. "Have at it."

Olive clapped her hands together. "You're gonna love what I got you." She stopped for a second as she bit her bottom lip. "Or you're gonna roll your eyes. Not sure yet. I guess we'll have to find out."

"All I need is you," Hank reminded her, his eyes soft as he watched her by the tree.

With a ridiculously wide smile on her lips, Olive dropped to her knees and crawled around under the tree.

"And maybe this view all the time," Hank grunted. "Shake your ass for me, babe."

Olive jerked her head over her shoulder to glare at him. "Do you always have to make everything about sex?"

"That's your job, not mine." His eyes twinkled like the lights all around them. "I just use my hose to extinguish objects that get too *hot*."

"Hank Parker, shut your pie hole or I won't give you your gift."

"Depends on what it is?"

Paying him no mind, Olive began going through each box searching for the one she'd wrapped for Hank. So far everything she'd picked up had been labeled Dog. When she didn't see her gift for Hank, panic rose as her heart raced. "You grabbed all of the gifts from the car, right?" Olive asked, as she moved a few more boxes coming up empty.

"Yep. I took everything out of the car when we got here."

"You're wrong. You have to be wrong."

Hank cocked his brow. "I'm not."

Olive turned to him, her heart pounding in her chest. "No, you must've forgotten some in the car."

"I might forget a lot of things, babe, but I got everything out. I promise. I'm sure it's here somewhere."

"No!" Olive sat back on her heels as tears welled in her eyes.

Great going, Olive. What a way to ruin the morning? How could it not be here? I know I wrapped it and—

Oh no.

Her stomach dropped.

Olive scrunched her eyes tightly closed as she realized exactly what happened. With all the commotion trying to get Dog in her crate, Olive accidentally left Hank's gift under the tree with the rest of them.

How could I have been so stupid?

Olive looked at Hank, her eyes watering. "I think I left it under the tree at home."

Hank put his coffee on the table as he cocked his head slightly to the side. "That's okay, Olive. You really are the only gift I need or want."

"No, you don't understand, it was the perfect gift. I was so proud when I found it," she groaned. "I can't believe I forgot *your* gift." Olive plopped onto her butt, absolutely defeated. "And when you find out what it is, that's gonna make it even worse."

"Was it something sexy, maybe a little skimpy?" His brows shot to the ceiling as the corner of his mouth lifted. "If so then, yeah, I'm a little sad."

"Hush your face." Olive shot daggers toward him. "You don't understand, it was perfect. I can't believe myself right now. I always remember everything. You're the one that forgets where you took your shoes off every day. Not me. I remember things." She pointed at herself with a pout.

"Hey!"

"It's true..." Olive slumped. "This sucks."

Hank pulled himself off the couch and kneeled in front of her. "Olive, don't be upset. It's not a big deal. This isn't about gifts. *We* aren't about gifts. Aren't you the one that explained to me the holidays are about being with the people you love?"

"Yes, but—"

"No buts. We don't have to give gifts ever. As long as I have you by my side for the rest of my life, I'm a very happy man." He cupped Olive's cheeks in his hands, kissing her gently. "I love you."

"I love you too." She melted into his embrace as she sighed. "And, I'm sorry."

"No need to be sorry. I'm sure it'll still be under the tree when we get home."

"If Luke opened anything, I'll kill him." Olive's eyes narrowed as her lips thinned.

"Yes, I know." He kissed the top of her head before he reached under the tree, pulling out a small box covered in red and green wrapping paper. "Here. This is from me."

Olive pushed it away. "No, I can't. If you can't open your gift, then I'm gonna wait until we get home."

"Hell no."

"Yes."

"Olive."

"Don't Olive me, I'm serious. It's not fair to you."

"The hell it isn't. I want you to open your gift." Instead of arguing with her further, Hank pulled Olive onto his lap. "Please, for me?" He handed her the small box again.

How could anyone say no to those puppy dog eyes? They couldn't. Giving in, she unwrapped the box. As she carefully opened it, tears sprang to her eyes as her heart skipped. "Hank..."

"It's a custom-made Christmas tree necklace," he spoke softly. "This way even when you aren't at home you can still feel free."

A tear ran down her cheek as she stared in awe at the gorgeous silver tree with hints of green scattered throughout the piece, all with a diamond star at the top. "I don't even know what to say."

A proud smile spread on Hank's face as he took the necklace from her. "You don't have to say anything." He unclasped the back. "Lift up your hair."

As Olive did as she was told, Hank placed a kiss on the back of her neck before he placed the necklace on her.

"There."

Olive's hand instantly went to it as she held it in her palm, willing her tears to go away. "I love it."

"Good." Hank kissed the side of her neck before turning her in his lap. "It looks good on you."

"It's beautiful."

He winked. "I can't wait to see you wearing nothing but that."

Olive chuckled as she punched him in the arm.

"Happy Anniversary and Merry Christmas, Olive Parker."

A sweet smile crossed her lips as she gazed at her husband. "Merry Christmas and Happy Anniversary, Hank Parker." Her nose scrunched. "There is only one problem, though."

"Oh yeah, and what's that?"

"This completely overshadows what I got you." She nervously laughed, making Hank's eyes twinkle.

"I doubt it."

"Trust me."

He brought his lips to hers. "I always do."

THE REST of the morning was full of Dog and Olive on the floor playing with their cat's new toys and Hank couldn't be happier.

He'd be lying if he said the best part wasn't seeing Olive absentmindedly grabbing her necklace to fiddle with it every once in a while.

Hank walked into the kitchen and pulled out the small cake his mom made them for their one-year wedding anniversary. Once he opened the lid, Hank laughed. His mom had made a small green cake and decorated it with a Christmas tree and two tiny Bigfoot prints.

A toothy grin spread across his face.

Olive was gonna love this.

As he put it on the kitchen island, Hank glanced over at the fire he'd built shortly after they opened presents. It seemed to be doing well, and he couldn't help but smile as Olive sat on the floor with Dog pulling along some shiny ribbon as the mammoth chased after it.

However, as he moved to the sink, he looked out the window and his heart skipped. "Babe."

"Yeah?" Olive looked at him with a lopsided grin on her face.

"Get dressed. Looks like Santa heard your wish after all."

"Huh?"

"You were right to bribe the big man." Hank jerked his thumb toward the window. "It's snowing."

Olive shot to her feet, Dog completely forgotten as she ran to the door and swung it open. She spun back to Hank before she pointed to the outside. "It's snowing!"

"It is."

Olive took a step out the door, but Hank stopped her. "No ma'am. Dressed and shoes. Then you can go outside."

"Oh, come on. It's snowing on Christmas. Just one second, that's it, I promise."

"I know you." Hank stared her down. "The moment you get out there I won't get you back in for hours. Go get dressed. *Now.*"

Olive protested as she closed the door, mumbling jerk and fuck face under her breath, only making Hank laugh as he poured another cup of coffee.

"Go put on your shoes, get dressed, blah blah blah," she mocked, walking past him.

"One."

Olive froze.

"Wanna make it two?"

And then out of nowhere, Olive did the one thing she was known to do best. She shocked the absolute shit out of him. "Maybe I do."

With that, Olive ran up the stairs leaving Hank with his mouth open.

Oh man, he fucking loved this woman.

But she was definitely getting at least two...

Hank swore it was less than thirty seconds before Olive made it back down the stairs and ran right through the door past him without even a wave.

Let her have her fun. He chuckled.

A few minutes later after he stoked the fire, Hank grabbed his coffee and headed toward the door. As he leaned against the frame sipping his drink, he couldn't help but admire how free Olive looked as she twirled around letting the snow fall on her.

There was just something about seeing Olive like this that Hank hoped he'd remember forever.

As Hank watched her spin, he felt something at his foot.

When he tilted his head down, he saw Dog gazing up at him with worried eyes. "I know, girl. It's too cold out there for us."

Dog meowed as she weaved in between his legs. "Are you having a good Christmas?"

Dog purred before she looked out the door toward Olive.

"She's a special one. Thanks for always trying to keep her safe. But let up a little, would ya?"

Dog huffed, but then began to purr again.

At least it wasn't an outright no.

He considered it a win.

Hank leaned against the door, watching Olive for about five minutes before he pushed himself off the frame. "We gotta get her in before she freezes her ass off, Dog. She'll stay out there all day if we let her."

The cat meowed in agreement. And Hank knew exactly how to persuade his wife to leave the snow.

He put down his coffee and went over to the table. After he picked up what he was looking for, he headed back to the front door. "Olive."

She turned to him, her smile wide as her eyes twinkled with delight. "Do you think Bigfoot's out here doing the same thing?"

"Maybe." Hank chuckled. "But the difference between him and you is, he's got a lot of extra fur to keep him warm, you pretty girl, do not."

"What are you talking about? I probably got enough excess blubber to let me last out here all winter."

Hank's eyes hardened as he stared at her. "Olive," he warned.

"What?"

"'Cause it's our anniversary, I'm gonna let that slide for right now but make no mistake I'm not gonna forget it."

Olive waved him off. "You forget everything."

His brow arched. "Says the woman that forgot my gift?"

"Hey!" Olive picked up the snow from the ground and made a ball.

"I wouldn't if I were you."

Giving complete disregard to Hank's warning, Olive tossed the ball directly at him. Which he of course expertly avoided as it swung past him into the cabin, triggering Dog to eagerly chase after it.

"Oh, you are gonna get it."

"Yeah right." Olive snorted. "You won't even come out here. What are you gonna do about it?"

Hank shoved himself off the frame and held up the duffle bag he'd been hiding out of sight. "That's not what I was talking about."

As soon as Olive spotted the bag, her eyes widened as she stood frozen.

"It's time for your anniversary gift."

CHAPTER TWELVE

Olive eyed the duffle bag in Hank's hand, causing her heart to race as lust formed in her lower belly.

Happy Anniversary to me!

Although, don't get her wrong, she was really excited about the duffle bag, *but...* it was snowing. And on freaking Christmas.

Her eyes moved from Hank to scan the scenery around her. It was truly breathtaking as the fresh snow began to cover everything. She honestly couldn't ask for anything more when it came to December twenty-fifth. As the snow fell, Olive's eyes drifted back to Hank.

Once their eyes met, a wolfish grin appeared on his face as he scanned over her body.

Fuck the snow.

"That's what I thought." Hank laughed as Olive ran toward him at full speed. "Don't know what took you so long."

"It's snowing. Give me a break."

Hank's eyes feasted on her like he was a man on a mission, and well, damn she was too.

"I'll give you a break."

Olive cocked her brow as she stood in front of him. She should've known better. Hank grabbed Olive around the waist, hoisting her onto his shoulder. "Do you always have to do this? I know you're a big ol' fireman dude with muscles for days, but can you chill? Like even for a minute. I don't want you to pull out your back."

"Olive."

"Pfft." She rolled her eyes. "Yeah, yeah... you know what? I'll say it for you...*one.*"

"Can't go stealing my line there, Olive Oil." Hank laughed as he squeezed her ass with the hand that was holding her in place.

"And what are you gonna do about it?"

Hank growled deep in his throat as he walked them into the cabin, slamming the door behind him. "I'm about to show you." Keeping the duffle bag in his hand, he ran to the stairs taking them two at a time as he made his way up to the loft.

Instead of arguing, Olive sat back and enjoyed the ride. Because whatever was about to happen, it sounded like a damn good time to her.

Hank tossed Olive onto the bed, making her bounce a few times. She swore he did that on purpose. Hank then flung the bag onto the end of the bed. After she righted herself, Olive couldn't stop from clapping her hands as she waited for him to open it. She could only imagine what goodies he'd packed away. Sure, they'd experimented a lot in their relationship, but he never ceased to keep surprising her.

Did she mention she was fond of his knot-tying skills? Oh boy, those were some of her favorite nights. The ones when Hank bound her to their bed, spread open to be entirely at his mercy.

Talk about out of this world.

As Hank opened the bag, her eyes widened further with

excitement. And the second she saw something sparkle, her heart raced.

Oh, hell yeah.

This was going to be better than aliens appearing right in front of her.

"On second thought," Hank stated, causing Olive to snap her eyes to him. "Maybe I'll save this for later." He closed the bag, pushing it out of the way.

"No!"

Hank cocked his brow at her as the corner of his lip rose. "You don't even know what's in there."

"I don't have to. I know I want it."

His smirk turned into a full-blown toothy grin. "You sure?"

"What do you want me to do, beg?" She arched her brow.

"That could be nice."

Olive's eyes hardened. "You either take out what's in there or I'm going back to the snow." She placed her foot on the floor. There was no way in hell she was headed back outside, but she knew her husband well enough to know exactly how to get him going.

"Stop."

His deep voice bellowed throughout the room, causing her pulse to race. *Heck freakin' yes!*

"Strip."

Who was she to argue? Well, her of course. But she was more interested in what was in the bag to keep egging him on.

Olive stood as anticipation ran through her body. If he was going to make her strip, she was damn well going to make a show of it. Turning away from Hank, Olive slowly removed her jacket throwing it to the ground.

She then bent at her waist, giving her tush a little shake in the air as she untied her shoes before pulling them off along with her socks. Olive kicked them aside all while keeping herself turned away from him.

Hearing Hank's groan as she stood sent shivers down her spine. And as her body heated from his sound, she glanced over her shoulder to him.

Olive wasn't startled to see he'd already removed the sweater he'd put on after they'd opened gifts. Nor was she surprised to see him openly palming himself through the pajama pants he wore. He hissed when their eyes met.

"Should I keep going?" she asked innocently with a slight pout on her lips.

His growl sent another shiver through her body. "You better."

Olive's heart pounded against her chest as she turned back around and grabbed the bottom of her sweater, pulling it over her head. She then reached behind her, undoing her bra.

Hearing another groan come from Hank urged her on.

There was just something about him making those noises that made her feel so damn sexy.

Seriously, it was almost too much to take. She could already feel the slickness between her legs and she hadn't even gotten her pants off yet.

Olive had always loved sex, obviously, since she was an erotic romance author. But throughout her entire life she'd never felt more comfortable with a person than she did with Hank. Maybe that's how it was always supposed to be.

Once you found your person, there was no hiding.

There was no judgment.

Just love.

And truth be told there wasn't a need for there to be any hiding. Hank loved her, Olive swore sometimes more than she loved herself most days. He loved every inch of her body. Every single lump, bump, and curve.

The thing is though, it wasn't just love. No, that was only part of it.

Hank lusted for her.

He was fully one hundred percent attracted to her in every single way.

Her.

The plus size, huge thighed, big stomach, double chinned in most angles, her.

And damn if that did not give Olive the biggest confidence boost in the world.

What Hank and Olive had was true, pure love. Something she never thought was possible but yet, here she was. Stripping down to nothing in front of by far the sexiest man she'd ever laid eyes on, made her hot.

Olive hooked her thumbs into the waist of her pants, making sure to hook her panties as well. And ever so slowly, she shook her ample hips back and forth as she pushed them down her body.

"Fuck yes," Hank hissed.

As she bent, removing the material, she spread her legs slightly giving Hank a perfect view of her center. She knew he'd be able to see just how ready she was for him.

And only him.

"On the bed," Hank commanded. "Close your eyes."

Yes! She loved this part.

Quickly she hopped onto the bed, waiting for his next instruction. She knew by now when Hank said 'close your eyes' she closed them.

Although, pushing back was always fun too. But right now, Olive was more eager to see what plans he had in store for her.

However, she fought rolling her eyes when she felt Hank's knee on the bed before lifting her head to place a blindfold over her eyes. "I would've kept them closed."

He snorted. "Sometimes you don't."

Well dang, he had her there.

Olive felt Hank move off the bed and heard him unzip the bag.

"Are you gonna tell me what's in there?" she asked, straining her neck to see if she could distinguish any noises she was familiar with.

"No. I'm gonna *show* you."

Oh, hell yeah! "Right now?"

"Not yet."

Before she could convince him to do just that, something wrapped around her wrist causing her brows to pull together under the blindfold.

What the...

This wasn't the regular rope they'd used when Hank would tie her down in the past.

No, this material was completely different. Almost itchy...

Olive listened as she heard Hank move off the bed, going to her other wrist to do the same.

Something was off. Usually, she'd feel Hank tighten the knots to hold her in place. But whatever he used this time, Olive knew with a tiny flick of her wrist, she'd get out of whatever it was.

"Holy fuck, you look perfect."

The bed dipped between her knees, which also surprised her since he didn't tie her legs apart.

What the heck? Just as she was about to open her mouth, something light caressed her breast as it trailed down her stomach. "What is that?"

"No talking." He did it again, this time going right over her nipples, causing a hiss to escape her lips. The sensation was like nothing she'd ever felt before. It definitely wasn't a feather. They'd done that enough, so she knew exactly how that'd felt against her skin.

"One of my favorite things is to see you bound to the bed open and ready for me," Hank moaned, moving the object lower, this time letting it fall between her spread legs as it brushed against her plump core.

Olive moaned low as her body hummed at the new sensation. She didn't have a clue what it was, but she wanted more.

"Do you remember what I said this morning?"

"Huh?" Her brain short-circuited as he danced the mystery object back across her chest.

"The only gift I'll ever need is *you*." With that, he removed her blindfold.

It only took Olive a few seconds to let her eyes adjust to the light in the room. When they did, she saw a naked Hank kneeling over her, a Santa hat on his head with gold rope tinsel in his hand. The same exact type of thin tinsel people used to decorate for the holidays.

Immediately, Olive's eyes shot to her wrist, and sure enough, that's exactly what he'd used to bind her arms. "Hank?"

"Shhh." He lowered himself between her spread thighs. "Let me enjoy my gift."

Hank kept his eyes locked on Olive's as he took one long lick of her core before placing a kiss on top of her mound. "It's the best kind of gift."

Olive's breath hitched as Hank let out a low hoarse growl when he flicked his tongue against her slit. He kissed her center once more, then lifted himself and crawled up her body to hover over her. "I heard you've been on the naughty list, Olive Parker."

Her body shivered as Hank grabbed the end of the tinsel, running it over her body. "Wh-who said I was on the naughty list?"

Hank's eyes darkened as he reached between them, placing his dick at Olive's opening. He pushed in with one deep thrust as he growled the word, "Me."

Olive's back arched to accommodate him. And thank everything, the tinsel he used to bind her wrists was flimsy since she broke free. She instantly wrapped her arms around Hank's shoulders, pulling him in tighter. "Hank!"

As his hips pulled out slowly, only to push back in just as slow, it was almost too much for her to bear.

Hank took complete possession of her mouth as he moved inside her. Kissing her with such need, she almost couldn't breathe.

When he tore his mouth from hers, pulling his body away to sit up, Olive wrapped her legs around him, begging him to stay.

Effortlessly, he unlocked her legs from around his waist, as his right brow cocked. "Oh no, no, no, people on the naughty list don't get to make the decisions."

"I'm not—"

To emphasize what he said, Hank grabbed her hips, flipping Olive onto her stomach. His hand went to the small of her back, pushing her down, forcing Olive's ass to rise in the air.

As Hank palmed her cheeks, another moan fell from her lips.

"You shouldn't tease me." His hand squeezed her ass. "You play a dangerous game when you do."

Olive looked over her shoulder as she wiggled her butt. "Maybe I like being on the naughty list."

A broad smile spread across Hank's face. "I have no doubt."

Before she could reply, Hank lined his member to her slit, thrusting into her, this time holding onto her hips as he moved.

"You always feel tight like this."

Olive's hands fisted the sheets as she pushed her ass into him, begging for more. Deeper, stronger, harder.

Just more. She needed more. At this point, he was going to kill her. "Hank!"

His hips moved faster as he reached for Olive's hands,

locking them behind her using the tinsel next to them to loosely bind her again.

Once she was in place, Hank kept one hand on her wrists as he pushed himself deep inside her center. Her body hummed as the tip of his dick hit her spot with each thrust.

She couldn't breathe. She couldn't think. She couldn't do anything other than feel.

Olive didn't know how much longer she'd last. But she knew for a fact she wanted him to explode with her.

As she panted, pushing her body back to him the best she could, Olive squeezed her center, causing Hank to hiss as he thrust again.

"Fuck!"

"I want to feel you empty in me," her words entered the room. "Fill me, Tank."

Hank's movements sped as he pushed harder. At this point, Olive was positive she'd have bruises later, but she didn't care.

"When you say shit like that, it..." He couldn't speak as his thrusts became erratic. "Fuck that was hot."

"I need to feel it. Now, fill me." Her whole body ignited only seconds from exploding. Knowing how close she was, Olive squeezed again.

A loud grunt came from above her and Olive instantly knew she was there. As her body vibrated, it only took one more push of his dick against her spot to send her flying over the edge. Thank God he was right there with her as he pumped into her, stilling as he emptied himself.

Holy freaking crap.

Olive was barely aware of Hank pulling out of her core, as she worked on gaining control of her breath.

Hank grabbed the broken tinsel from her wrists, tossing it to the side, as he fell onto the bed beside her. He plopped onto his back, his chest rising and falling with rapid speed. "Best damn gift I've ever gotten."

Olive had to agree with him there. However, she flipped onto her side as she smiled at him. "You don't know that. You still haven't opened my gift yet," she joked, knowing damn well nothing she'd get him could ever compare to their times together.

Hank laughed as Olive continued. "I do have to say I'm a little surprised tinsel was in the bag. I was positive there would've been more."

"Who said that was the only thing I packed?" He stared at her, his eyes filling with heat.

Olive's mouth opened for a split second before she bit her bottom lip, trying to stop the moan that wanted to escape. She should've known better. "Well, then, Happy Anniversary to me!"

Hank beamed as Olive scooted closer to his side.

"And me." He laughed.

Olive gently placed her head on Hank's chest, hearing his heartbeat. Everything about their time away had been more than she ever expected. She wanted to go home, but in moments like this, she never wanted to leave. "I don't want to go back tomorrow morning," she sighed into his chest.

"What if we come back?" he asked, his arm moving around her shoulders holding her close.

Hearing his words, Olive propped herself onto her elbow and eyed him. "Really?"

"Or better yet, why not look into buying a cabin of our own? That way we can get away whenever we want."

A wicked smile appeared on Olive's face as her eyes traveled down his body. When she saw his dick twitch, she looked at him. "Keep going..."

Hank's eyes darkened as his hand went to the small of her back, urging her to move closer to him. "Field trips for research. Research is fundamental. Especially, in your line of work."

Olive's tongue shot out as she licked her bottom lip. "I

have to agree." She flung her leg over Hank's waist straddling him, his member coming to full attention under her.

"And zero people." Hank's hands caressed up her sides before seeking out her chest.

Those were the only words Olive needed to hear. "Sold!"

CHAPTER THIRTEEN

HANK THANKED every fucking thing out there the drive home had been uneventful. Even most of the snow had melted or was plowed off the roads by the time they'd left that morning.

Which made the drive exactly how Hank wanted it to go.

As smooth as humanly possible.

But that was only the drive...

Hank just hoped whatever he and Olive were about to walk into as they pulled into their driveway wasn't World War III or worse.

"You ready?" Hank placed their vehicle in park and put his hand on Olive's knee, giving it a light squeeze.

She'd spent most of the morning as she did on their way to the cabin, her eyes glued out the window.

Olive tilted her head slightly as she gazed back at him, her smile wistful. "As ready as I'll ever be. I loved our cabin adventure more than anything. And even though I don't want to admit it, I kinda missed everyone." Her eyes narrowed on him as her lips thinned. "Don't ever tell them that."

"I missed them too."

She shuddered causing Hank to laugh. "I even missed Luke."

Dog meowed from the backseat, agreeing with her.

Hank moved his hand to her crate sticking his fingers in the holes. "None of us want to admit it but we all missed them. It's good to be back home."

However, the moment Hank opened the door of the SUV to hop out, he heard shouting.

Fuck me. It was three freaking days. They had got to be kidding him. Hank turned his head back to Olive only to see her eyes round as she listened to the commotion.

"What did Luke do?" she asked, as she stared at their front door and then back to Hank.

"Luke? It could've been Miranda."

As they stared at each other the silence only lasted a few seconds before they both burst into belly laughs. "Nope, it was definitely Luke."

Deciding it was best to stop whatever the hell was going on, Hank jumped out of the car, Olive right behind him. As they dashed up the front steps, they heard the voices grow louder.

Was it too late to turn around? I'm sure I can call the owners of the cabin and extend the trip a few days...

"I'm telling you, *Lucas.* I don't care how pissed you are, you don't do that."

Hank turned to Olive. "Glad we didn't make a bet on who caused the trouble."

Olive chuckled as her hand went to the doorknob. "That's cause we both knew who it was."

They opened the door and walked in to see Miranda and Lucas toe-to-toe screaming at each other in the living room.

"Stop yelling, the neighbors will hear you," Lucas whisper-shouted.

"I'm not the one yelling, you're the one that's yelling. You're the reason that—"

Hank cleared his throat, causing Lucas and Miranda to jump back from each other and snap to his direction.

"You're back!" Miranda ran to Olive, hauling her into her arms. "I missed you."

"No, don't you dare give in, Miranda," Lucas shouted. "We were in this together."

Olive pulled out of their hug to point at Lucas. "What's he talking about? Did he hurt you? Do I need to kill him? I can do it."

Lucas jerked his attention to Hank, his eyes hard with his nostrils flaring. "How could you?"

Okay, that was not what I was expecting. Hank crossed his arms over his chest as he stared back at his best friend a little confused. "I have no idea what you're talking about. I thought you'd be happy to see us?"

"Oh, I am all right. Since we had no fucking idea if you'd even gotten there okay!" Lucas was pissed. Actually, pissed was an understatement.

Oh, shit. Hank's eyes rounded as he realized he'd forgotten to let them know they'd arrived safely. With Lucas's face hard and glaring at him, Hank wasn't sure if Lucas was about to throw a punch or pull him into a hug.

"You were supposed to let us know you got there okay. That was the deal."

Hank nodded, swallowing. "We got there okay."

"I will fucking deck you."

"Luke, it's fine." Miranda tried to calm him. "We knew they were okay once we finally got Olive's phone to ping." She held her hands up as if trying to tame a wild animal.

"How are you so calm now?" His eyes flew to her. "You were right there with me freaking out that first day. Everything was fine. Then out of nowhere, we *both* got the feeling something bad had happened. We were—"

"That's probably 'cause we almost died on the way there," Olive answered without thinking. "But I'm not entirely convinced we weren't brought up to the mothership," Olive stated matter-of-fact, causing all eyes in the room to shoot to her.

"You what?!"

"That's not what happened," Hank groaned.

They should've talked about this before they got home. You know ease into the almost car crash, not just blurt it out. Hank was going to have to speak to her about it before his parents got there. Lord knows his mom would have a freak out.

Olive's hands snapped to her hips as she narrowed her eyes at Hank like *he'd* done something wrong. "You don't know that for sure. I understand that your phone said we didn't lose any time. But maybe the aliens have some time machine device thingy and they forgot to fix the clock on the dash—"

"Someone better start talking right now," Lucas interjected, cutting Olive off. "What the fuck is going on?"

"I have to agree with him this time. What do you mean you almost died?" Miranda stepped closer to Lucas as if picking sides.

Hank wanted to roll his eyes, but seeing the panic and worry on not only Miranda's face but Lucas's too, he knew he needed to explain. He really didn't mean to forget to inform them they'd arrived. He lost his mind when they ran off the road. "I take full responsibility for not telling you. I'm sorry. I said I would and didn't. Not letting you know we arrived safely must have scared both of you."

"Damn straight it did. I was ready to get the guys and go searching for you myself. The fuck, Tank?" The hurt in Lucas's eyes almost killed him. "I only didn't when Miranda *finally* got Olive's fucking phone to ping. It's the only reason we knew you'd made it safe."

"Those first few hours were pretty stressful," Miranda added. "And we both had this horrible feeling."

"That's why we were arguing when you came in. I wanted to fucking deck you and Miranda said we should wait to hear your story. You scared me. I mean us."

The hurt was prevalent on his face, which made Hank feel even worse. "I'm sorry, man."

"Stop saying you're sorry and explain the almost dying and alien thing." Lucas waved his hands in the air. "I really am about to hit you."

And Hank would have let him.

But before he could explain, Olive jumped in.

"I think it really could've happened." She bounced on her toes, excited. "See, I was looking out the window for Bigfoot as we turned off the interstate. I mentioned how we were making great time and *bam!*" She slapped her hands together causing everyone in the room to jump. "There was this bright light and Hank lost control of the car. And get this, when I looked back to the clock, we'd lost twenty minutes!"

As Hank opened his mouth to try and calm the fury he knew was about to come from his best friend and his sister, Lucas shock the shit out of him.

"Like the episode with Mulder and Scully on the dark road?"

"Yes!" Olive jumped for joy as someone understood her. "That one. I bolted out of the car to see if there was a tracking device, but came up empty," she pouted, her excitement dwindling.

Silence filled the room until Lucas swung his attention to Hank. "Are you fucking kidding me? You let her get out of the car?"

"You don't *let* Olive do anything," Hank replied, the exact time Miranda yelled, "You almost got in a car accident?"

A slight throb formed behind Hank's left eye as he tried to figure out the best way to explain everything. And get Olive to dial the alien thing back a notch or two. At least for right now. "Let's take a step back, so I can explain."

"You can take a step directly into my fist."

"Luke," Miranda hissed. "I'm just as pissed as you are, but violence won't solve anything."

"You threaten to punch me all the time."

"That's different."

"No, it's not. And, I *am* pissed." Lucas glared at Olive for a split second. "Although the alien thing sounds cool and all that, but this is huge." He looked back to Miranda. "We both had that feeling that something bad happened. And something bad *did* happen. They ran off the road."

"You know what, he has a point." His sister spun around to Hank, her arms crossed over her chest. "Care to explain?"

"I'm trying." Hank pinched the bridge of his nose. "Let me get Dog in the house. We don't need to add her to the people who are pissed, since she's still in the car." With that, he turned on his heel and headed through the front door, but not before he heard Olive going off about the aliens again.

Part of him wanted to laugh, but there was a bigger part of him that felt like an ass. He didn't mean to forget to send Lucas a message. It just slipped his mind.

And he knew he was one hundred percent at fault for their extra stress and worry.

Deciding to leave their bags in the car, Hank only grabbed Dog and headed back into the house.

Once he was inside, he gently put her crate down, opening the door. Dog immediately walked out, sniffed the air and trotted over to Lucas to rub against his leg.

"Did you tell her to do that so I wouldn't be as mad at you?" he asked, arching his brow.

"Nope, that's all her. She missed you."

"Okay," Lucas grumbled as he eyed him not sure if he told the truth or not. Figuring it was best not to piss Dog off though, Lucas reached down and scratched under her chin.

Now that Dog was in the house, and for the most part, things were a little calmer, Hank walked over to their couch and sat down. "We were pulling off the interstate and the road was pretty dark. A truck came around the corner and blinded us. I lost control of the car for a second and we ended up on the side of the road. No one was hurt. Hell, Dog didn't have a care in the world. And well... Olive thought we were abducted or some shit like that since a wire on the dash must have loosened screwing with the time." He rubbed his temples. Hearing it come out of his mouth sounded just as crazy as he thought it would.

"You forgot about the static."

Hank sighed. "There was static 'cause we were in the middle of nowhere." Hank closed his eyes trying to ward off his headache. However as he opened them, he saw Lucas nodding at Olive.

"With the twenty minutes disappearing, I would have thought the same," Lucas interjected.

Hank was all for listening to Olive's theories but with Miranda glaring death daggers his way, maybe it was best not to enable her right now. "I should have messaged you then to let you know what happened, but to be honest, it freaked me out. I thought I'd lost Olive again and my brain kinda short-circuited. My only goal was to get us there safe by that point. I had every intention of messaging you once we got there. I'm sorry I didn't."

"But you guys are good now?" Miranda asked, the worry still in her eyes.

"Yeah." Hank nodded. "And no issues on the way home. Olive kept her head glued out the window and there was almost no traffic."

Lucas let out an audible breath. "I'm glad you guys are safe. We figured as much once we saw you'd made it, but it's still nice to hear. Not so nice to hear about the crash—"

"Or abduction," Olive corrected.

Lucas chuckled, shaking his head. "Or abduction. I'm glad you're both okay."

Hank watched as his best friend's shoulders relaxed. He knew they would probably need to talk about it again later, but at least for now Lucas seemed satisfied enough.

"We were both so worried about you. It actually forced us to get along on the first day." Miranda looked to Lucas and then back to them.

"That's good. It's about time, honestly." Olive got up from her seat next to Hank and walked to their tree as the tension in the room began to dissipate.

"Other than the one mishap, did you enjoy your time away?" Miranda asked, sitting further onto the chair, curling both legs underneath her.

"Yeah," Hank replied. "Other than that, it was perfect."

"And the squirrel," Olive calmly added, making Hank groan.

Lucas's eyes widened. "What squirrel?"

"It was nothing."

Olive spun on her heels from the tree to face the room. "Not true, it tried to kill me."

When Hank saw Olive failing to hide her smile, he cocked his brow. *That little shit.*

Staring her down, Hank mentally added *one* to his ever-growing list of punishments she'd be getting as soon as they got the chance.

Olive must've seen it in his eyes since her smile disappeared as she cleared her throat. "It was in the Christmas tree."

"No shit."

"Yeah," Olive huffed. "Made me burn my cookies."

"Not your cookies for Santa?" Miranda gasped. "That's horrible."

Olive pouted. "I know!"

"They weren't that bad, and once we got the squirrel back outside, everything was fine," Hank elaborated before Olive and Miranda went off on one of his wife's adorable tangents about cookies for Santa.

Lucas's hand went to his stomach as he burst out laughing. "I'm surprised Dog didn't chase it."

"She did."

With another laugh, Lucas pulled out his phone and began texting.

"What are you doing?"

"Messaging the guys. I know there'll be here soon, but I gotta let them know they owe me fifty bucks."

"For fuck's sake. You can't tell me you bet on there being a squirrel in the cabin? There is no way in hell you knew that."

Lucas's eyes shined bright as a playful smile spread across his face. "Nope. But I did bet the guys you'd fuck it up somehow."

"How did I fuck it up? I didn't put the thing in the tree."

Lucas stared at Hank like he was crazy. "It's your fault the squirrel was there."

"That's what I said." Olive nodded vigorously.

Hank's eyes swung back to his wife. *Oh yeah, you are just racking up those points now, aren't you, babe?* Deciding it was best to let Olive think about it, Hank picked up a throw pillow and tossed it at Lucas's head. "At this point, we should've just stayed in the cabin."

"Nah, you'd miss me too much." Lucas puffed his chest.

"Doubt it."

Hank flicked his eyes to the ceiling as Olive went back to the tree. He was sure she was searching for the gift *she'd* forgotten to bring. Before he could tell her not to worry about it though, Olive spun back, glaring Lucas down madder than he'd ever seen Olive.

And that included when he messed with her books that one time.

"Why is one of the presents half open?"

"Shit!" Lucas instantly held up his hands. "I can explain!"

CHAPTER FOURTEEN

IT HAD BEEN a few hours since Olive and Hank arrived home, and thankfully everything had calmed down for the most part.

At least Olive was considering it calm.

She had to admit though, once Lucas and Miranda knew they were safe, and they'd apologized, she couldn't help riling up Hank a bit as she kept adding to the chaos.

That's what he deserved for rearranging her books when they lived in the apartment. She wanted to pat herself on her back.

Olive: one.

Hank: Okay, still like two million and ten but whatever.

As Olive sat on the couch, her eyes trailed to Lucas who sat on the smaller loveseat in their living room.

She wanted to be mad at him but seeing as they'd unintentionally worried him and Miranda, Olive decided to let it slide.

Although, she didn't quite believe his excuse of, *it was an accident. I stopped and fell and it just happened to rip open.*

Plus, she'd be lying if she said him knowing about the *X-*

Files episode didn't give him brownie points. Who knew Lucas was a fan of the show?

As Olive looked at him with the same ol' goofy grin on his face he always had, she couldn't help but wonder if there was more to Lucas than anyone knew.

Honestly, though, right now she didn't have the time to deal with thinking about it. Instead, she pushed it off to revisit later as she watched everyone settling into the living room around the tree.

Jim and Robin had arrived about an hour after Hank and Olive got home. And as soon as they walked in the door, Robin started preparing the meal along with the help of her and Miranda.

Then came Rick and Tim, who weren't far behind as they were the last to arrive.

Which led everyone to right now. Olive's whole face beamed as her smile ran from ear to ear.

It was finally time.

However, before Olive could get the show started, Lucas jumped from his spot next to Miranda and stood in front of the Christmas tree. "I'm Santa."

Oh, heck no.

"It's my house." Olive shook her head as she pointed to herself. "I should be Santa."

"You want me to tell everyone about the cras—"

"Let him have this," Hank interrupted, with a twinge of panic in his voice.

And Olive understood Hank's worry. After they'd told Lucas and Miranda about the drive, they figured it would be easier if they held off telling Hank's parents about it, at least until after the holiday.

It seemed less chaotic that way. And Olive had to agree. There was no use in freaking Robin or Jim out, but man she couldn't wait to tell them about the *possible* abduction.

"Besides," Hank continued, "you were Santa at the cabin."

As her attention focused on Hank, a smug smile emerged on her face. "I thought I was Mrs. Claus."

"Ewww. I don't wanna hear about whatever the hell you all did while you were there." Miranda's fingers flew to her ears as she shook her head. "Again *ewwwww.*"

"Shut your face." Olive glared at her for a moment, and then turned her attention back to Lucas. Truth be told, she was fine with him being Santa, but she wasn't gonna let him win too easily.

That just wasn't her.

After all, riling up the guys was one of Olive's favorite pastimes. And she could blame Hank for that. Now she understood why he liked to mess with them.

It was kind of fun.

"Luke only wants to be Santa so he could hide the presents that were damaged by the smoke." Rick laughed as he leaned on his elbows as he sat on the floor.

The smile that instantly appeared on Rick's face told everyone in the room, he damn well knew exactly what he'd just done.

What the hell was he talking about?

Olive's eyes shifted around the space as her heart rate picked up. When she didn't come across any visible damage, she focused her sights on Lucas and Miranda. "What does he mean smoke damage?"

"I thought we agreed not to tell them?" Miranda groaned.

Hank pushed himself to the edge of his seat, his eyes full of concern. "Tell us what?"

Tim happily chimed in all too eager to continue the conversation, "We were called out to the house on Christmas Eve."

"You were called out?! Did we have a fire?!" Olive shot out of her seat as she spun around the room, seeing if she'd missed anything. Coming up empty again, she darted her eyes to Lucas. "What happened?"

"Dude, really?" Lucas stared flabbergasted at their friend Tim.

"Yes, really."

"If someone doesn't tell me what happened right this minute, I swear to everything I will kick you all out and then murder every single one of you in my next book."

"Actually, I'd like to know what happened too," Robin interrupted, with her brow cocked just like Hank and Miranda did so expertly. "I don't think anyone bothered to mention that to me when I called to make sure you both hadn't killed each other and wish you guys a Merry Christmas Eve."

"Thanks for checking in on them, Mom," Hank ground out through gritted teeth, trying to be as sincere as he could, but refusing to peel his eyes from Lucas.

And Olive couldn't blame him, she was seconds from losing it herself if people didn't start talking.

"You're welcome, love."

Hank's hands fisted at his sides. "Luke, you've got two seconds to start explaining before I murder you and *not* in a book."

"Ugh, fine. Okay, but you're making this a big deal for nothing." Lucas flung his hands through the air. "I fucked up and almost burnt your house down from the fireplace."

"What! Holy shit, Lucas, that's a huge deal! Are you guys okay?" Olive's whole body flew into a panic as her blood pressure skyrocketed.

Oh crap, this is it. I'm about to have a heart attack and on freakin' Christmas. At this rate, Hank's never gonna open my gift, 'cause I'm gonna be dead.

"Wait..." Hank sat back, completely confused. "That's not possible. You're more careful than anyone I know. Hell, you take fire safety more seriously than I do."

"This time I wasn't. Mistakes happen." Lucas snapped his eyes to Hank almost as if to silence him. "It was all good. And no one would've known if you didn't have that stupid sensor that sent a signal right to the station if there is even a hint of smoke in your house."

Olive's head was going to explode. Hank was right though, this didn't sound like the Lucas they knew. At this point, Olive contemplated if they really *had* been abducted and for some weird reason the aliens sent them back to the wrong parallel Universe.

Olive's eyes moved to the ceiling. *Uhh, Universe, or aliens whoever is in charge, I'm cool if you want to take me back. Just take me back with Hank, that's all. Oh, and I guess Dog.*

After a few seconds with no reply, she took a deep breath focusing back on Lucas. "None of this is making sense."

That's when Miranda cleared her throat grabbing everyone's attention. "It's okay, Luke, and it's very sweet of you to try and cover for me."

"What do you mean cover for you?"

"Luke was in the shower, and I didn't want to bug him. The thing is I really wanted to start a fire. I mean it was Christmas Eve and I thought it would be nice to sit with a glass of wine and just watch the fire crackling. I didn't realize your flume was installed weirdly. I *thought* I opened it, but I somehow actually closed it instead."

"Oh no." Olive's head swung to Hank. "I told you that was gonna be a problem! You didn't listen to me."

"When I heard the smoke detector go off, I ran out of the shower and down here only to find Miranda freaking out," Lucas continued. "I fixed it in a few seconds, but there was a lot of smoke. And since you installed those special sensors to go off at the station if anything were to happen to your house, the guys came running."

"I have to make sure Olive is safe at all times," Hank stated matter-of-fact.

"Yeah, I get that." Luke rolled his eyes. "But they're so

damn sensitive, I'm surprised burnt cookies don't have the whole damn station running over here all the time."

Olive gasped as her hand flying to her chest like she'd been shot. "Don't bring up burnt cookies!"

"Luke's forgetting to mention that when we got here, he was naked," Rick added, his smile running from ear to ear.

"You were what!" Olive's eyes widened even further as her jaw hit the floor, gawking at Miranda. *Sister, you and I are gonna have a* long *freakin' talk.*

"Ummm, you see, uh, that's my fault." A deep blush crept up Miranda's cheeks as she diverted her gaze from Lucas to the floor.

That settled it. Olive and Miranda were going to have a huge freaking talk as soon as their gifts were opened.

"I didn't mind." A cocky smile appeared on Lucas's face as he winked at Miranda.

To make the situation that much better, Rick chose that exact moment to continue. "Apparently, after Miranda opened the windows and doors to get the smoke out, she looked for anything that could help do it faster and I guess Luke's towel was her best option."

"I didn't look at him!" she shouted in her defense. "I focused on using it to fan out the smoke. Plus, I was hoping we'd gotten it out in time before your stupid sensor went off."

Tim laughed. "You didn't."

"Yeah," Rick agreed. "Sure was fun storming in here to see a butt-ass naked Luke running around, while your sister screamed put clothes on and her eyes were gonna need bleach."

Not being phased in the slightest, Lucas turned to Olive. "That's why the gifts were moved and one ripped."

"*Ohhh...*" Olive nodded, still a little confused as her brain worked on piecing everything together.

Holy freakin' crap on a cracker.

Hank burst into a hearty laugh, breaking the complete

chaos of the room. "All right. I can deal with the fireplace thing. It's happened to Olive more than once." He looked at her, his eyes sparkling. "I'm glad no one was hurt and that you didn't cause the issue. I was a little worried there for a second. I thought I needed to have a talk with the Lieutenant and send you back to the fire academy."

Olive twisted to face Hank, her hand on her hip. "How can you joke at a time like this? There was almost a fire in our house. The only thing worse would be if the zombies came and we weren't home to see it."

Hank sat back with an amused look on his face. "The house was always in good hands—from a fire *or* zombies. I might screw with Luke for the rest of his life about this, but him nor any of the guys would've ever let anything happen. Besides, now we'll finally have something else to talk about at the station other than me always losing shit."

"Nope, that's still gonna happen." Rick's face brightened as the corner of his mouth turned up.

"Ahh. That reminds me!" Olive ran to the tree, grabbed the gift she'd forgotten and rushed back to Hank tossing it at him. "Here! Open it!"

"I thought you gave presents to each other at the cabin?" Jim asked, quirking his brow.

"Yeah," Robin added, pointing at Olive's neck. "The necklace Hank had made for you looks stunning."

"Thank you," Olive replied, as her cheeks slightly heated. She bit her bottom lip as her hand went to the necklace, hoping it would give her strength. "But, umm, you see—"

"Olive *forgot* my gift," Hank cut her off, sitting up a tad straighter in his seat. Hank then moved his attention to Lucas. "You might lie to protect Miranda with her fuck up, but rest assured I am never letting Olive live this down."

"Hey!" Miranda and Olive both said at the same time.

"Bastard." Olive's eyes hardened on her husband, but even

if she wanted to, she couldn't be mad. Not when he had that goofy grin on his face.

Again bastard, but he was her bastard.

"What?" Ignoring them, Hank opened his gift with a smirk.

Olive contemplated if she should make her own punishment countdown thing for Hank... Because right now he'd definitely be getting a *one*.

Once Hank removed the gift wrap, he held it in the air, examining it. "What is it?"

"It's a finder!" Olive grabbed the box from him, showing the pile of tiles on the cover. "These tiles here are tracking devices. You know like what aliens put in you—"

"They put something in you all right," Lucas snorted.

Olive cut into him with her eyes daring him to continue, which immediately caused Lucas to hold his hands in surrender.

With one more hard look at Lucas, Olive focused her attention back on Hank. "As I was saying, before I was so rudely interrupted. You download this app onto your phone and load in all the trackers. Then you just stick them to all the things you lose. It'll always tell you where your stuff is. And get this..." She flipped over the box. "I got the really fancy ones. They'll even make a sound to help you find what you lost. They come in all different sizes, so you can put them anywhere, your wallet, keys, hell even your shoes." Olive's toothy smile spread across her face. "I figured this way the guys can't keep making bets at your expense."

Hank's whole face lit as he examined the gift. "That's really sweet, babe. I do hate when those assholes use me for their betting."

"I know!"

"But, let me get this straight," Hank continued, his smile even brighter as he looked at her. "You bought me a box full of tracking devices so I wouldn't lose anything, and *you* forgot it at home."

Olive's jaw hit the floor for a split second before she glanced at the ceiling and groaned. It didn't help that Hank had his hand on his stomach as he laughed uncontrollably. "See, this is why I knew it would be even worse that I forgot your gift here."

Hank tried to control his laughter, but failed as Olive crossed her arms over her chest glaring at him.

"Oh, Olive Oil, I'm never gonna let you live this down."

With a pained sigh, Olive stared up at the ceiling again. *I'm glad you're enjoying this, Universe.*

"There is one problem, Olive," Lucas chimed in. "You didn't take into account one major flaw in your plan."

Olive's lips pursed as her right brow cocked at him. "Yeah, and what's that?"

"We're still going to bet on him and *I'm* going to win. You said he needed an app on his phone. Too bad, ol' Tank here loses his phone at least five times a day."

Olive tilted her head as a cocky smile appeared on her face. "Good thing more than one person can have the app."

Lucas gasped as his hand went to his chest. "And here I was gonna share my winnings with you."

"Yeah, right." Olive rolled her eyes. "That reminds me, I've been meaning to ask how much have you made off Hank over the years?"

"I'll never tell."

"I think Olive is right. How much have you made off me?" Hank asked, eyeing Lucas. "After the holidays we're gonna have a little sit down."

"Don't worry, Luke," Miranda spoke, a sly smile on her lips. "He'll probably forget to ask you."

Olive didn't know whether to interfere or grab some popcorn and sit back and watch. Sibling fights, especially between Miranda and Hank, were the best fights. Besides, it wasn't like she'd pick sides or anything, so she might as well enjoy the soon-to-be show.

"Olive called me her 'person,'" Hank proudly stated, toward his sister's direction, his shoulders straightening in triumph.

Oh, fuck me. I should've intervened. Damn it.

Olive knew better.

"She wouldn't," Miranda gasped as she shot her eyes to Olive, her hand over her heart.

"I—"

Hank puffed his chest as he smirked. "She did and there is nothin' you can do about it."

"If we're picking people, I'm calling Miranda as my person," Lucas announced as a matter-of-fact.

Instantly Miranda flung her hands in the air. "I'm Olive's person, not yours."

"Sorry, Sis, that's me now." Hank barked out a laugh at their fun.

"Children," Robin hollered, grabbing the room's attention. "It's Christmas. Can we all just say everyone is everyone's person and leave it at that? You can argue about it later."

Lucas snorted. "Ha. You guys just got in trouble by your mom." He laughed again. "What are you, five?"

Robin arched her brow at Lucas, crossing her arms over her chest. "Care to repeat that, Lucas?"

Instantly Lucas lowered his head, as he mumbled, "Nothing, Momma Parker."

"That's what I thought."

However, Lucas winked at Hank before focusing back on Robin. "Did Hank tell you him and Olive almost got into a car crash on their way to the cabin?"

"Luke!" Olive was going to murder him.

"What!" Robin and Jim both yelled at the same time as all eyes in the room fell on Olive and Hank.

"It's not what it seems!" Olive rushed out in a panic as Robin propped her hand on her hip, staring them both down.

"Don't believe her," Lucas continued. "She'll just tell you they were abducted by aliens."

Olive shot an evil glare toward Lucas. "We could have been. We don't know for sure. And you, buddy, just sealed your fate. You're dead in my next book."

Unfazed, Lucas shrugged.

"Did you really just blurt that out so my mom would focus back on us rather than you?" Hank stared at him with his brows cocked to the ceiling.

"You gotta do what you gotta do to stay on Momma Parker's good side." That stupid cocky smile was back on Lucas's face, and if he didn't remove it, Olive was going to remove it for him.

"You owe me twenty bucks," Rick announced as he grinned at Tim. "It was a toss-up between Hank and Luke. And I just couldn't pick."

"For fuck's sake."

"What?" Rick took the twenty bucks from Tim's hand. "I bet you'd both fuck it up today. Tim thought it would just be Luke. There, in fact, I win twenty bucks."

Robin threw her hands in the air. "Universe, give me strength because all..." She pointed at everyone in the room. "Of my children, will send me to an early grave."

"Mom!"

"Don't you dare Mom me, Miranda. Now all of you get your asses in the kitchen, present time is over. We'll try again when you've all had a time out. Right now, we're gonna enjoy this family meal so help me God, or I'll lose it. I brought you into this world, I can take you out."

"Can't take me out, I didn't come out of your hoo-ha." Lucas stood a little straighter.

Hank punched him in the arm. "Don't talk about my mom's hoo-ha."

"That's my job," Jim joked with a laugh.

Robin scowled at Lucas, her eyes daring. "Wanna bet?"

"Not on your life." Lucas immediately shook his head.

"Eww," Miranda shouted as she faked a gag. "Can we just stop? You know what? I'm not moving back here if we're gonna be talking about Mom's va-jay-jay."

"You're moving back?!"

The whole room froze as Lucas snapped his attention to Miranda, his eyes impossibly wide as the shock paralyzed him.

"Uhh..." Miranda let out a nervous laugh. "Umm, Merry Christmas."

As soon as the words were out of her mouth, Lucas grabbed Miranda by the shoulders and brought his lips down to hers in a kiss. It only lasted a few seconds before Miranda shoved him away.

"No. Eww. Abso-freakin-lutely not." Miranda stomped toward the kitchen, only turning back to glare at Hank and Olive. "Not a word."

With that, Miranda spun on her heel and ran out of the room.

"Well, okay then," Rick was the first to speak. "Guess I owe Hank a hundred bucks."

"You all owe me a hundred bucks," Hank replied. His eyes shot to Lucas who sported a shit-eating grin on his face. "Including you."

Without looking at him, Lucas pulled out his wallet, walked over to Hank, handed him the money and went in the direction Miranda had taken off in.

"For the love of all things." Robin shook her head as she walked toward the kitchen after them. "Death of me, I swear."

Holy crap on all the damn freaking crackers...

As everyone migrated out of the room to the kitchen,

Olive's head spun. This was not how she planned their family holiday going. Not even in the slightest.

Olive's eyes caught the sight of Dog who sat at the base of the tree. The poor girl had the same dumbfounded expression on her face Olive was sure she had as well.

You and me both, kitty. I bet you kinda wish those aliens did take us now, don't cha?

Deciding it was best to assess the damage she was sure was happening in her kitchen, Olive took a step in that direction.

However, Hank grabbed her elbow stopping Olive. Instantly, she tipped her head to the side as she looked at him.

"Before we go in there to whatever hell awaits us, I just wanted to say I love you." The soft loving smile on Hank's face filled Olive's heart. "I love you too."

Hank pulled her into his arms, melding her to his body. "I can't wait to spend every anniversary and Christmas with you by my side."

"Ditto." She nodded as a toothy grin appeared on her face. "I hope you liked your gift."

"I loved it." He leaned forward placing a kiss on her lips. "And I promise, New Year's Eve, it'll just be us. You, me, and Dog sitting on the couch watching the ball drop. Not another soul in sight."

Olive's whole face broke out into a massive grin as she wrapped her arms around Hank. "Thank freakin' Bigfoot!"

THANK you so much for reading Teased by Tinsel! I hope you enjoyed it. Lucas & Miranda's story is up next. Subscribe to my newsletter, or join my reader group to get updated on their release.

DID the hairless cat intrigue you? If so check out Abbie & Hunter's story *Nothing But a Dare*, an enemies to lovers, second chance romance.

DO you want to know if Lord Waffles will rule the world? Did you enjoy the very opinionated Corgi, his accident prone mom, Holly and her Adonis veterinarian husband, Ben?

If so check out their story in **Stumbling Into Him**.

Look for a sneak peek on the next page.

STUMBLING INTO HIM SNEAK PEAK

Chapter One

"WATCH OUT!"

Holly Flanagan heard a commotion coming from the other side of the park.

Figuring it was best to ignore the shouting, she bent over to focus on picking up her Corgi—Lord Waffles's—most recent deposit. Although, with Holly's track record, she should've known anyone yelling "watch out," "take cover," or "that's about to fall" was directed at her. Even after years of being the unofficial spokesperson for unlucky, klutzy, and clumsy, she still ignored the shouting as she carried on with her dog parent duties.

Unfortunately, for her before she could register what happened, she was knocked onto her back with pain radiating from her mouth and nose.

"Well, at least the sky is pretty today," Holly mumbled as she tried to get her bearings. Looking away from the sky, she reached for her mouth as the pain spread.

"Miss, I'm so sorry. Are you okay?"

With a heavy sigh, Holly closed her eyes.

Was she okay? Wasn't that the million-dollar question?

She'd just been hit with something and she was pretty

sure some part of her face—she didn't know which part—was bleeding. Waffles hadn't stopped barking, and her head hurt.

So, was she okay?

Holly groaned with a heavier sigh escaping her lips.

Yeah, she was fine. This was just another normal day in her life. And so far, if being hit by an unknown projectile to the face was the worst thing that happened to her, she would considered it a good day.

Deciding to face the music, she opened her eyes.

Holy shit!

Above Holly, only a few inches from her face, was by far the most handsome man she'd ever laid eyes on.

He should be on the cover of a magazine hot. He had dark brown hair and deep blue eyes that were richer than the ocean. His jaw was chiseled, with a light dusting of scruff—in the alpha male, I'm in charge here kind of way.

Wonderful. Freaking wonderful...Okay, let's add embarrassing yourself in front of a Greek God to your list of accomplishments for the day. Hey, it can only get better from here, right?

When Holly realized she'd been staring at him for what might have been considered too long, she quickly jerked her head forward, trying to right herself. Sadly, for her, though, she slammed her head right into the guy's forehead.

Really!

Great. Not only did her mouth hurt, now her head hurt... and well, let's not forget she'd just head-butted the hottest man in the world.

Absolutely freaking wonderful!

"Shit," the Greek God grunted.

Slowly, Holly opened her eyes only to see her Adonis holding his head. *Great. Could today get any worse?*

As if the Universe heard her, Waffles barked loudly in her face, looked at the pile still on the ground, and then back at her.

"For the love of all things, dog. I was about to pick it up," she growled. As she took her hand away from her mouth to deal with his majesty, *Lord* Waffles, she screamed when she saw blood on her hand.

"Oh shit. Lady, you're bleeding." The man grabbed her chin moving it from side to side as he examined her face.

"Oh, God, what happened?" As she looked at the blood, her heart raced. *Did I break my nose? Wait, am I unconscious? Am I dying? I'm dead right and to add salt to my wound I'm greeted with the hottest man alive?*

The man tilted Holly's chin back to get a better look. "I was tossing the Frisbee with Ripley and it somehow veered off course. I tried to warn you when I yelled *watch out.*"

Typical. Holly groaned. *Hot guy throws a Frisbee. Said Frisbee hits me in the face. Hot guy then insinuates it's my fault for not getting out of the way fast enough. I mean, I know I'm generally invisible to men like him, but, damn. You'd think these extra wide hips would make me be seen.* Her eyes darted to the Frisbee sitting next to her as she glared at it. *I don't know why, but I'm blaming you.*

With one last huff directed at the Frisbee, she glanced back at the man.

"I can't tell if it's just a busted lip or worse," he remarked while he tilted her chin upward even further.

That's it. This was already embarrassing enough.

Holly ripped her face from his hand. She'd be able to tell if it was only a busted lip. She'd had them more than enough to count in her life—from falling down, objects to the face, and even falling *up* the stairs a few times. She reached into her pocket and pulled out the napkin she had stuffed in there to wipe her mouth.

"Let me see," the man demanded, as he took the napkin from her and dabbed it on her lips.

In an instant her eyes widened as she froze.

Well, Holly. This is the most action you've had in months. And, if some hot guy is all over you, you might as well enjoy it while it lasts.

As the man inspected her lip, Waffles crawled onto her lap

and started kissing the underside of her jaw, demanding attention.

Holly rolled her eyes. *Great. Thanks, Waffles, for bringing the attention of my double chin to McHotPants.*

"Thanks for trying to help me clean up your mom," the man remarked before quickly abandoning his job of cleaning the blood off her mouth to scratch Waffles on the head.

"He's not trying to help you," Holly grunted. "He's *trying* to remind me I still need to pick up his poop and give him a treat."

"Shouldn't your mom be the one getting the treat if *she's* the one picking up your shit?" The handsome man cocked his head at her dog.

Waffles, ever the one to argue, looked at the man—who now had a mischievous grin on his face—with the most judgmental side-eye he could muster.

No one came between him and his treats.

With a small chuckle he ignored Waffles's glare, and gave him another quick scratch, this time under his chin, before moving back to Holly's mouth dismissing the dog. "I think it's just a busted lip, but your front tooth..." The man coughed as he sheepishly looked away.

"My front tooth?!" Holly ran her tongue along the front of her teeth. *Fuck!* The jagged piece was unmistakable. "Crap." She quickly pulled her phone from her pocket and launched the front-facing camera. As soon as she saw herself, she jerked back.

Holy shitballs. Her hair was all over the place, her face was red, and there was still blood on her...

Well, you've definitely had better days, Holly. She took a deep breath before he hastily opened her mouth to see the damage.

"Oh, no..."

Staring back at her was a chipped front tooth, the damage matching her busted lip. *Wonderful. Absolutely wonderful. Thank you, Universe. Thank you so freaking very much.* She didn't know whether to laugh or cry. *Clumsy Holly strikes again.*

As her eyes flooded with tears, a cold nose hit her arm. Realizing it wasn't Waffles since he was still in her lap, Holly looked to her left and saw one of the most beautiful gray and black Australian Shepherds she'd ever seen.

"Aren't you a cutie?" Everything going on was instantly forgotten as her love of animals overrode everything.

"That's Ripley." The Greek God chuckled, his eyes twinkling in a way Holly thought was only possible in movies. "I'd thought you'd be more concerned about your mouth than a dog?"

"Well you don't know me." Ignoring him, she reached out to scratch Ripley's chin. "You're so pretty. Aren't you?" Ripley must have agreed, because she barked once before kissing Holly's hand.

"Uhh, miss? I'm not a human doctor, but I think we should pay more attention to your injuries instead of the dogs."

"Human doctor?" Holly snapped her head to him with her right brow cocked. "As opposed to what, an alien doctor?"

"I haven't worked on any aliens that I know of, but I did neuter a cat named Alien once. Does that count?"

Holly's eyes widened. "You have got to be kidding me? Of course you've got a body of a Greek God, and are also a vet. Which means you love animals. *Freakin'* wonderful. You're like the most perfect guy and here I am on the sidewalk with blood pouring out of my face with a chipped tooth and a pile of poop a few feet from me." She pushed Waffles off her lap and stood. "Please excuse me while I find a place to die of embarrassment."

"You're funny." The corner of the sexy man's mouth quirked upward.

"And you're hot. So, we've now successfully established

which groups we belong to." Annoyed at herself more than anything, she angrily started to stomp away from him.

"Hey, wait up!"

She spun around to glare at him. It was his fault she was in this mess to begin with. It was his dumb Frisbee. However, the moment Holly saw Waffles sitting at the foot of the man looking up at him, her left eye began to twitch.

Of course, her dog would betray her. She wouldn't expect anything less from him. "Waffles, come." She gently pulled on the leash, but the dog wouldn't budge. "Lord Waffles, get your butt over here."

The man cocked his brow. "Lord Waffles?"

"Yeah," she answered. "He thinks he's a freakin' king. Hence the 'lord' and I love waffles. Do you got a problem with that, buster?"

The man burst out laughing as he scratched Waffles on the back. To make matters worse, her betraying Corgi rolled over asking for belly rubs.

The audacity! That's it. No more treats for you! She glared at her dog.

"Who's a good boy?" the man cooed. "You've got a weird name, but you're the best boy, aren't you?"

Holly's eye twitched harder.

As she stomped back toward her bastard of a dog, but out of nowhere, her foot hit an invisible rock causing her to trip. Within a split second, she ended up falling right into the arms of the bane of her existence at the moment.

"Whoa, are you okay?"

"I'm fine," she grumbled as she righted herself. *Go ahead and add this to the, "it can only happen to me" list.*

"I feel like you need to walk around with a warning sign or at least a crash helmet."

"Not the first time I've heard that." Quickly she bent down and scooped Waffles into her arms. "If you'll excuse me. Not only do I really need to find a secluded place to die of embarrassment, I also need to call my dentist or go to the walk-in clinic. Maybe both." She turned on her heel and began power walking down the sidewalk.

The moment Holly passed the spot she'd tripped at, she examined the cement coming up empty. Figures, there'd be absolutely nothing there. If there were a sporting category on tripping over invisible objects, she'd win gold every time.

"Hey!"

Holly kept walking doing her best to hide her humiliation while ignoring the Greek God who now chased after her.

"Hey, I want to make sure you really are okay." He caught up to her in two point three seconds.

Stupid short legs! "I'm fine."

"Your lip's still bleeding."

She glared at him. "Thanks for the heads up."

"Hey..." He reached for her arm stopping her next attempted escape.

"What?" she snapped.

"Let me help you. My practice is only a block from here. I've got all the supplies to clean up your lip and I can get a better look at your tooth."

"You're a vet." Her eye twitched again. *Could today seriously get any worse?*

"I'm pretty sure if I can surgically remove nuts from an animal I can look at your busted lip." He shrugged, sending her a smirk.

Crap on a cracker, he does have a point. He'd at least be able to see if anything was really bad. But no. She shook her head. This was already too embarrassing and she really didn't need to add this to her list. "Thank you for the offer—"

"Ben," he cut her off. "My name's Ben Richman." He held out his hand, which Holly stared at like it was her mortal enemy.

"Thanks for the offer, Doctor Richman, but there's a walk-in clinic not far from where I live."

"Please call me Ben. And let me do this. Trust me, you'd be doing me a favor."

"How would I be doing you a favor?"

"I'll be able to sleep tonight knowing the woman I maimed with my Frisbee is somewhat okay."

Holly watched as his eyes pleaded with her. In her arms, even Waffles—the jerk—looked up at her and whined. "Oh, for the love of... fine. Lead the way, *Ben*."

"Thank you." His mouth curved into a smile. "Follow me."

When Ben whistled, Ripley sat instantly by his side as he bent down and fastened her leash before walking toward the street.

Holly stood there for a second and looked at the man and then back at Waffles who was clearly enjoying being carried. "Guess you get an extra trip to the vet."

She burst out into a deep laugh when Waffles closed his mouth and glared at her.

*Continue Ben and Holly's story in **Stumbling Into Him**.*

ALSO BY MOLLY O'HARE

Stumbling Through Life Series

Stumbling Into Him

Stumbling Into Forever

Stumbling Into the Holidays

John & Emma's story – *Coming soon*

Teased by Love Series

Teased by Fire

Teased by Tinsel

Lucas & Miranda's story – Coming soon

Hollywood Hopeful Series

Hollywood Dreams

Risking It All (Danny and Lexi's Story) – *Coming soon*

Standalone Novels

Nothing But a Dare

Learning Curves

Tents & Tights

Just a Batter of Time

Stay Connected

Sign up for my newsletter or check out my website.

If you just want to hang out, come join my reader group: Molly's Badass Babes.

ABOUT THE AUTHOR

Molly O'Hare is a USA Today Bestselling author of curvy romance books.

She's obsessed with all things animals, mainly Corgis, and body positivity. She grew up with severe dyslexia: trust her, spelling is not her strong suit. Over the years, she's become a huge advocate of "just because you learn something a little differently than others doesn't make you less." To help herself fall asleep, she'd create stories in her head, always picking up where she left off the night before. Molly figured if she got enjoyment out of her imagination, others might as well. So here we are.

Fun Facts:

I went to a Bigfoot museum once and it was the best thing in my life.

My husband and I converted my office to one right out of Olive's dreams... I legit have three Christmas trees up (I have a video on TikTok). It's the office of my dreams.

Peppermint Bark is my favorite holiday candy.

The X-Files is my favorite show.

I sing more show tunes more than anyone should, and super loud at that.